THE REWARD

"Hey, why don't you guys come along?"

"No," she interceded. "I think it's time for O'Malley to be rewarded for his wonderful work on the case."

...They dined on fruit by candlelight for an hour, and then they dined on each other in darkness for two more. They lay in bed naked for half the night talking of their lives together.

O'Malley's legal career then had seven weeks to go.

SPECIAL CIRCUMSTANCES

BRIAN LYSAGHT

AVON
PUBLISHERS OF BARD, CAMELOT, DISCUS AND FLARE BOOKS

AVON BOOKS
A division of
The Hearst Corporation
1790 Broadway
New York, New York 10019

The St. Martin's Press Inc., edition contains the following
Library of Congress Cataloging in Publication Data:
Lysaght, Brian.
   Special Circumstances.
   I. Title.
PS3562.Y4498S6   1983   813'.54   83-2938

First Avon Printing, July, 1984

To JFL, and the woman and boy he didn't know.

1

At dawn they came again, sneaking over the garden wall and past the open drapes. It had been the same for each of the four days since the grand jury indicted him. Since the first grand jury indicted him, that is.

Fine bolts of solar energy were slinking under his eyelids and setting up staging areas like commandos somewhere near the medulla. From there they attacked, killing without mercy whatever innocent brain cells they found. There seemed to be more this time and the body's defenses were routed earlier than usual. Either that or the cumulative effect of four days of Jack Daniels was taking its toll. His skull was, as usual, doing all the wrong things. Heads are not designed properly, he thought. They should give a little when invaded. Like the Russian army.

For a time he lay motionless, letting the pain and nausea pass over him in waves. He tried to keep his mind a blank, void of the familiar visions. But it was impossible. His ultimate curse was a fecund imagination. And so he saw again how it would be—poverty, public humiliation, imprisonment in a federal penitentiary—visions that had haunted him for months as a developing possibility and for the last five days as a staggering reality. Visions that bore principal responsibility for all those empty bottles of evil Jack.

But even jail was far off compared with the problem of the commandos. Survival required standing. Standing required transmitting electronic signals through the cerebral cortex via a series of synapses to the top junction box of the spinal column. He ran a test pattern—moved a finger—and he could feel the sparks, the overheating, the beginning of the process of implosion.

The system needed cooling. Outside, attached to his brand new house, was his brand new swimming pool. Neither would be his for very long. But for the moment it was salvation. He leapt up, sprinted for the door, and fell staggering into the water. At first he almost drowned, but soon the blessed liquid cooled the distress centers long enough for his lungs to begin gulping in equal parts of smog and green chlorine. He wound up only half dead, retching on the aquamarine plaster of paris dolphin.

2

Most of the law students at NYU thought Benjamin Aaron O'Malley was slightly unusual. The name, and the disparate cultural genes it connoted, were the least of it. More important, he looked so out of place, like a worker, a man who used his hands to earn money. The hands were thick and hard. The face was the same. It also seemed older, with lines around the eyes and mouth. Yet at that time he was only twenty-six.

The horn-rimmed glasses seemed an affectation, a camouflage. He put them on only to read the thick books. When he wore them he stared at the books intently for hours. The only movement was the four full fingers of his right hand moving the pages from right to left.

The index finger was a source of discussion. The prevailing view was that he had mangled it in a factory accident.

On the weekends he invariably left the Washington Square flat with the thick books under his arms. The subway ran crowded and noisy on Friday evenings, but for only thirty blocks it didn't matter. At Forty-second Street he left with the others and rode the escalator up to the cavernous lobby. Four escalators later and he was at the bus level, watching the black effluent wrap around the blinking Port Authority sign. As he sat coughing, he always wondered the same thing: Why didn't they ever turn the buses off?

O'Malley never minded the hour-long ride through the tunnel and down along the wrong side of the Hudson. For one thing it was quieter on the Jersey side. The tunnel seemed to capture the noise and grit of the city. Once on the other side the bus would pick up speed, leaving the chaos of rush hour behind. There was a highway to travel on, which didn't exist in the city, and a chance for O'Malley to close his eyes and listen to the steady hum of the engine, broken intermittently by the crash of the tires bouncing off the holes in the concrete.

The late September sun in 1973 was extraordinarily hot and for once he didn't enjoy the bus ride. When it finally ended in the shade of the Bayonne refineries, he walked off sticky and dark with grime. A patrol car was parked next to a ten-year-old Plymouth. A rust-haired cop sat hatless behind the wheel, watching O'Malley approach. As O'Malley got near, the cop threw him two keys held together with a paper clip.

"Try to keep it in one piece tonight, A.J."

O'Malley laughed. "Don't I always. Or almost always."

"No," said the cop. "What do you got planned?"

"The usual." He held up the books. "This is for Saturday. Tonight I'm meeting Elaine." He hesitated and looked at the cop. "Sunday we ought to talk."

His father nodded, then leaned over and turned down the squawking radio. "You found something out?"

"Yeah, it's what we expected."

"Good," his father said. "Save it till Sunday. Your mother will want all the details. Where are you heading tonight?"

"Well, Elaine has found this interesting lecture on gardening at the high school and we thought . . ." The roar of the starting engine cut him off.

"Ask a stupid question," the cop said as he pulled away.

O'Malley parked the Plymouth gingerly between the polished Corvettes lined behind the brick building. Across the street the factory clattered with the efforts of the dead man's shift. Inside the Town Tavern the noise was only slightly lower. The owners of the Corvettes sat young and strong at the bar, shouting challenges and insults, howling laughter and pounding backs, drinking straight Seagrams or Canadian Club with beer chasers.

The bartender shouted when O'Malley walked through the door. "Hey look, it's fuckin' Audie Murphy." O'Malley shook a dozen hands and drank two shots before he made his way across the room to shake his brother's hand.

"Welcome back, lawyer man."

"Thanks. Looks like you're doing well."

His brother shrugged. "Same as always. Lunch and Friday night. Otherwise I die." As he talked he worked, pouring the rye with his left hand, pulling the white stem over the beer keg with his right. The patrons kept their cash in front of them; most had an allowance from their wives and an uncashed check in their wallets. A few, the very old and very young, had wads of cash and no wife to give it to. They would be broke again by Monday. "So what's the word?" the bartender shouted over the din.

"It all worked out," O'Malley hollered back.

His brother brightened and slid a Jack Daniels down to him. At a break he came over with one of his own. They clicked glasses, the bar owner and the new lawyer, both doing well. "To California," his brother said. They drank and put the glasses down, then said nothing for awhile, drinking in the sounds of the celebration around them. The bartender was especially intent on the sounds.

"No need to wonder why you're going," he said.

O'Malley drove the Plymouth around to the other side of town. There was a half hour yet before she got out of work and he wanted to let the city wash over him again. It was dying, of course, as everyone knew. The factories were now old and unprofitable, kept alive only until the corporate parents could sell out or build others in places like North Carolina or Texas. Two centuries earlier, in the days of Alexander Hamilton and the Society for Useful Manufacture, the rivers had brought a flood of entrepreneurs and jobs. The wrong side of the Hudson had lived off that capital ever since. Now the city, indeed the region, was fast becoming an enormous industrial ghost town, the only new industry the service of the government-subsidized dark-faced poor.

And always the refineries. The ubiquitous, filthy refineries.

O'Malley was neither resentful nor mournful. The city was a parent and he loved it for that alone. And, like a visit to the grave of a long-dead parent, his time in the city was made pleasant by thoughts of the past. Equally pleasant was the reality that this graveyard would not be his.

The diner was in the good part of the city, meaning that the men who ate there were white. Because of that the parking lot was again sprinkled with Corvettes, the white boys' Cadillac. He lit a cigarette and waited for her in a dark corner of the concrete rectangle.

Her shift was over at midnight and she came bouncing down the stairs ten minutes later, smiling as the groups of men parted to let her through, throwing back a laughing reply to the hurried suggestions. Her shiny black uniform was slick and tight, the dark stockings appearing at mid-thigh and running down the slim exposed legs to heeled sandals. Purple tinted glasses sat precariously on top of her head; the brown leather bag trailed in her wake, occasionally tapping her round bottom suggestively as she pranced to the passenger side of the Plymouth. Elaine had always had a very clear idea of how to get a man to look at her.

O'Malley laughed as Elaine hurled herself across the vinyl seat to wrap his face in a deep, tongue-enhanced kiss. Her heels were still on the outside of the car, the inside light still shining brightly. O'Malley was trying to return the kiss and at the same time search for the now dropped, lit cigarette.

"Elaine," he began before getting cut off again. He was laughing through the kiss as the girl tried to wedge herself between his chest and the steering wheel. The horn sounded and he smelled burning vinyl. In the mirror he saw men pointing at the well-lit interior of the car.

"Elaine," he said again. "Wait . . . please, there're people watching."

"Where?" she asked excitedly. She broke the kiss and leaned to see through the back window, which at least stopped the horn from blowing. O'Malley used the respite to dispose of the cigarette. Elaine pouted. "They're too far away to see," she said.

"Look," O'Malley said quickly, "if you're a good girl and sit over on your side we'll go over to the park."

"And after that to your brother's place?" she bargained.

"Sure." O'Malley grinned and kissed her.

"O.K.," she said.

O'Malley could have driven to the spot in his sleep, which was fortunate. Elaine sat quietly on her side, as promised, making no effort to attack him as he drove. She used the time to good purpose, however, hiking the tight black skirt above her waist, squirming out of underclothes and stockings, folding the unneeded garments neatly into her purse. That done she started on the blouse, unbuttoning the clasps and letting the thin material fall away. O'Malley gripped the wheel tightly with both hands, trying to ignore the tension in his groin and the sudden desire to lurch to a stop at the side of the road. Once comfortably seminude, Elaine sat back smiling, enjoying immensely her effect on the driver.

6

At the park O'Malley was as ready as she was. He grabbed her hand and began walking hurriedly into the trees, her giggles trailing behind him in the night air. Once hidden he quickly stripped her of blouse and skirt, then backed her against the rough bark of a tree. He entered her like that, standing. In response to the lack of romance she bit hard into his thick shoulder.

"Ow, goddamn it, Elaine," he complained, but didn't stop his thrusts.

Elaine relented and wrapped her arms around his neck and her legs around his waist, pulling him close into her breasts. "Benjo, that feels great. I can't believe how much I missed you. It's been a week. And I've been *so* good you wouldn't believe it." As punishment for the obvious lie he began rubbing her bare skin against the tree.

"It's true," she protested. "All the guys say so." A moment later they both lost interest in the debate.

Afterward he carried her still squirming body to the grass. He lay beside her, rubbing her breasts with his right hand. She took the hand and examined it, then began licking the top of the one-inch stub.

"I love this little guy," she said. "Tell me again how many Viet Congs you got."

She was teasing again; she knew the story well. She was the first at St. Albans on Long Island when he was carried back. She and the old man, still in his work blues. The old man held his bandaged hand and walked next to the rolling bed into the operating room. Elaine, overcome with patriotism, stayed in the ward to give succor to as many of the wounded as time permitted.

"If someone's not careful, someone's going to find her bare ass up against that tree again."

"What'd I do," she complained. "It's just that I was so proud. A hero. And all those medals." They both laughed. There was no medal. And no Viet Cong. Just seventy-two hours as an S.P. in Saigon. Then his first ride on assignment with his pretty new armband, a Saturday night spent cruising the ubiquitous bars. He had stopped the jeep officiously when

7

he saw the metal table fly through the closed second-story window and had grabbed baton and hat when he saw the Marines dangling the hooker by her feet through the jangled shards of the former window. What he never saw or heard was the live grenade. He remembered staring dumbly as his partner leapt screaming into the brackish gutter water. The next thing he remembered was vomiting in a C-130 heading east.

There was a nice legal question of whether he was entitled to a Purple Heart for getting blown up by the Marines, and ultimately it was decided it would hurt morale to decorate Americans made casualties by their countrymen. But that wasn't important. What was important was the right hand. No index finger, no force. No blues like the old man's. Instead, blues like the guys with the Corvettes wore. He did it for a year, in the factory across from his brother's bar, a year of transforming flat sheet metal into round cans. A year of Elaine's body and free Jack Daniels. At the end of the year he made a vow to the Virgin Mary that he would never again feed his face with the labor of his hands.

"Be happy," he said to Elaine. "It's all worked out for the best."

"That's right," she said, firmly and proudly. "You're gonna get out of here."

The sign over the bar was dark by the time they got back. All the Corvettes were gone from the parking lot. Inside his brother was trying to lead the hard-core drunks to the door. There was the usual complaining, like that of children being sent to bed. Two went easily. The third, as happened every night, refused, claimed his change had been stolen, and threw a punch. O'Malley didn't interfere; his brother was a compassionate man. The punch landed on a chest that didn't give. Shaken, the man retreated, now sober with fear. O'Malley's brother wrapped him in a friendly embrace and led the sobbing drunk to the door.

Elaine stood on tiptoes and gave the bartender a genuine, sisterly kiss.

"You're a nice guy, you know that, Terry."

He grinned. "If I hurt that man I lose half my gross."

"Sure," Elaine said.

They sat at the bar, now a family, and drank Jack Daniels while O'Malley told his tale. Elaine and Terry listened intently, the way prisoners must listen to the fancy plans of a short timer. That O'Malley would someday, now soon, be a lawyer was old news. That he would live in California was a different sort of plan. They made him repeat himself over and over, as though by hearing it again they might make sense out of it. It was the how and the what that interested them. They all knew the why, or thought they did. Of course none of them, including O'Malley, had ever seen the place.

When the questions were done O'Malley poured another Jack Daniels and looked at Elaine. She was staring at her image in the glass, happy in a dream. She was not going to go, but it hadn't been said yet.

"Elaine," he said.

She looked up from her reverie.

"You can come with me, you know."

She smiled and kissed him. "Is that what you want?"

"Sure," he lied.

She was happy at that. Her eyes were down and she was playing with her glass.

"There's something I have to tell you."

"O.K."

"It's about Joey."

"Joey," O'Malley said. "You mean Joey De Mica? Little Joey? My best friend in all the world? That Joey?" O'Malley suddenly knew it was all going to come out fine.

"Yes. Joey told me to see you tonight. And to be as nice to you as . . ." She looked at Terry and grinned, ". . . as I've ever been."

"And why would little Joey be in a position to tell you what to do, Elaine?" O'Malley stood up and began rolling up his sleeves. Terry took the sap from under the bar and walked around next to her, tapping the wood against his palm. She was now surrounded by well over four hundred pounds of

O'Malleys. "Because . . . because we . . . we got married Tuesday night."

She sprinted squealing for help but the brothers tackled her, wrestling her to the floor with congratulatory kisses.

3

O'Malley arrived in Los Angeles in late summer, that dream-killer time when the desert sun cooks the upper atmosphere to a temperature higher than that of the air on the ground. The superheated air acts as a lid, joined by the equally impenetrable barriers of the northern mountains and eastern desert. With no place to go the air sits motionless, a breeze simply a wintertime memory. But temperature inversion is only the first of the city's problems. Millions of badly tuned internal combustion engines continuously produce nitric oxide to join the trapped oxygen. Then an unusual photochemical reaction with the beaming sun lets the residents see the air they breathe. If it weren't so lethal, the combination would be one of the wonders of the world.

O'Malley's DC–10 seemed to buckle when it hit the brown lid, then slid through it like a spoon through pudding. Once under the chocolate top the plane entered a whiteout of horizon-to-horizon haze. At about five hundred feet it was possible to make out some surface features, primarily vast tracts of undifferentiated single-family houses sometimes relieved by a few blocks of tall buildings, always crisscrossed by wide, linear, fifty-mile boulevards and highways. This is already different from the dream, O'Malley thought as he followed his four hundred fellow New Yorkers gasping and weeping to the baggage line.

He wasn't naive, of course. He had read of the city, of it's environs, and of Jenkins & Dorman. The history was fascinating and unnerving.

Easterners have no notion of how new the West is. In 1870, when Lincoln was long buried, the Civil War won, and the North full steam into an industrial revolution, Los Angeles had a population of 5,614, 80 percent Mexican. California had been a U.S. possession for only twenty-two years, and LA was little more than a booze-and-whore desert town.

It took time for the white man to discover the outback, and when he did so he quickly eliminated the resident Spanish elite. In so doing he found most helpful the skills of two young criminal lawyers who shared space in a converted livery stable on the town's one legitimate street. When the white man came to Los Angeles, Albert Lee Jenkins and Jeremiah Dorman were there to serve.

The first whites to immigrate were embittered and disillusioned Southerners fleeing the demise of a slave economy and the unaccustomed egalitarianism of Reconstruction. They enlisted the aid of refugees from the San Francisco Vigilante Committees and set about taking over. There was some resistance, of course, but lynchings were common sport and good politics besides. The Chinese massacre of 1871 slaughtered twenty-five men, women, and children in a single night of rape, looting, and murder, and resistance to the newcomers became quiescent.

Control of government was worthless without control of the three items that would dominate southern California's politics for fifty years: land, water, and the rails. The first task was securing the railroad, without which LA would remain a farm town doomed to dominance by the land-grant rancheros. The railroad demanded over a million dollars in tribute, an impossible sum for a barrio town to raise. Dorman led the prorailroad forces. On the morning of the election on the bond issue, his vigilante horsemen took to the streets. The Mexicans were herded into corrals and led to the polls like steer. Included were the daughters of the Spanish rancheros with land holdings adjacent to the proposed right-of-way, although they weren't brought there to vote. By evening the bond issue had been approved overwhelmingly, and in an unprecedented civic gesture, the antirailroad Spanish had dedicated the tracts of land necessary to close the deal.

The trains brought people; the people, wealth. Each added to the coffers of J & D. By 1885 a thousand people a day were pouring into the town and the little pueblo began its first real estate boom-and-bust cycle. The two young partners profited at all levels, selling to the newcomers during the boom, foreclosing the mortgages for their bank clients during the bust. By 1890 the population was 130,000 and Jenkins and Dorman were, with the exception of the railroad and the Spanish, the largest landholders south of the Tehachapies.

Third was not good enough. The firm, now swollen to the unheard-of size of twelve lawyers, made good use of the depression of 1893. Through Dorman's control of the political machine, property tax ordinances were passed, taxes that the appraisers made sure did not affect the holdings of either Mr. Dorman or Mr. Jenkins. The rancheros stood it for awhile, but by the turn of the century even their vast wealth, diminished by depression and taxation, proved insufficient. The breakup began. Jenkins, the financial genius, was there to pick up the pieces, some through foreclosure, some through probate and estate challenges.

Neither Jenkins nor Dorman lived to see the results of their labors. In 1908, for reasons described in the *Los Angeles Times* only as "financial and personal," the two partners and their seconds met in a cattle pasture on what had formerly been a rancho known as San Fernando. Jenkins was still taking the obligatory ten steps when Dorman shot him. Jenkins' second, one Mr. Blanton, then shot Mr. Dorman. Dorman's political machine, incensed at the cutting down of their leader, tried and convicted Mr. Blanton and he was hanged in Spring Street in 1909.

Dorman and Jenkins died childless but not without progeny. The firm continued, battling with Mr. Gibson's firm and Mr. O'Melveny's firm for dominance. J & D's champion was Theodore Duff, who had never set foot in a law school in his life, nor a college for that matter. He "read" for the law under Jenkins' tutelage and was admitted to the bar by acclamation in 1907 at the age of forty-eight. Duff was a businessman, exclusively concerned with natural resources: oil, gas, land, water. Under Duff's guidance water came to Los Angeles to cool the oil derricks, and the second great boom began.

Oil, gas, water, land, and munitions were lucrative. But there was yet another way to make money. At the time of his death Jenkins was fully into the process of enticing moving picture makers to move to Los Angeles, the primary attraction being proximity to the Mexican border in case of injunction or criminal prosecution arising from stolen films. J & D represented the studios from the beginning, and through their advice and counsel the studios dominated all aspects of the industry by 1930. When television came it wasn't a threat, just another client.

Just as sons of rumrunners become president, remembering the parent with fondness born of the flattering cloud of time, so too did Jenkins & Dorman ultimately become a symbol of gray, somber professionalism. Its new leaders, children during the early days, recalled their founders in huge, sentimental oil renderings in reception areas. Neither J & D nor the city of Los Angeles ever looked back. By 1970, a mere sixty-one years after the hanging of Mr. Blanton, LA had become the third largest city in the United States, sporting a population of almost three million and controlling a population three times that large. Its metropolitan area sprawled over eighty-eight thousand square kilometers, four times the size of the state of New Jersey.

J & D did almost as well, swelling to three hundred lawyers and presiding over all financial affairs west of Chicago from the top fourteen floors of a fifty-story downtown bank building. The city spread west to the ocean, north and east to the mountains, south to the headquarters of white supremacy known as Orange County. Those who pursued the manifest destiny of the city tried to wrench the financial center with them, but J & D was an anchor. It profited from the cancerous growth, and though certainly a little upset when Spring Street, its ancestral home, turned into skid row, it never released its hold on the city's innards but simply picked up its skirts and moved a few blocks from the drunks and the Mexicans, creating a new downtown from the rubble of urban decay, acting as a lightning rod to bring the money back. And back it came. In floods. In a decade LA had its first skyline, dozens of bank buildings radiating financial power from the J & D nucleus. The challenge to its authority had strengthened it. The white shoes and white faces had moved south. The western Wall Street stayed where it had always been.

Randall Elliott Marks sat behind a lucite slab the size of a billiard table with his head buried in his phone messages, occasionally grunting and crumbling one up, otherwise silently placing them in stacks on colored spikes surrounding his multibuttoned phone. He studiously avoided meeting the gaze of the large, red-haired young man sitting motionless in a cane-backed chair across the room. O'Malley had been sitting in that chair for a full half hour now and was starting to get a little sick of it.

That morning he had driven into the bowels of the bank building to the Mercedes dealership that passed for the J & D parking area. From there he had stepped into the private elevator with five identically dressed males for the rocket ride to the forty-eighth floor. It was an instructive elevator ride. Talking was apparently forbidden, but there was a stance that seemed to be required: eyes up watching the flashing numbers, both hands holding briefcase square to the body. Then at the destination a rush to flatten against the wall so the partner in the back could get off first.

He had walked off the elevator into a black marble and mahogany antechamber, lit only by the glare of arc lights trained on gargantuan oils of the founders, each looking young and virile behind black, bushy, turn-of-the-century handlebars. Beneath the oils a strict receptionist sat behind a curved counter inlaid with blinking electronic equipment. She had stared at him with an insolence born of trifling authority. He had become immediately irritated.

"Name?"

"O'Malley, Benjamin A., not in that order." She began fumbling through a list. Then she raised her head.

"You're late."

"Pardon?"

"You're late. The letter from the employment committee asked that you arrive at eight-thirty. It is now eight thirty-five."

"I see. Well, I apologize. Promise you won't report me to the other receptionists." Her eyes got narrow, and her head cocked a little to the side.

"Why don't you just have a seat, Mr. O'Malley, and I'll *see* if Mr. Marks is *still* available."

"Sure." He sat down, picked up *Forbes,* and tried to concentrate on an article about how Saddam Hussein was eventually going to take over the world. He didn't know then that Iraq was a J & D client.

After a time someone named Mildred came out and led O'Malley past a succession of offices to the great man's corner suite. Then it was time to sit quietly again, this time without his magazine, while Marks silently instructed him on the differences between them.

It gave O'Malley time to study the man. He knew of course that Marks was one of the great Brahmans at J & D, a true brother in the fraternity of the powerful: member of the Management Committee; gold share partner; member of the boards of an aerospace company, the largest bank in the world, an oil company, a steel company, and a host of mediocre enterprises, meaning a standing lower than twenty-five on the *Fortune* list. *The Wall Street Journal* had done three feature pieces on Marks in the past year, each beginning the same way: "Randall Marks, powerful securities specialist at the prestigious West Coast law firm of . . . etc." Like the Ways and Means Committee, Marks was never mentioned without a prefatory reference to power.

O'Malley had to admit that the man fit the metaphor. Marks was elegantly tall, six-four or more, with a well-nourished plumpness that looks ridiculous when a man is naked and prosperous when the excess flesh is encased in the expensive tailoring Marks favored. The eyes were clear and blue, seemingly picked from a display case to dispel any notion that the surname denoted unacceptable roots. The lines of the face were appropriate, as if they'd been penned in by a service. They ran as streams from an ice cap of academically disheveled white hair.

When O'Malley tired of playing with his tie, he tried clearing his throat, then coughing, any sound to get Marks' attention. Marks raised his head when the hacking reached tubercular proportions.

"Are you ill, Brent?"

"Ben. And no, sir. Just a bit of a frog in the throat, I suppose."

Marks obviously wanted to go back to work but then seemed to decide that there was no graceful way to do it. "Well, let's get you a sip of water before we begin." He touched a buzzer and Mildred was at his side before his finger had left the button.

"Mildred, a little water for Mr. O'Malley and I'll have my morning cup. Will yours be black, Brent?"

"Ben, and regular water's fine, thanks." O'Malley smiled back at their stupefied stares, pleased that he was able to carry it off so far, only slowly realizing the obvious. "I mean . . . on the water that is . . . uh, regular's fine. On the coffee, uh, black's fine, too." Marks' mouth and eyes were wide but he recovered, flicking an imperious index finger at the door. Mildred fled from the room like she was filling the lane on a fast break. Marks went back to his little green slips of paper.

Mildred had the water in and out of O'Malley's hands with the finesse of a pickpocket. The water was replaced by a lovely bone China cup and saucer. O'Malley was trying to balance everything on his knee when Marks deigned again to speak.

For a half hour Marks held forth, talking from a script, explaining the hours required, the salary offered, the performance expected. The speech was meant to intimidate and it worked to some degree. Marks' message was simple. To exist in his company at all was an honor. To remain would require nothing less than the undiluted dedication of all waking hours.

When he finished the speech, he buzzed again for Mildred. "I think we're ready for Mr. Evans now."

Mildred left and was soon replaced by an anemic-looking guy with bad skin. He stood in the doorway with his hands folded and smiled, perfectly comfortable with the fact that Marks was now ignoring him, too. He kept that pose until Marks saw fit to raise his head.

"Mr. Evan Evans, I'd like you to meet Mr. Benjamin O'Malley. This is Mr. O'Malley's first day with us and I'd like you to take responsibility for showing him about."

"Yes, sir. I'll take care of it." Evan Evans. Lord, give me strength, O'Malley prayed. Evan Evans extended a hand limp and cool to the touch.

Marks now moved on to his dismissal speech. "Brent, I'm glad we've had the opportunity to talk and I hope it's been helpful. Feel free to stop in any time you have any questions. Remember, we have an open-door policy at J and D and I'd like you to consider me your, ah"—his mind began fighting the concept—"friend and confidante." He seemed to shiver a little at the thought.

In the hall Evan Evans' head was bobbing in wonderment. "Quite a guy, our Randall, isn't he? They just don't make them like that anymore."

"Yeah, they must have thrown away the mold after they made old Randall," O'Malley agreed.

Evans began nodding excitedly. "And this place is filled with people like Randall. You'll see. It's what makes it so interesting."

"I'm sure," O'Malley said. "Look, I've heard all the recruitment speeches. Why don't you tell me about the geography. I understand there's more than just this one floor."

Evans laughed. "That's right. We couldn't very well fit all these eggs into one little basket. Ha, ha."

"Ha, ha."

"We actually occupy seventeen floors," Evans explained. "That's if you count the computer people, accounting, and the word processing center. The lawyers have fourteen floors, from thirty-five to forty-nine, with our evening restaurant on fifty and our informal dining on ten. All the floors are the same: receptionist area at the private elevator exits; senior partners in the corners, executive offices they're called; junior partners next to them, in the ambassador offices; then the senior associates, in the collegiate offices; and finally the junior associates like yourself in the . . ."

"In the stalls in the head, right?"

Evans shook his head seriously. "No, at the end of each wing, in the standard offices." He flapped a skinny hand at each one. "Lawyers on the outside, with windows. Secretaries and paralegals in the clerical wall. Each floor houses a different department: general securities, tax, probate, general litigation, labor, entertainment, government bonds, antitrust, government contracts, real estate, debentures, commercial paper, and some others I'm probably forgetting. Anyway there're fourteen all told, each on its own floor. Are you okay? You look a little pale."

"No, I'm okay, just overwhelmed by the glamour of it all. Tell me more."

"Well, as you know, new associates are assigned to work in one of those departments. After awhile you'll move to another, just so you get to meet and work with as many people as possible. Then on to another and so on."

"How long does that go on?"

"About four years."

"Four what?!"

"Four years for the orientation program. Then you'll be asked to join a department and from there it's just a straight shot to partnership."

"And how long does that take?"

"Ten years, give or take. For a junior partner, that is. But I'm sure you've been told all this."

O'Malley was trying unsuccessfully to stop his eyes from rolling backward. "Who decides which of these departments I work in?"

"Your choice. As long as it's consistent with the needs of J and D, of course."

"I see. That kind of choice." The remark was lost on Evans. O'Malley had never really paid much attention to these details during those lovely dinners at The Palace. It wasn't much more important now. Except Evans took it so seriously.

"So let me understand this," O'Malley said. "Four years of orientation, which I assume means carrying briefcases and making coffee. Then six years in a slot doing God knows what kind of work. And then . . ." He hesitated. The concept was staggering.

Evans shook his head sympathetically. "It's a very sad thing. Nine out of ten people who arrive will be asked to leave in the tenth year. As Randall likes to put it, it's 'ten and up or ten and out.' Of course the ones who leave do very well elsewhere."

"Oh yeah? Like what?"

"They're usually picked up by one of our clients and join a corporate legal department."

"How exciting. Maybe they can even get into the debenture department, whatever that is." What a system, O'Malley thought. It was no surprise that Evans was such a toady. Nevertheless, it still didn't matter. A year, maybe two, and he'd know the territory well enough to get out and find something worthwhile. They'd get their money's worth, he'd make sure of that. But that ten-year tricky track was insanity. He glanced up from his thoughts to find Evan Evans looking slightly hurt.

"I'm in the debenture department," he said.

At noon Evan Evans took him to the private elevator again and they dropped like a brick to the tenth floor. Lunch introduced a refinement to the required elevator posture; those not carrying briefcases could fold their hands decorously over the crotch. At ten the doors opened like a stage curtain and they emerged onto a deep, maroon pile rug supporting fifty white-draped tables, each set with gleaming crystal and china. Black and brown attendants scurried around placing flower arrangements at each table.

"This is our informal lunch room," Evans explained. "Another opportunity to let our hair down and meet the lawyers from other departments."

O'Malley could tell this wasn't going to be any fun either. The elevator doors kept opening and closing, disgorging more and more dark suits. Evans took him over to the table to meet some of his debenture pals. O'Malley grabbed a chair in the corner.

"Hi. I'm Harrison Adams," a voice boomed. O'Malley looked up to see a beefy hand. He shook that and the nine others that were offered. Each hand was attached to a man with a first name that should have been a last.

After the introductions he was free to hide again, this time behind the large, gold-embossed menu. Of the three hundred people in the room there were only four blacks that weren't serving food. And about the same number of women. At one point the elevator opened and a tan, taut, attractive woman emerged, obviously self-assured, easily chatting with various of the diners as she worked the room on her way to her table. Mr. Adams of the booming voice grinned and whispered to the man next to him. The woman continued on, oblivious to the insult. O'Malley was sure it was hard for her here.

But O'Malley had his own problems. His only anchor in this sea of dark suits was Evan Evans, and that was a most insecure mooring. Evans had been conscripted and tomorrow he'd be gone. O'Malley would have to face this room alone every day, thinking of clever things to chat about with people like Marks and Adams. But it really didn't matter, he told himself. The year or two would fly by and they could remember him as that quiet guy who missed lunch a lot. That pleasant dream was shattered by Adams' booming voice.

"So how are you liking it so far?"

O'Malley looked up to see eighteen eyeballs staring in his direction. He had a paranoic vision of six hundred more doing the same. "Fine, thanks." They all waited expectantly. O.K., something clever. "J and D seems to be a very, uh . . ." A very what? ". . . well-furnished and large law firm." Brilliant. Everybody squinted slightly.

"Did you say 'well-furnished'?" Adams asked.

That was obviously wrong. No one called a law firm well-furnished. "No, I said 'well-burnished,' " O'Malley explained. He heard menus dropping all over the table. Don't panic, he told himself. "You know, well-polished. The stairs and chandeliers, for example. Very shiny. Most impressive."

The waiter came and took the orders. Adams ordered his meal without taking his eyes off O'Malley. When the man left, Adams leaned on the table. His voice could be heard all over the room.

"So, Ben, tell us a little about yourself."

O'Malley looked up at the smiling face. Adams was playing games.

"Well, I got out in '71," O'Malley said.

"From law school, you mean."

O'Malley shook his head and took a bite of lettuce. "Prison." Adams laughed heartily and the rest of the table, after an instant's hesitation, did the same. O'Malley munched stone-faced. "I'll always be grateful to J and D for this opportunity," he said sincerely. "It's progressive programs like this that enable inmates to make a fresh start in life." He looked intently into Adams' face, which wasn't laughing any more. "I just hope I'm equal to the challenge."

"That's impossible," Adams said. "What were you in prison for?" The question was softly stated.

"The usual. Armed robbery, assault, cunnilingus with a minor." O'Malley put his hands on the table where Adams could see them. The hands looked like the hands of a felon. "That last one was a bad rap, though. We were in love." He opened his mangled hands apologetically. "How was I to know she was twelve years old?" The eighteen eyes were now wide with horror. Evan Evans began surreptitiously moving his chair.

"I don't believe it," Adams said, the voice now angry, the game going the wrong way. "Where were you in prison?"

"Trenton," O'Malley said. "That's in New Jersey." Then he started telling them about prison, which wasn't hard. When little Joey De Mica went off to college he went to Trenton State so that he could be close to his brother Dominic. Dominic was matriculating at another Trenton State, the one where they called the dean "warden." O'Malley and Joey would visit Dominic whenever possible; it was exciting and Dominic could tell great tales. As O'Malley told the same tales to Adams and his pals he saw, incredibly, belief register in their eyes. O'Malley decided to keep his money out of debentures.

O'Malley was prevented from further entertainment by the arrival of a latecomer, a white-haired, distinguished-looking man. The nine debenture people forgot about prison and leapt to their feet until the old guy sat down. Then everyone's voice changed. The tone became obviously, affectedly formal and the words became polysyllabic. No one talked to anyone but the newcomer.

The white-haired guy seemed to enjoy the sycophantism, thanked the group for the kind welcome, and embarked on a little speech on something called reverse triangular mergers, an issue of great moment in the world of debentures. When he stopped he smiled, and everyone nodded, gazing at him with great affection and respect. Then each of the debenture-adventurers talked on the subject and the conversation be-

22

came—O'Malley couldn't believe it—*spirited*. But at least they left him alone.

The chattering became a buzz, then a drone, finally simply a background hum. The faces in the room blurred too, dissolving like a movie fade. Except for one. As O'Malley quietly ate he watched her—the woman from the elevator. Her eyes and lips were animated, yet serene and confident. She talked and listened, cocking her head a little to the side at this one, smiling at that one. Once she raised her head and met his look through the sea of dissolved faces. Her eyes flattened for an instant. Not reproving, just quizzical. Then a man touched her arm and her gaze returned to her table.

4

Because he was new he watched and listened closely to the city. Like many before him he found the city to be a dissembler, a tease. But illusions are for tourists. Those who live in Los Angeles are not long deceived.

The first illusion to go was the illusion of community. Los Angeles County is nothing more than a loose political union of towns—disparate, frequently small, geographically isolated by mountain and desert. Some—like Beverly Hills, Watts, the San Fernando Valley—are stereotypes of distinct classes of economic life. Others, twenty or fifty others, are anonymous. They share three things: transient residents, the Board of Supervisors, and an almost complete lack of information about one another.

But that was an easy illusion. Others are insidious and the ultimate loss horrible.

The travel brochures show the lovely waves crashing on hundreds of miles of broad, free public beaches. Pretty young bodies, healthy and strong, lie on the sand twelve months a year. But the millions have already fouled the waves. In one year in the 1970s five Santa Monica lifeguards contracted leukemia.

The local politicians pride themselves on the relative honesty and competence of elected officials. The judiciary is liberal, intelligent, and progressive. The illusion is a well-run, crime-free, major urban area. The reality is a per capita homicide rate that is the highest in the country. The reality is a city whose police annually kill more citizens than do the police of any other city in the land.

Then there is the climate, the warm Mediterranean-like sun. The reality is the air, the filthy air. The year 1962 was the worst, the records show. In that year there were two hundred days when visibility was less than three miles.

Perversely, once the illusions were stripped away O'Malley began to like the place a bit more. It was more like home.

For one year O'Malley lived and worked uneventfully, becoming expert at the pleasures of the city, otherwise beavering noiselessly if unenthusiastically at the dreary tasks J & D offered. That first year passed effortlessly for him: He didn't get indicted for anything and not a single client was murdered. All that began to change around the fourteenth month. He was again in the familiar, straight-backed chair and Mildred was again slipping him a cup. After the obligatory fifteen minutes of silence Marks looked up.

"Ah, Brent, so nice to see you again."

O'Malley remembered to be polite. "Ben. And thank you."

"Quite so," Marks agreed. Then his eyes were down again and his hands were fumbling through the cards.

"Brent, the reason I've asked you in is because we'd like you to accept another assignment in the securities department. It involves a relatively minor acquisition for one of our medium-sized clients."

O'Malley stiffened. In the year at J & D he had worked for Marks twice and each time had liked the man less. The first time he wrote off his dislike as irritation at Marks' pretentions. During the second project, preparing an annual report for an aerospace company, O'Malley realized that Marks was a very dishonest man.

The aerospace job should have been simple, tedious but simple. Go into the bowels of the corporate file room, Marks had ordered, and check to see whether all the formalities have been complied with. O'Malley did as he was told, ready to scream with boredom but remembering that the way out was a simple walk to the door, getting closer with each passing day. But as it turned out the files weren't boring at all. As he hacked through the foreign military aircraft files, he came upon a thick one, carefully indexed, marked simply, "Cumshaw." It had no stamped serial number and looked as if it had landed in the open files by accident. Inside, separated by country, cross-referenced by individual recipient, was a concise history of twenty years of bribery and corruption, all as yet unmentioned in the company's glossy annual report.

O'Malley checked out the file and laid it on Marks' desk. Marks never even opened it; he just looked at the title and thanked O'Malley for his care and attention. The next day O'Malley was given a litigation assignment that took him to Spokane, Washington, for sixty days.

Six months after O'Malley's meeting with Marks a general sales manager named Ralph Parks testified before the Senate Foreign Relations Committee that for years he had been making "questionable payments" to overseas consultants in order to sell military aircraft. Marks, on behalf of the company, expressed "shock and dismay" at the revelations and announced an immediate internal investigation. The investigation concluded that Parks, undergoing personal problems, had acted alone. Marks issued a press release announcing that Parks had been terminated.

"Something wrong, Brent?"

"Not a thing, sir." What could be said.

"You'll be reporting to Ms. Radnowski, a senior associate officed on the thirty-seventh floor."

"Really!" That made all the difference in the world.

Marks raised his eyebrows slightly at the unexpected enthusiasm but went on. "She will tell you all the details about the client and the specific transaction you'll be working on. As I say, it's only a moderate-sized client and this is a fairly routine divestiture of a subsidiary. I'm sure that after a brief period of familiarization you will be free to devote some percentage of your time to matters you may consider more, ah, desirable."

They locked eyes for a moment, and the look said all that could be said. Yet for some perverse reason O'Malley thought the situation was funny. Here was Marks trying for all the world to maintain the appearance of propriety. But they both knew! Knew all about poor Parks and the Cumshaw file. O'Malley couldn't hide a smile. It was so funny to him that they both knew that it was a game. The fact that Marks stared back at him stone-faced just sent him into most impolite giggles.

5

She was always known at the firm as "Rad," and every male in the building whose blood was still moving knew exactly who she was. Rad was thirty-five and had become, through dint of relentless effort, one of the most important women in

Los Angeles. Now, after nine and a half years at J & D she was on the verge of breaking through that very special barrier that had traditionally separated the merely successful from the truly powerful, the one that for over a century had required every partner in the institution to have a white penis And Rad wasn't going to slide under the gate as a probate or family lawyer, gently leading the recently bereaved or divorced through the minefield of postcrisis procedure. Rad was a securities specialist like Marks. Her days were spent in boardrooms advising the powerful. No one had the slightest idea where she spent her nights.

The rap on Rad was predictable: icy, cold, asexual, ambitious, probably screwing the entire Management Committee if it got her an inch of ground. O'Malley didn't buy any of it. For almost a decade the woman had lived in a fishbowl and was smart enough to keep her private life out of public view. Rad was also an intimidating presence, and in O'Malley's mind the tales were told because the young lions were, at bottom, simply afraid of her.

O'Malley was as bitten as any of the others, but to him her strength and presence were great sexual assets. She also had a lot more. She wasn't a beautiful woman in any rosy-cheeked sense. She was no longer nineteen years old and didn't look like it. Nevertheless, she exuded sensuality. The eyes and face had the look of an experienced woman. The body was tight, tan, and athletic, kept in top form by constant exercise yet retaining a female roundness that no amount of jogging or strict, tailored business suits could hide. More than simply looks, however, Rad had a style that was commanding and graceful. She moved well, spoke well, and saw the world through laugh-lined, sparkling gray eyes.

She was just getting off the phone when O'Malley was ushered in for the first time. She held out her hand and shook vigorously, then pointed to a chair. "I take it you've met Marks, so there's no need for me to talk about the school colors. I'm also sure you've been told absolutely nothing about this case."

O'Malley nodded and tried to think of work and not how

nicely her voice went with her eyes. "That's right. He just said it was a matter that shouldn't take too much time."

"That's sort of true," she said. "This deal is easy enough. The client itself is anything but simple."

"What do you mean?"

She reached behind her and picked up a ten-inch sheaf of paper and dropped it in front of O'Malley. "Here's my working file. I'll give you a narrative now but it's important for you to become familiar with this. There's a whole roomful of paper on this company in the file area but this has all the important documents." She paused and looked at O'Malley. "Forget whatever Marks told you. For your own protection become as familiar as you can with this client."

The tone and expression were ominous. O'Malley was surprised to have his impressions of Marks validated so quickly. He resolved to be very, very careful around anything that touched the man. "O.K., I will. What can you tell me about it now?"

"Everything. Although today I'll keep it straight and simple. The client is Associated Computer Research, Incorporated, or ACR, as it's usually known. It's a new company that has grown at an astounding rate over the last decade. It began as a simple computer servicing operation and now has a spot on the Big Board. It's a totally diversified enterprise with a piece of anything that will stand still long enough to be grabbed."

O'Malley began scribbling furiously. "Who are the founders? They must be impressive."

"The founders are, or were, two young research engineers by the names of James Hardwick and Allen Friedrich. They've been together forever, same hometown, roommates at college, that sort of thing. They're an inseparable pair and everyone refers to them collectively as 'the boys.' After graduate school they both went to work for Brandon Electronics Federation, which as you may or may not know is on the verge of becoming the biggest in the country. After two years with BEF they went over the side to start ACR. Only they left with more than their slide rules."

"What did they take? Money?"

"No, something much more important. Drawings and plans for the next generation of computer peripheral equipment. It's never been proved, but the allegation is that they copied everything that wasn't made of wood. Customer lists, patent specifications, budget analyses, the works."

"Is it true? The allegations, I mean."

She shrugged. "Let me just tell the story for now. I think when I'm through you'll be able to guess my opinion."

"O.K. So what did BEF do?"

"Nothing at first. Threw them a nice party and wished them well. Six months later they got the announcement of the opening of ACR. They thought it was a big joke. The Chairman of the Board even wrote a memo about it." She went fishing in the ten-inch stack. "Here it is. It's supposed to be funny." O'Malley took it and read it quickly. It had all the earmarks of a very embarrassing document for BEF.

CONFIDENTIAL
MEMORANDUM

Date: January 26, 1969
From: D. Hensley
To: Board Distribution
Subject: Operation CRUSH

As you are all aware, agenda item 69–24 represents BEF with the most significant challenge faced in the fifty-five-year history of the corporation.

I'm troubled by the lack of respect given this most important matter. Board discussions and memoranda discussing this issue are uniformly void of positive responses to this assault on our walls.

For the past fifty-five years this corporation has enjoyed a well-earned position as the number one domestic supplier of electronic devices to American business. From the adding machine to the floating magnetic head we have led the field; we invent, others copy.

Are we now to sit back and become complacent, watching while our profits flow like the mighty Mississippi into the coffers of ACR? Who are these upstarts who would invade our territory and pillage our fields? Who among us will explain to the stockholders of BEF that we must turn the keys of our domain over to Messrs. Hardwick and Friedrich, gentlemen who but one year ago were not entitled to the keys to the washroom.

No, I say, a thousand times no! We will fight them in the basement parking lot, in the first-floor tobacco shop, in the third-floor cafeteria, in the ninth-floor washroom, even in the forty-second-floor boardroom (although all personnel should be aware that the table in the boardroom is quite expensive and should not be scratched in the fray). All personnel are on notice that these interlopers must be driven into the sea. We will destroy them by means fair or foul. Our efforts, our very lives and honor, must be devoted to the cause.

He handed it back to her. "Not only is it not funny, it's not very smart."

She nodded. "It was probably the biggest mistake Hensley ever made. Anyway BEF wasn't laughing for long. In the fourth quarter of 1969, ACR announced a joint venture with a major West German manufacturing firm. The press reported the Germans would contribute quote an undisclosed amount of cash end quote and the boys would contribute quote certain technical material end quote."

"The Germans were buying the stolen documents, in other words."

Rad shrugged. It was too obvious to say out loud.

"Anyway, things got really interesting after that," she continued. "A year later, that would be the fourth quarter of 1970, ACR announced its first full product line. Not only in the press. But also in a beautiful brochure mailed to every BEF customer."

O'Malley nodded. "They got the customers from the stolen customer list, of course. And I assume their product line was identical to that of BEF."

She smiled. "Good guess. But it was better than that. First, BEF hadn't even announced yet. Second, the ACR line was actually cheaper, by about twenty-five percent. That's because ACR's only cost was the Xerox charges. Third, and most important, the ACR line was better than anything BEF had on the drawing board. With the boys' drawings and the Germans' engineering expertise, ACR had actually improved on the unimprovable." She paused for a moment. "So tell me, Ben, what do you think happens when a company markets a product that's technically superior and significantly cheaper than the nearest competitor's?"

"They sell a lot of widgets."

"Exactly so. ACR took off like a rocket and has never looked back."

She fumbled again through the stack and came up with a sheet of paper. "By the first quarter of 1972, ACR was reporting quarterly sales of thirty-seven and a half million dollars and was listed on the Big Board. BEF had lost twenty-nine-point-eight percent of its market share in the western United States and was trading at fifty-six, off from its 1969 high of eighty-seven. ACR was a go-go glamour stock and was trading at twenty-one times earnings." She dropped the paper on her desk. "So what happens next, O'Malley?"

"BEF goes to the cops?"

"No. Cops have enough trouble catching robbers. Their eyes glaze over at words like 'patent specifications' and 'quarterly earnings.' No, BEF sued ACR, which is something they should have done much earlier." She pulled out the complaint, which looked to be about an inch thick. "This tells the whole story. What it boils down to is a suit for about a hundred million dollars. That's when ACR became a client of J and D."

"Why J and D? I thought J and D only represented the big boys."

She shrugged again. "Who knows. They were Marks' cli-

31

ents from the start. Nobody's bothered to ask how that happened for a long time now."

"Well, I'm sure Marks has never been in a courtroom in his life. He didn't represent them, did he?"

"He didn't. Do you know Armington Bishop?"

"Sure." Bishop was a firm institution, one of the most famous corporate trial lawyers in the country. With each new administration Bishop was rumored as first in line for a Cabinet post or a spot on the Supreme Court. He hadn't gotten either yet, but everybody assumed that it was only a matter of time. Bishop was a quiet man—mild-mannered, soft-spoken, and slightly effete. He was said to approach every case the same, big and small, like a hungry cat happening upon a disabled antelope.

"Marks and Bishop go way back together," Rad went on, "back to Harvard in the late 1940s, I think. So when Marks asked his old pal to take it on, Bishop was delighted. I was a mere slip of a girl fresh out of law school at the time and was assigned as the corporate liaison on the case. It was quite a show."

She glanced up and smiled, remembering the case. "Bishop ran the case like a symphony conductor. First he sent the best young litigators in the firm to rummage through the BEF files for months. Then they computerized all the documents and asked the computer to spit out every piece of paper authored by any BEF Board member that related to ACR. What do you think popped out?"

"Hensley's joke memo?"

"Exactly. That and all the other ones. But Hensley's killed them. A one-page memo that has probably cost BEF a half billion dollars in lost earnings over the years. Bishop took it and rammed it down their throats. All of a sudden no one cared about the boys' theft; all anybody wanted to talk about was Operation CRUSH. I watched Bishop take poor Hensley's deposition and it was sad. For three weeks the man did nothing but drink milk, take pills, smoke cigarettes by the carton, and answer Bishop's questions. Then one day he stood up and began screaming at Bishop. Uncontrollably. Bishop just stared at him in that quiet way of his. His lawyers led him off and the next day the settlement discussions began."

It wasn't hard for O'Malley to predict what happened next. "I take it the settlement was favorable."

She nodded. "Very. All BEF got out of it was some saved face. ACR paid a nominal sum, about fifty thousand dollars, in return for a complete release. That meant it could keep the stolen—I mean allegedly stolen—files and continue to do business as before. As I say, those files have meant about a half billion dollars to ACR."

O'Malley was quiet then, the ethical question so obvious it didn't need asking. Rad answered it anyway. "Yes, it bothers me if that's what you're thinking. When I first came it bothered me a lot. Now . . ." She spread her hands and smiled, ". . . less so."

Even later O'Malley could never remember arguing with her about that.

They talked for a long time that evening, until well after the bulk of the bodies had left for home and hearth. He thought he knew her well when they finished, although not nearly as well as he wanted to. He was sorry when decorum required that he pick up the file and leave.

"Well, thanks for the help. I'll look at all this and we'll talk again when I know some more background." He studied his shoes for awhile. "To be frank, I've always wanted to work with you."

Rad smiled easily and warmly. "Why, O'Malley, that's positively gallant. I like you, too, and I'm sure this case will be fun."

He looked back at her, emboldened by the warm, slightly flirtatious smile. "Well, maybe sometime . . . I mean if we're working late or something . . . we could, uh, have dinner?"

Her smile beamed a laugh, which was not the reaction he wanted. "Why, O'Malley, is it possible that this is a round-about pass? Right here in my own office?"

"It's only roundabout because I don't know what the rules are. Actually I'd prefer being much more direct."

The smile stayed, not exactly receptive but clearly grateful.

"O'Malley, I know you won't believe this, but in nine plus years at this place you are the first associate to make a legitimate, unabashed pitch for my, ah, affections. And believe me, I appreciate it."

The kiss of death. "Nevertheless, it couldn't possibly work for all the obvious reasons," O'Malley said.

She nodded gently. "Yes, I'm afraid so. As you've probably learned, J and D is nothing if not prudish. An internecine flirtation is the surest road to the door. I hate to use that as a reason for my decision but the fact is that next October I will, barring some embarrassing seduction of a new associate or equally untoward event, be selected as the first woman partner in the history of this firm."

"I know that. And I know how hard you've worked for that and what it must mean to you." He reached for the door again. "I won't bring it up again."

Rad looked thoughtful. She rubbed her chin for a moment and then looked up, an involuntary smile returning to play across her lips. "No need to go that far."

Fantastic.

6

It was already dark on Sunday night when O'Malley finished hacking through the first half of the ACR file. It was slow, tedious work. He was home and on his third Jack Daniels when the phone rang. It was Rad. His headache went away.

"How's it going, O'Malley?"

"Fine. I'm up to 1975 and I now understand how to build up a multimillion dollar business from scratch. No need to invent the wheel—just steal it off the other guy's car."

She laughed and he wondered if she was alone—and if there was any way he could change that. "Don't be so moral, O'Malley. I told you the boys are sharp businessmen. Occasionally they bend the rules."

"What rules?"

"Fair enough. Let's say the only rule that we're concerned with is an accurate bottom line on a quarterly income statement."

"Do the boys bend that, too?"

She became quiet at that, the laughter gone. He could sense her thinking about the remark. "That's an interesting question, O'Malley. Are you sure you haven't come across something you'd like to tell me about?"

There were lots of things he wanted to tell her, and lots of places he wanted to be with her. He could imagine her exchanging a business suit for a bathing suit and lying by the pool in Cozumel waiting for a white-coated waiter to bring something in a glass with rum. He could see her clearly in a hotel room overlooking the sea in the Yucatan with the whiteness of the sheet setting off a brown tan on slim athletic legs. He could think of a million places he wanted to talk to Rad. Even here and now. But nothing yet about ACR and prison; after all, he was only up to 1975. "No, I'm just talking."

She seemed to relax and brighten.

"Good. I just never know with the boys."

Even at this stage O'Malley had a definite dislike of "the boys" and their curious way of doing business. "Why the hell is a blue chip firm like J and D still screwing around with these guys? It just doesn't make sense."

"Call Marks and ask him. He's real accessible and just loves to chat with new associates about his personal affairs." The remark was sharp and her voice lost some of its warmth. "Anyhow, O'Malley, I called for a reason. The boys are coming in at nine-thirty on Wednesday to talk about the new deal. Marks' office. You're to be front and center, fresh-faced and clear-eyed, fully prepared. Marks will introduce you as the new lion on the team."

"Terrific." That meant that he had to digest the second half of the ACR file in two days. The first half had taken ten. Welcome to the real world.

"Any questions?"

"What are you doing later?"

She giggled in spite of her irritation. "Don't stop, O'Malley. I love perseverance."

Terrific.

7

Mercifully the second half went faster than the first. Nevertheless it took him a pair of eighteen-hour days to get through it all. He decided it would be paranoia to suppose that Marks had it timed that finely.

There was a real shock in the second half of the ACR saga. O'Malley had anticipated that with BEF out of the way the boys and their Aryan brothers would have blue skies ahead, the glamour stock becoming simply more glamorous. Not quite. ACR was effective at delivering a better mousetrap off the stolen BEF drawings. Yet its internal memos showed it was failing miserably in its attempts to design anything new. It would take some time for customers and Wall Street to wake up to that deficiency, but even a rookie like O'Malley could see that ACR was in trouble.

But no one would be able to tell of the coming disaster

from ACR's reported earnings. Every quarter ACR's net rose at a perfectly respectable 17 percent annualized rate. Neither antiquated technology nor lost sales was having the slightest effect on ACR's reported income.

The magic seemed to come from the accountants. Each year there would be some minor "adjustment" in the accounting system tucked away in a footnote, each one changing a break-even quarter into an excellent one. One year ACR kept the shipping department working twenty-four hours a day in December so that "sales" for that month were five times the normal rate. The next year the depreciation schedule was amended, resulting in a vast increase in the value of the ACR inventory. The following year ACR increased its "assumed" rate of return on the money it held in trust for employee pensions from 6 percent to 8 percent, thereby adding $2.5 million to income. But nothing illegal—simply "polishing the profits" a bit, as the accountants like to say.

The problem with this sort of tinkering is that, like a pyramid scheme, it can't go on forever. If next year's earnings are mortgaged to make this year look good, then next year there has to be a new scheme. O'Malley wondered what ACR would pull out of its hat next. He should have wondered more.

On Wednesday morning he arrived at Marks' office at 9:25, all three pieces of his new suit in place and his graduation briefcase in hand. Mildred was her usual polite self, barely nodding to a chair while she clicked away. O'Malley wondered again whether there were any more dignified ways to make $30,000.

Rad came out about fifteen minutes later and interrupted his reverie. She smiled warmly and led him by the arm into the King's Chambers. There were more people in the room than he had anticipated. On a ratty-looking brown sofa—undoubtedly antique mohair—sat a pair of bookends in identical business suits that could only have been the boys. In real life Friedrich and Hardwick looked anything but the commercial geniuses they were said to be. Friedrich was a stocky, swarthy runt who looked slightly unclean. He had fat little legs and a fat little balding head set off by a lovely bushy mustache that appeared to curl under his upper lip and keep going back to the tonsils. He also needed a new blade in his razor. O'Malley wondered where he had hidden the tusks.

Hardwick looked like a fourteen-year-old British schoolboy who had just been caught with a few million sperm in his hand by the headmaster. His little squinty eyes were never at rest, yanking the rest of his head around and around, up and down. He was constantly rubbing his sunken cheeks with long, witchlike fingers. His complexion looked as if he had died about four days ago. The pencil-thin lips, always pursed, were the color of a slate sky on a winter morning.

Set between the two like a king amidst pawns was a man who had undoubtedly been a major in the Wehrmacht. O'Malley suddenly understood clearly why the French were scared stiff of the Germans, how the master race myth got started, why they won more gold medals and made better cars, and why for the rest of recorded history it was crucial to keep Germany divided. The German's blond hair was almost white, and the blue eyes were the palest shade pigment allowed. His perfectly tailored light gray suit was punctuated by a silk tie the color of his eyes. The tanned head looked as if it were carved from unfinished oak and it might have been, because only the mouth and the glistening ivory teeth ever moved. The frame was roughly the same as that of an outside linebacker on the Rams. There was a slight bulge underneath the left side of the jacket that O'Malley hoped was an over-developed pectoral.

To complete the picture there was Rad, of course, looking ravishing in a tailored beige business suit and burgundy cravat, and Marks, looking like Marks. Armington Bishop was also on hand, looking slightly bored. Finally there was a thin, pale man who stood quietly in back of the German.

Marks started the meeting with the introductions, identifying the Wehrmacht major as one Klaus Rendt, executive vice-president of a company with eighteen letters, two vowels, and AG on the end. O'Malley was introduced as a "brilliant young associate" who had made a specialty of the legal devices necessary to consummate the "arrangement" that ACR was contemplating. The pale man wasn't introduced.

When he finished, Rendt mouthed—literally—some appropriate pleasantry, Rad flashed a grin, and Bishop still looked bored. The boys went into their act—Hardwick stroking his ashen pan with the wires he called fingers and Friedrich munching on his mustache as if it were a soda cracker. Marks pointed at O'Malley with a pen.

For an hour O'Malley regurgitated everything he knew about ACR, its past glories and present troubles. He couldn't understand the purpose of the recitation, but Marks seemed to want to show off the goods. O'Malley deferred to Bishop a few times on technical litigation points but otherwise went on uninterrupted. When he finished he could tell Marks was impressed, and Rad was wearing a proud little smile. Even Bishop was nodding sagely. Only the boys seemed put out.

Hardwick whined first. "Allie, to listen to him it sounds like we did something wrong." Friedrich soothed him. "No, Jimmy, I'm sure he's just repeating what those insufferable creatures at BEF have said." He turned to O'Malley.

"But really, Benjamin, I think your assessment of the future of ACR is a bit dark, isn't it? Wouldn't you say so?"

O'Malley couldn't speak for a moment because his mouth was open. His realization that the boys were lovers was only partially responsible for his shock. The stranger part was how obvious it was that they were incompetent to have pulled off the corporate maneuvering that had made ACR great.

Rendt jumped in and saved him the trouble of responding. "In our view the future of ACR is bright. We expect continued earnings commensurate with past performance." When he finished, the boys literally sank back into their sofa.

Marks took over, soothing the two with his dulcet tones. "ACR is in a fine position, ably led by competent management. To be sure, ACR has suffered as we all have in recent bad times. Nevertheless, it is, ah, unwise to emphasize those negative featues of recent performance in predicting the future. It is more appropriate to consider them as aberrations in a pattern of sustained growth. I'm sure Mr. O'Malley's remarks were more, ah, descriptive than, ah, anticipatory. Isn't that right, Ben?"

O'Malley didn't say, "Whatever you say, boss," but something close to it.

Marks' words seemed to be a signal for everyone to make a long speech about ACR's bright future. When that nonsense was over Marks suggested a break for lunch and Bishop used the excuse to claim other pressing appointments. The rest of the cast trooped to Genevieve's, an overpriced restaurant in the bottom of a nearby bank building whose food passed for haute cuisine in downtown LA because the waiters wore tuxes and affected bad manners.

They were shown to Marks' regular table and everyone chatted amiably till the food came. O'Malley was trying to moisten the sand dabs with sauce from his carrots when a man approached the table from behind Rendt. Rendt reacted instinctively; his right hand moved to straighten his tie, then slid under the left lapel of his jacket—and stayed there. The man came up and grabbed Friedrich by the shoulders.

"Your office told me you might be here. I must speak to you. It's urgent."

"Allie" was frightened and grabbed "Jimmy's" arm. Rendt's arm had not moved.

Friedrich squealed. "What is it? Can't you see we're having lunch? See me in the office. I'll be back around four."

"I don't give a shit about your lunch. I tell you it's urgent."

The unknown man seemed to notice the lawyers for the first time and became flustered.

"I . . . I'm sorry, ma'm, it's just that a . . . a matter of some importance has come up."

"No problem," Rad said.

He turned back to Friedrich and changed his tune. "What I mean to say, sir, is that a problem has arisen with the Genoa account." He glanced at the table again, then back to Friedrich. "And knowing your desire to remain personally on top of this account I felt it would be important to bring this matter to your attention at once."

Rendt didn't relax, although his right hand returned to straighten his tie and from there to the table. The oak head never moved.

"Please accompany this gentleman and resolve the difficulty."

The pale man walked over and stood next to the boys. Friedrich stared at him for a moment, then nervously wiped his face and rose from the table. He bowed to Rad stiffly and departed, leaving his Coquilles St.-Jacques behind. The pale man left with him.

O'Malley's mind was in a fog bank somewhere off the Mendocino Coast when he heard Marks chatting amiably with Rendt about a series of Carolingian tapestries that were passing through LA. Just as if nothing had happened. Rad's lips were tight and she was staring at her food as if it were alive and moving. Hardwick was trying to eat yet had to use two hands. Klaus Rendt looked as shaky as a large rock.

Allen Friedrich never returned from his emergency. The rest trooped back to Marks' office and spent the remainder of the afternoon talking about ACR. Marks left early, saying it would be "inappropriate" for him to remain for the meeting, whatever that meant. O'Malley's eyes kept darting back and forth among the people in the room, as he wondered why no one else seemed to care that Rendt carried a gun.

8

The central nervous system at J & D is a spectacular mahogany spiral staircase that winds itself in serpentine splendor around a brass and cut glass light pole. The pole and the staircase extend for the full fourteen stories of the J & D domain. At any hour of the day or night dark-faced men and women in pale green wraparounds pass zombielike up and down the walkway carefully carrying pieces of paper as if they were unburnt offerings. Jackets were unnecessary to distinguish the messengers from the lawyers.

The stairway to heaven was O'Malley's favorite architectural feature of J & D and he usually bounded up and down the risers, weaving through the greencoats like a driver at Indy. He did this both for the exercise, which was all he got, and to tweak those who regarded the display as unseemly. He also did it for Bridget, the matronly receptionist on his floor who rightly regarded every associate as a working stiff like herself and whose eyes lit up when she saw him charging around the bend before vaulting the last few steps. She'd give him the same line every time: "Mr. O'Malley, one of these times you're going to land in Bridget's lap and then where will we be." He'd pinch her cheek and tell her that's where he wanted to be. They'd laugh and both feel better for thirty seconds.

When he completed his descent following Marks' meeting, he turned the last corner in lockstep with the greencoats, even down to the approved J & D facial expression for the help. Bridget knew something was up. "Trouble, Mr. O'Malley?"

"Huh . . . uh, no, I'm just . . . ah, thinking. Is Baird at home, by chance?"

She consulted her electronic monitor, which gave precise information on the comings and goings of each of the twenty-seven lawyers in the three wings of her floor. "Yes, sir. As far as I know he's not left yet." She looked concerned.

"Thanks." O'Malley started away and then went back. "Oh, by the way, Bridget," he began sternly.

"Yes, sir."

He pinched her cheek. "Call me Benji, like the dog." The grin he gave her in response to her relieved laugh fell like a deadweight as soon as he turned the corner.

Jerome Baird was a third-year litigation associate with an

office next door to O'Malley's. Baird was without the slightest clue why he was spending his days at a major corporate law firm, a trait that endeared him to O'Malley immediately. He was also a very strange-looking person. Each day he wrapped his six-foot-six Ichabod Crane form in the same rumpled, undersized dark suit. With feathers and claws Baird could be gliding over the desert searching for carrion. He was also lazy, brilliant, dissolute, organized, and efficient. He did twice the work of others in half the time and spent the rest of the day staring out the window walking roads known only to him.

The partnership did not know what to do with him. He was too smart to fire and too strange to keep around. The prevailing wisdom was he'd be shown to the door in the tenth year.

Baird's door was closed, which was a sure sign he was in one of his trances. O'Malley went in without knocking and found him standing at the window. He joined him there and for awhile the two stared at the tens of thousands of engines sitting immobile on the Santa Monica Freeway burning thousands of gallons of precious fuel for the privilege of powering single-passenger vehicles at ten miles per hour over the twenty-mile route between the city and the west side. The drivers would arrive home in an hour or so, secure in the knowledge that the same poisonous journey had to be made twice again the following day. But it was important to live on the west side. Everyone said the air was better.

They watched for awhile without comment and then O'Malley turned to him. "You got a minute?"

"For Benjamin O'Malley—always. Have a seat. Promise me only that you do not intend to bore me with the details of one of your tedious little cases." Baird hated to talk about law even when he was getting paid for it. As they sat, Baird extracted a brown bag and two lovely pewter jigger cups from his desk. From the bag he pulled an even lovelier bottle of Remy Martin Champagne Cognac.

O'Malley accepted. "You know, for a slob you've got excellent manners."

" 'Slob' is a lower-class word, Benjamin. If you are to make it around here you must think of my style as 'dishabille.' " They toasted the freeways. "But you did not come merely to insult me. What else is on that one-dimensional little brain?"

"What if I told you I went to lunch today with some clients and one of them—a West German who looks like a blond Mafioso—had a gun."

"More precision, Benjamin, more precision. What do you mean—'had a gun'? Over the mantel at home? At his hunting lodge? Brandishing at Genevieve's?"

"The latter—sort of."

"Explain, please."

O'Malley did and it quickly became evident that even with analytical embellishments there really wasn't much there. Baird's cross-examination made it sound even thinner. When the tale was finished Baird sighed and poured another cognac.

"It's clear to me that the tedium of securities law has over-stimulated one of the few imaginative sectors of the brain left to you. One of your many boring clients has an unflattering habit of scratching under his left clavicle with his right hand. Another was called away from lunch by a business problem. Two look unusual and may have a presently atypical but increasingly popular sexual orientation. From these few threads you weave a fabric of intrigue, conspiracy, and potential violence. Two questions. First, have you identified the nature of this intrigue? Second, have you passed on your observations to the glorious Ms. Radnowski or the vainglorious Mr. Marks?"

"No—to both."

"Ah, so your suspicions are at this point embryonic and you do not wish to appear foolish to your superiors. In my case such an appearance has long since been cast in stone so you do not have the same concern." He spread his hands. "What shall we do then? Find out where the German is staying and 'case the joint'?"

"No." Baird was right—it was a stupid concern. O'Malley

changed the subject. "I have another question. What do you know about securities fraud?"

"Everything, of course. Do you have something specific in mind."

"Yes, how can I get fucked by doing work for these clowns."

Baird sat back and stared at the ceiling and let his incomparable mental computer digest the question and retrieve the precise response. "Securities fraud is essentially no different from any other fraud. However, in the case of securities one must look first to Section 10(b) of the Securities Exchange Act of 1934—passed in a time of considerable sensitivity to fraud on the New York Stock Exchange—and to the Securities and Exchange Commission's implementing Rule 10(b)(5), each of which is codified respectively at—"

"Baird, I can't stand the suspense. Can we please move this along?"

"Ah, so you wish only generalities. All right. The elements of a basic fraud are simple. First, one needs a material misrepresentation—a lie about something important, if you prefer—or a failure to make known an important fact. Second, one needs reliance on the lie by an innocent purchaser, say, someone who buys the stock on the strength of the misrepresentation. Third, the bad guy must have intended that the innocent lamb rely on the lie. Last, the innocent must have sustained damage."

"How about phony financial statements?"

"Of course. Phony financials are the classic securities fraud. The financials are a lie and the maker of the report intends people to rely on them. The reports are received by Wall Street and on the basis of the lies securities analysts advise grandmothers in Iowa to buy the stock. The grandmothers buy the stock and when the lie is discovered the stock price plummets and the grandmother loses all the insurance money that grandpa left when he passed beyond this vale of tears. Then a class action lawsuit is filed, we represent the company and settle for ten cents on the dollar. The Justice Department

45

begins grand jury proceedings and sends the corporate officials to Terminal Island for six months."

"So, how can I get screwed? I'm not a corporate official."

Baird leaned back and again began quoting from a mental printout. "An attorney participating in a securities fraud is an aider and abettor. There are only three elements and they're easy to show. First, one must have a fraud. Second, the lawyer must have knowledge of the fraud, or at least enough information that any reasonable person in his position would have begun asking questions. Third, the lawyer must make a contribution to the scheme."

"Like doing the legal work on a fictitious transaction that finds its way into the financials?"

"No question about it if he knew what was going on."

"How much do I have to know?"

He shrugged. "Hard to say. The cases are all over the lot because obviously every defendant tries to use the 'I didn't know what was going on' defense. It's basically a question of fact. How much did the guy know, how close was he to the facts, how much confidential information did he have access to, that sort of thing."

"What can happen to me?"

"If you're involved? All the standard nasty things. You get sued along with everyone else, except unlike the corporate officers, you're not insured. The bright side is that the plaintiffs' lawyers know you don't have enough money to chase, so they'd probably settle with you early in return for your cooperation."

"What about jail?"

"That's the kicker. The Justice Department couldn't care less about your relative poverty and would love nothing more than to indict a lawyer at a big-name law firm. Once the grand jury indicts, you'd have the option of going to trial and taking your chances or working out a deal where you plead *nolo contendere* and accept thirty days in the jug."

"Anything else?"

"In your case, sure. You'd lose your ticket."

"Disbarment?"

"That's right."

O'Malley held out his cup. Baird poured solemnly, and they drank silently as the gathering darkness created two brilliant points of light for every stacked engine on the Santa Monica Freeway.

9

Looking back on it all later—the first few thousand times he looked back on it all later—he thought that this was the last time he might have gotten out unharmed. When he left Baird's office late that evening he had a healthy, instinctive fear about the whole affair, a fear that led him to give serious thought to resigning. After that both the strangeness and the concern grew. But the way out was never as clear. Or, as it turned out, as available.

O'Malley didn't resign. Instead, he did what they told him to do, which was to put together the paperwork for the sale of a subsidiary, a subsidiary whose strange workings made ACR look as straight as the Sisters of Charity.

Video Enterprises was owned by ACR and had been hanging around the corporate neck like an albatross for five years. In the early days, when the boys were at their most ambitious, they had formed it to diversify into the entertainment business. For the first year after its creation the company lay dormant. It had no assets, no offices, no employees. All it was was a piece of paper in a government office in Sacramento. At the time of the marriage between the boys and the Germans it was thrown into the deal like an old refrigerator.

The twist came six months later. Suddenly Video Enterprises had money—lots of it—and spent it like the proverbial sailor. It opened new offices; had a new president (one Frank Pisano, of unknown origin); hired clerks, secretaries, and salesmen; printed pretty stationery with the corporate logo; and looked from the outside like a perfectly legitimate operation.

At the beginnng Vid Ent even had revenues and more or less broke even. There was a film editing lab, which made a bit of money, and a film school that weekly collected $12.97 from each of the twenty-three waitressess and auto body repairmen from the San Fernando Valley attending it. In return they received acting lessons from an aging alcoholic who had appeared as a minor black hat in fourteen Westerns between 1947 and 1961. The black hat came cheap and the school was only slightly in the red. There was also a dubbing studio, a color lab, a mastering and replication facility on Sunset, and a billboard printing shop that specialized in "junior panels" for the film industry. These enterprises were scattered in storefronts and second-floor walkups in seven locations on Hollywood Boulevard and Sunset—not the glamorous Strip but the part where the adjoining tenants are Denny's restaurants and working girls.

The profits from all these operations were tiny, but overhead was small and the company stayed above water. It was its final activity, begun two years later, that established Video Enterprises as one of the great all-time losers: the financing of theatrical motion pictures.

As O'Malley pored over the records of Vid Ent it became clear to him that Frank Pisano was perhaps the worst judge of talent in the history of the entertainment industry. In three years Pisano invested tens of millions in film production and had yet to have a picture that recovered ten percent of its negative cost. Most of his films never hit a screen in the

United States. They must have been big in Tel Aviv, Zurich, Auckland, and Barranquilla, however, because that's where they were made, where the talent came from, and without exception, where the money went.

Yet notwithstanding his losses, Frank Pisano steadfastly refused to take one krone from an outside investor. He was religious about it. Vid Ent even had a standard form letter that it used to reluctantly decline to discuss participation in film financing from the occasional eager and embarrassingly cash-rich seeker of the tax shelter. It was not Frank's style to take others with him. He seemed maniacally bent on proceeding down the toilet alone.

The net losses were staggering. In only three years Vid Ent lost $53,745,642.23. Yet the checks kept coming. Every quarter for three years an ACR check in the amount of $7 million traveled from the ACR offices in Beverly Hills to a Video Enterprises account in Caracas, and from there to a series of Leichtenstein *anstalts* that actually produced the films. And every quarter a check for $2.5 million would come back to ACR from Pisano. That left a shortfall of $4.5 million per quarter, $18 million per year, $54 million for three years.

O'Malley's first question was why would anyone buy a company with these losses. He posed the question to Rendt at a meeting at ACR's opulent offices on Wilshire in Beverly Hills. Rendt gave O'Malley one of his wooden stares and without separating his teeth, moved his lips enough to mouth, "The motivations of the principals to this transaction need not concern you."

That wasn't good enough, but O'Malley let it slide for the moment. "All right. Who are the buyers?

"Messrs. Hardwick and Friedrich. Or more precisely, a holding company that they control."

O'Malley had his mouth open in shock when there was a brief knock followed by the entrance into the room of a man whose appearance alone demanded immediate attention. Frank Pisano looked like a man who bought a new suit every morning, right after he finished his daily visit to the barber, manicurist, and tooth polisher. O'Malley lowered his eyes to shield them from the glare of Pisano's rings and was almost blinded by the light refracting off the gleaming black shoes. Only the olive face—tanned by the rays from a wall socket—and the white shirt and perfectly coordinated silver tie set off the unsettling impression of darkness that Pisano created.

When he stood between Rendt and Pisano for the introductins O'Malley had a sudden irrational urge to run home and change clothes. Friedrich and Hardwick looked like two clowns, playing court jesters to two well-tailored princes. The notion that the boys were Pisano's superiors was ludicrous.

Rendt sat everyone down and took charge of the formalities. "Frank, Mr. O'Malley is with the firm of Jenkins and Dorman. He's a lawyer and he'll be taking care of the paperwork on the sale of Video Enterprises."

Frank was intently inspecting his manicure. He never looked up. "Happy to meecha." O'Malley couldn't believe it—right out of the old neighborhood in Bayonne.

O'Malley decided to be ingratiating. "Let me guess. North Jersey, clearly. Not upper Bergen County, more like Jersey City maybe?"

Frank brightened. "Yeah, howja guess. You from there or somethin'?" It wasn't a difficult guess. With Frank the "th" sound was always a hard consonant.

Rendt cut it off before it got too friendly. "Perhaps you can continue this at another time. For the moment I think it would be more efficient to concentrate on the matter at hand."

Pisano shrugged. "No problem, it's your nickel—you just tell me where to sign." He turned to O'Malley. "Let's have a drink sometime, pal, we'll talk about the old country." He laughed at his own joke. So did O'Malley, although a bit nervously.

Rendt began talking again. "Just to bring everyone up to speed, we are here to discuss the sale of Video Enterprises, a subsidiary of Associated Computer Research, Incorporated, to F and H Holding Company, Incorporated, for the sum of thirty-seven and a half million dollars."

O'Malley had a sip of hot coffee in his throat when the number came out and he almost choked to death. He was wheezing and turning colors with Frank pounding on his back for ninety seconds before he caught his breath. It was another minute before his normal office pallor returned.

O'Malley turned immediately to the boys. "You're going to pay thirty-seven and a half million dollars?" They nodded.

"But the thing's not worth anything. All it's ever done is chew up money."

Rendt flushed with anger and spoke quickly, regaining control immediately. "I think we're getting off the mark again. Neither the cost of the acquisition of this company nor the value of its inventory is of any concern to you. Your firm has been engaged to render legal services. You have been assigned to perform those services, presumably because you are capable of doing so. You are not a party to this transaction; you are a servant of the parties." He stopped and stared at O'Malley. "It is tedious to be compelled to continue to emphasize the distinction between client and lawyer. If you persist in failing to understand the difference, I will be compelled to request that Mr. Marks assign someone to the case who does."

O'Malley returned the stare. "You mean someone you can control."

"No, sir. I mean precisely what I said."

Pisano was back to inspecting his nails. "I think he wants you to be quiet and do your job, pal." The "pal" was no longer friendly. O'Malley didn't think they were going to have their drink after all.

"Not possible," O'Malley said. "After I finish drawing up the deal I have to explain it to the auditors. What am I going to tell them?"

Rendt again. "You'll tell them the truth, of course. What else?"

O'Malley had no rejoinder to that. As long as they were willing to describe truthfully what was done, the strangeness of the transaction was irrelevant. O'Malley decided to cave for the moment. "O.K., so these gentlemen are going to acquire Vid Ent for thirty-seven and a half million dollars. How will the purchase price be paid?" He picked up his legal pad. Rendt continued.

"The new corporation that will make the acquisition will be wholly owned by these two gentlemen." He indicated the boys, who were paying no attention to what the adults were doing. "Each of these two shareholders will contribute ten thousand dollars on behalf of the new corporation."

O'Malley wrote the number down. "O.K., that leaves thirty-seven million four hundred eighty thousand to go."

"The balance of the purchase price will be in the form of a note from the buyers to the sellers."

O'Malley laughed at the obvious fraud. It was a classic tax dodge. Sell a subsidiary for one hundred times its true value—or in this case 37.5 million times its true value—to a shell corporation controlled by the sellers. Take back a note for the purchase price. The seller records the transaction as a sale and has millions in paper profits to show to Wall Street. The note is a so-called nonrecourse note, meaning that the seller cannot sue anybody but the shell corporation. The shell corporation never pays a dime and goes bankrupt. The only person "hurt" is the seller. The seller gets a huge tax writeoff when the note fails and receives 40 percent of the value of the phony note in tax savings.

"What's the collateral for the note?" O'Malley asked smugly.

Rendt looked at him with a faint, complimentary smile. "A fair question—indeed, an excellent question. The collateral will be three hundred sixty thousand shares of ACR stock." ACR was then trading at about 104 per share. O'Malley couldn't do the math fast enough, but he knew that two zeros added to three hundred sixty thousand came out damn close to 37.5 million. He was stunned, beginning to feel way out of his league. To gain confidence he looked at Friedrich, who was taking apart his pen and putting it back together with a look as if he'd discovered special relativity. O'Malley felt safe again. "Where does the stock come from?"

"These gentlemen will provide the shares."

The butterflies came back with a rush. Their own shares. It wasn't possible.

"You mean they're really going to put up their own shares?"

"No, they don't have that much yet. ACR will deliver one hundred thousand shares of treasury stock to them in return for twenty-five percent of the new corporation."

"Twenty-five percent of nothing is still nothing. You mean if they default on the note ACR just gets its own shares back. Doesn't sound like collateral to me."

"What does the remaining two hundred sixty thousand shares sound like to you?"

O'Malley had absolutely no answer. Those shares were owned by the boys and were solid gold, Bank of America, Crown Jewels collateral, representing 12.5 percent of the outstanding shares of ACR and worth about $28 million on the open market. If the boys defaulted, they'd lose everything. And they didn't seem to care. They just sat on the couch bleating at each other in muffled giggles. O'Malley couldn't believe they were going to do it. But Rendt was right. There was nothing he could do about it. His only job was to put together the paperwork and tell the truth to the auditors. Nevertheless, this was too complicated; there were too many angles he didn't understand. He resolved to confront Marks and force him to get involved. He finished writing and folded up his file.

"Well, I hope for their sake they're heavily insured."

Rendt said nothing. Frank Pisano discovered a piece of lint on his coal-black pants and was inspecting it with the care a biologist would take over a rare snail.

10

O'Malley grabbed Baird as soon as he got back from ACR
and talked him into sliding out for an early Friday afternoon
libation at the Bonaventure. Baird claimed to hate the Bonaventure—an immense, penta-cylindrical hotel done entirely in
concrete and mirrored glass with a one-acre, six-inch-deep
lake on the first floor. It had all the warmth of the German
battery positions at Calais. O'Malley loved it. LA architec-
ture should not pretend to good taste.

They settled in seats in the rotating top-floor bar and for a
time watched the city turn around them. On one side were
three blocks of fifty-story towers. On the other three sides
were fifty miles of three-story towers. O'Malley waited while
Baird commented on the city, the hotel, and the hats of the
conventioneers, then tried to get him to pay attention. Baird
half-listened while O'Malley talked about the deal, Pisano's
appearance, the boys' stupidity, and the fact that the whole
thing smelled and was getting fouler by the minute. Baird
punctuated O'Malley's dramatic embellishments with studied yawns.

"I take it you're not impressed."

Baird shrugged. "I think I've heard this tune before," he
said. "I'll take your word for it that 'the boys,' as you call
them, are making a bad deal. But what does that mean?
These guys are sophisticated businessmen. They know far

more about what they're doing than you or I; that's why they're making the bread and we're the hired help. Maybe there's some bizarre tax angle involved. I think your friend Pisano is right. Do your job, make sure your ass is covered, and go home and sleep like a baby."

"Just like that."

"Well, I don't see what the problem is. Do you have any doubt that the boys are aware of what the deal entails?"

"No, they know what's going on. They were sitting there listening—sort of."

"And have you ever been asked to phony up a document, or lie to the auditors, or cover up any wrongdoing whatsoever?"

"No. Rendt told me to tell the truth."

Baird spread his hands, using one of the fingers to signal for another round. "So you're home free. You draft your tedious little contracts, write a couple of CYA letters and memos to the file and have a nice closing party when it's all done." CYA was "cover your ass," a time-honored, self-serving device to insure that when the shit hit the fan it landed on others.

Baird used O'Malley's troubled silence as an excuse to change the subject. "Speaking of parties, are you going tomorrow?"

Tomorrow's "party" was the elaborate conclusion of a string of more or less mandatory affairs that J & D put on to introduce new lawyers to the affluence that would soon be theirs. The affairs began with the "New Associates Clambake," at which white-coated attendants cooked various exotic fish on an electric grill on the sands of a probate partner's beachfront home. This was followed by the "New Associates Fiesta," described as a "fete with a Latin twist" and held on a real estate partner's four-hundred-acre Santa Barbara ranch. It featured hordes of Chicanos, more than a little embarrassed at being dressed in gaucho outfits, who passed among the J & D elite and spouses carrying trays filled with every conceivable Mexican delicacy. Fourteen separate mariachi bands held forth at stations scattered throughout the grounds, each next to an ad hoc bar serving Mexican beers, exquisite full-bodied red wine, and nine variations of the piña colada. Then there were the *intime* dinners, small catered affairs for fifty or so at which a partner's wife guided a select group of new lambs through her home like Jackie Kennedy at the White House.

These gigs were a lot of laughs. The partners stood around talking about law and the wives talked about their husbands. The new lawyers approached the fun with the casualness of men bound for IRS audits. O'Malley hated the fucking things. He and Baird usually snuck into a corner and got drunk with the help.

Tomorrow was special, however. The New Associates Ball. Black tie. Ballroom at the Dorothy Chandler Pavilion at the Music Center, right where they present the Oscars. Dinner for four hundred, music by a chamber group from the LA symphony, a welcoming address by the chairman of the Management Committee, and speeches by the mayor, the deputy secretary of defense, and the quarterback for the Raiders, the latter an aging, recently injured, off-season law student who was pining for a J & D offer. Following dinner and speeches, the chamber group would be replaced by twenty guys dressed like Guy Lombardo who claimed to play everything from Cole Porter to New Wave. It sounded wonderful.

"I don't think so, Baird."

Baird studied his drink, working on the timing. "That's too bad."

"Why? You'll be able to find someone to get ripped with."

"I wasn't thinking about me."

"Who, then?"

"The delicious Ms. Radnowski. She was asking for you before you came back. My guess is she desires an escort."

O'Malley cut a swathe through some conventioneers like Moses through the Red Sea. He had the number dialed while his beer was still shaking on the bar.

"O'Malley, you sound winded."

"I've been jogging. I heard you were looking for me." Please, God, he prayed, I'll give up cigarettes, alcohol, and drugs. I'll work harder and make friends with all the partners.

"O'Malley, I realize it's late to ask, but I was wondering whether you had plans to take anyone to the . . ."

"Yes."

"Pardon?"

"Yes, I'd love to go with you. I adore these parties. They're terrific. I was just telling Baird how much I was looking forward to tomorrow night."

She was laughing and her voice came across the line soft and warm, like a log fire in a ski chalet, like warm cognac and a bearskin rug. "Can you come by around seven? We'll have a drink first."

"Terrific. I mean sure, I'll be there." She hung up before he got the address. So what. He shook the hand of a conventioneer waiting for the phone and asked him where he was from. Bismarck—great town! O'Malley clapped him on the back. Baird had a smug look on his face when O'Malley got back to the bar. So what. He clapped Baird on the back, too, bought a round for everyone he could see, and told the bartender to keep the change from a twenty. They immediately had five new friends and within an hour O'Malley was telling Baird what great guys the North Dakotans were. They didn't talk abut ACR anymore.

O'Malley decided he looked great in a tux, sort of an ashen Frank Pisano. The thought of Frank brought the case back, but he chased the thought away, splashed on a little Old Spice, and jumped into the freshly washed Jensen-Healey for the ride to Rad's.

The Jensen was getting old now and was never very expensive even during the two years it was made. But it was still a great car. He bought it used for $4,500 because the lines were beautiful and he knew it could perform—it had a lovely little transverse-mounted Lotus-four that took an hour and a half to get off the line and jumped from sixty to ninety in a millisecond. O'Malley rocketed out of the hills at fifty in second gear and the tach never got halfway to the red line. He hit the flats and popped into third for the two blocks to the Hollywood Freeway, then swung into the traffic flow heading north. The wind was in his face and he kept it in third until the needle crept up to seventy. When he dropped into fourth the little beauty slid down to two thousand rpm's and the engine sounded as if he had turned the key off. O'Malley patted the dash and began singing into the wind as the little red convertible tore past Universal City in the fast lane.

Rad's place was up in Laurel Canyon, a rustic, densely wooded residential community peopled by young professionals and moderately successful rock stars. It was a short hop from the hills over the Cahuenga Pass, down into the Valley for a ways and then back up into the hills. Once into the hills the two-lane road twisted and turned in pitch blackness through the trees. The Healey loved it and so did he.

Rad was ravishing, the tailored suits and sensible shoes only a downtown, daytime memory. She greeted him at the door in a long, plain black gown that clung to her lean body. Her hair was clean blown and full and those laughing gray eyes were, like the streaks of gray in her hair, set in black. The gown was vintage '40s, held to her body by static electricity and two thin straps. The straps left bare her full, tanned shoulders and back. Her only jewelry was a plain silver choker and matching Mexican bracelet. Her heels forced her body forward, causing the thin material of her gown to follow faithfully the curve of her breasts, the flatness of her stomach and the lean, athletic hardness of her hips. Thirty-five years old: simplicity, beauty, and intelligence to boot. O'Malley was stunned.

She smiled gratefully at his rather obvious admiration and turned slowly. "You like?"

He found his voice. "I love." Then he found his manners. "I couldn't find a corsage so I thought this would do as well." O'Malley handed her a bottle of Mumms. She accepted the champagne eagerly.

"Perfect. Flowers belong in window boxes, not on dresses. I'll chill this and we'll save it for later. Come in and we'll have a real drink to fortify us for the ordeal."

The room was as he thought it would be, eclectic and cheerful. The walls were covered with primitives from Rousseau prints to Delacroix lithographs to pale, exotic Balinese masks. The gleaming hardware floors were dotted with Dhurrie rugs. The furniture was a melange of high-tech pieces and American antiques. An enormous burgundy camelback sofa faced the fireplace. The entire room was dominated by a squeaky-clean floor-to-ceiling plate-glass window letting in the city lights below. All in all, a room to live in and laugh in. Maybe, if you're lucky, even to love in.

Rad came over with a couple of Scotches and they sat in front of the window watching the lights twinkle like stars against the blackness of the canyon. They were as nervous as kids in a drive-in and kept giggling, talking too fast and too loud, bumping into each other's words, and apologizing with new laughs. It didn't matter; the subjects were nonsense. The important thing was they couldn't stop staring at each other. O'Malley was transfixed by those gray eyes, except when his attention would slide past the full untouched lips, over the silver clasp and olive throat and down to the thin straps on bare shoulders, straps that with a touch would themselves slide down to uncover the full breasts below. He'd catch himself and jerk his vision up past her knowing smile and back to those warm pools of gray.

They spent an hour sipping Scotch and babbling and then it was time to go. She laughed with delight when she saw the Healey and ran back into the house, emerging with an exquisitely embroidered black lace shawl. She snuggled down in the seat with a happy smile as the little red car blew down the canyon and out onto the freeway for the ride downtown.

The ball itself was a haze. O'Malley screeched in front of the Music Center and flipped the keys to the attendant, who let his eyes roam over Rad's lines to the complete exclusion of the Jensen. O'Malley quickly gave him a five and told him to park it near the front of the line. A J & D partner with a pink and flowered spouse was arriving as they were and gave O'Malley, the car, and Rad a quick disapproving look. But this was a new associates' party and O'Malley was a new associate, so Rad's incomparable ass was covered. They had a long walk to the table and Rad caused more than a few male heads to follow their progress. They made it to their seats just as Everett Danton, the esteemed chairman, was rising to deliver his welcoming remarks.

Danton was followed by applause, chamber music, a prime rib dinner, an incongruous yet perfect Montrachet, and a lovely parfait. Rad and O'Malley tried to avoid making moon eyes at each other and for the most part succeeded. Then came the mayor, who seemed awed, and the deputy secretary of defense, who was actually a former Jenkins partner. The Raider quarterback spent a long fifteen minutes equating a goal line stand and a trial, then completely blew his chances by openly expressing the hope that he, too, would one day be part of a "Super-Bowl team" like that before him.

The speeches were followed by dancing, which was actually very nice. O'Malley was enjoying himself for the first time at a J & D party and was even chatting amiably with the partners' wives, typically about such heart-stoppers as hubby's recent rise to greatness in the Naval Reserve. The dances with Rad were widely spread out so she could work the room and each time they danced they barely touched, like children investigating flowers, or more precisely like new lovers refusing to let a ball take credit for anything so important. Baird looked lost and slightly hurt because there was no one to get ripped with. O'Malley hoped he understood.

He was feeling pleasantly warm about midnight when the band outdid itself and broke into some perfectly passable vintage Cole. Rad appeared at his side and took his hand and led him to the door. They began dancing on the outskirts of the celebrants. She placed her head on his shoulder.

"O'Malley, please take me home."

He nodded. They danced over to the door and then bolted, giggling like kids sneaking from class.

Outside there was some commotion as other early departers tried to get the attention of the attendents. The attendant winked at Rad and came screeching around with the Jensen to the chagrin of those queued up trying to get someone to take their tickets. O'Malley gave the kid another buck for his good taste and then roared away, achieving exit velocity on the on ramp to the Harbor Freeway.

The Healey got quiet again at seventy-five and the only sound was the swirling wind. The noise and light of the ball seemed harsh and far away. It's possible to catch LA just right, notwithstanding the millions and their nonsense, when one enters a pocket of peace and the city switches off and becomes little more than an extension of the Mojave. It doesn't often happen on a freeway, but that night even mice were footmen.

He opened the door and she asked him to pour the Mumms. It was the first words either had spoken since they left. They toasted each other silently. The light came in pinpricks through the plate glass from the faraway city. He reached for her hand and she came smiling and eager. Her kiss was warm and unhurried.

Yet behind the warm kiss there was still tenseness and hesitancy; slight, rapidly departing, but still there. He stood back, leaving her alone in the middle of the room, naked in her beautiful, form-fitting gown. He poured himself another glass but didn't offer a prop. Instead, he simply stared at her. Her head was slightly bowed and eyes slightly hurt. Then her lips parted in a half-smile and her breath began coming quickly.

He waited till she whispered his name before returning to her. He stood in back of her gently massaging the tense muscles of her bare neck and shoulders. Her eyes were closed and she rocked softly when she spoke. "Benjamin," she said.

"Yes."

"This is probably a bad idea. You know that, don't you?"

"What idea is that?"

She smiled and relaxed a little under his fingers. "The idea in your mind. The idea in my mind," she said softly.

"I don't know what you're talking about," he said, his fingers continuing their gentle manipulation. "I thought I might have a glass of champagne and then head home. That way I'll feel rested and refreshed tomorrow. Maybe even go in and do a little work. Why, what's on your mind?"

She giggled a little and ran her tongue around her full upper lip. "My idea was that you might like to sleep with me." Her neck muscles were relaxing. But O'Malley continued his probing.

"You don't want me to sleep with you at all, do you?"

"No," she said.

"But you would like me to push the straps of your gown aside and . . ."

"Yes."

"And push the gown down over your beautiful breasts . . ."

"Yes."

"And then remove your . . ."

"I'm not wearing one," she said, smiling again. "I decided while dressing that I'd save you the trouble."

"I see," O'Malley said. "And what else did you decide?"

She turned and kissed him. "I decided that I wanted you to make love with me. To take off my gown and see me naked. To touch me." Her eyes got mischievous and her hand dropped to the buckle of his belt. "But more than that, Mr. O'Malley, I decided to put you to work tonight on a very important project. One that will take all your energy and resourcefulness to accomplish correctly."

"Is that right," he said. He pushed her other hand down, then moved the straps of her gown aside. The straps fell and the gown followed, collecting with the speed of snowfall over her marvelous ass. He kissed her bare breasts until the dark points rose in response. She reached for his belt again but he gently pushed her hand away, then turned her so that she was facing away from him. She closed her eyes as he came up close behind her. He pushed the gown down to her ankles, then held her close, letting her feel him hard against her bare ass.

His black tux emphasized her bare tan and white skin. When he massaged her breasts she moaned slightly and her chest rose and fell. He whispered in her ear, telling her explicitly what he wanted to do to her naked body, what he wanted her to do to his. She began rocking, straining to hear. All the while he massaged her breasts, first gently, then harder.

The sexual tension built. She spun out of his grasp and turned to kiss him deeply. He held her tightly until the rhythmic shudders came, like a child coughing. She relaxed like a doll against the smooth material of the dinner jacket. His eyes traveled softly over her eyes, her mouth, the dark, excited tips of her breasts. Her eyes were surprised. Rad had for too long been admired for her brain.

He told her that. "You're beautiful. Tonight I want to show you how beautiful you are."

Her face was flushed. For once she was making love without fear as a silent partner. "Benjamin, I'll do all the things you want. And more. Just tell me and I'll do it."

"What are the rules?" he asked smiling.

She shook her head enthusiastically. "There are no rules tonight." Her gown was still collected around her ankles. "I know men like my body and I'd like to show it all to you. Would you like me to remove all my clothes?"

"Almost all," he said.

She smiled and stepped out of the black fabric, then pulled her sheer panties down over her tan legs. She folded the dress neatly on a chair and returned to him clad only in pumps and her twin pieces of jewelry. Without ceremony he led her by the hand to the burgundy couch.

She stretched like a cat and reached for him. O'Malley ignored her arms and ran his hand dispassionately over her body. Her breath caught with slight indignation. He waited for it to become long and slow again, then kissed down the front of her body. When he reached the soft hairs between her legs she laughed and moaned simultaneously with anticipation. He kissed and entered with his tongue. She stiffened and cried out, raising her hips to help. Her spasms came faster.

He stopped only when she relaxed again. He kissed her deeply, letting her taste the moisture from her own body. She wanted the taste and ran her tongue over his lips, drinking in the new sensation. As they kissed he ran his hand roughly over her beautiful ass.

She smiled at his touch and turned onto her belly easily and submissively. Reflective beads of moisture were caught in the fine hairs of her neck. He kissed the salt wetness and stroked the damp skin on her lean back. Her glorious bottom was naked and vulnerable. She thought she read his thoughts. "Are you going to beat me?"

He laughed. "Would you like that?"

"No . . . I don't . . . at least I don't think so. But if you would like that?" She took the silence for direction and brought her knees under her, elevating the tight white ass in offering, awaiting the insult. But O'Malley didn't cause her pain. Instead he reached between her legs, to the hard little point already made tender by his tongue. His fingers knew where to go to create maddening sensation. She buried her face into the coarse fabric of the couch and began moving her body to the rhythm set by his hand. The pleasurable irritation fueled her shudders. Her mind wanted relief, her voice and body wanted more of the delicious spasms. He kept up the relentless massage for a long, long time, through innumerable shudders. He stopped when her cries for more had become hoarse sobs.

She was easy to relax. Soon the breaths were even and the eyes closed. She woke with a start and seemed to recognize the room for the first time. She jumped up and began smoothing her hair.

"Jesus fucking Christ." Her eyes and face were wet. O'Mal-

ley was still sitting in his tux like the headwaiter at Genevieve's. Her naked body was glistening. She tried to fix her
eyes. He had never seen anything so beautiful. "O'Malley,
where did you learn that?"

He grinned and tenderly kissed her palm. "Misspent youth.
That was before I devoted my life to J and D."

Her body was giving little twitches like aftershocks. She
closed her eyes to enjoy them. "Mm. New York. Are there
many like you back there?"

"They're all back there. Except for me and Frank Pisano."
She nodded. "I know."

He took her hand and led her to the bedroom. She stopped
his hand on its way to the tie. "No. Let me do that. It's my
turn now." While her fingers worked she came up close, whis-
pering to him as he had to her. "I'm going to make you very
happy tonight. You must think of everything you've ever de-
sired. Everything that a woman can do to please a man." Her
face was serene and calm. "As for me, I'm now going to enjoy myself immensely. Unless I'm greatly mistaken, Mr.
O'Malley, you're soon going to be making some very undig-
nified sounds. Two can play that little game, you know."

She was right. Now relaxed and confident, she moved like
the woman of beauty, intelligence, and experience she was,
taking O'Malley to dreamlike places he had never visited
with the girls in Bayonne. They made love together until the
pinpoints of city lights were swallowed by the pale predawn.
When he offered her a cigarette, she took it hungrily. They sat
naked and drank Mumms while the sun warmed the room.

She spoke without looking up. "Benjamin, will you stay
with me today? And make love?"

"I'll stay with you forever if you want."

It was an easy question, and the right answer. She grinned
and went running for her purse. When she returned she held
a silver key. "Here. I want you to have this. Use it whenever
you want. Day or night. Just as you may use me. I *know* I can
make you happy."

There was no doubt. O'Malley accepted the gift gratefully but couldn't think of a thing to say. Or a thing to think. So he kissed her again.

11

Monday mornings have a way of destroying dreams. He woke about six when the low sun threw javelins of light through the canyon trees and into the room. His bedmate was curled up, naked and breathing softly under a thin sheet. He removed the sheet and kissed the little valley formed by the hills of her hips and ribs. She purred softly. He hoped the kiss added something to her dreams. He dressed quickly and stole out without waking her.

If he hadn't known where he was going, the ride down would have been beautiful. As it was, the peace of the early morning canyon did no more than dull the sharp distaste he felt at the thought of another week at the fifty-story monument to wealth and tedium. Nevertheless they were paying him to do a job. He was suited up and at his desk at 7:45— number seventy-three on the guard's list.

Because everything was different for him, he expected it to be different at J & D. It wasn't. The help came in at nine, as always. More importantly the ACR file occupied the same place on his desk as it had when he left to join Baird for that watershed drink at the Bonaventure.

Soon there was no doubt he was back. His secretary arrived

at 9:15 with an inch-high stack of directives from the Management Committee, Baird's door closed with the same slam at 9:30, and Mildred called at 9:45 to demand that he appear for a meeting in Marks' office at 11:00. The mention of Marks reminded him of the case, which made him think of Rad, which made him lean back with a cup of coffee and a cigarette and think of all sorts of things he shouldn't have during working hours at J & D. He again considered calling her and saying, "I love you madly and I've decided to leave the firm, sell my house, and cook, clean, and make myself handsome for you in Laurel Canyon." He didn't, of course, but it made for a wonderful hour-long fantasy.

O'Malley arrived on schedule for the audience. Marks was on the phone as usual and O'Malley spent the time in quiet despondency at Rad's absence. When Marks was finished he stared at O'Malley. His voice was flat and hard. "I understand you had a meeting with our clients," he said.

O'Malley was lost in his thoughts and Marks had to ask twice. "That's right. On Friday," O'Malley said finally.

"I was not informed."

It wasn't a question so O'Malley didn't give a response. O'Malley's unanswered phone messages were stacked on a spike on the corner of Marks' desk.

"In the future, please inform me before initiating any contact with our clients."

O'Malley laughed slightly. They played the game of stares and O'Malley lost, as he knew he would. "In the first place I did not initiate any contact. I received a call from Rendt's secretary—"

"Mr. Rendt."

"All right, Mr. Rendt. His secretary asked that I come to a meeting at ACR. I called and told Mildred about it." He pointed to the spike. "It's right there with the rest of them."

Marks ignored that. "What was the purpose of this meeting?"

"To tell me further details of the sale. Also to introduce me to Frank Pisano."

That inspired Marks. "Pisano was there?"

"Yes. Mr. Pisano was there."

"And what did you and Mr. Pisano discuss?"

"We didn't discuss anything. Nothing except pleasantries, that is. Rendt . . . Mr. Rendt did most of the talking."

"And who else was there?"

"Hardwick and Friedrich—more or less." O'Malley was tired of the "Mister" game.

Marks became lost in thought. It was awhile before he spoke. "I'd like you to tell me everything that transpired at this meeting. Do not edit your thoughts. Do not leave anything unsaid. Please begin."

O'Malley gave him as much detail as he could recall. Prominent in the report were his observations about Rendt's motivations and the boys' collective intelligence. Marks listened intently without interrupting. When O'Malley was through Marks stared at the ceiling, erecting a church with his fingers.

"And that's *all* that was discussed. Nothing else. Nothing about the funds that Video Enterprises lost? Nothing about where those funds are today?"

"That's right." O'Malley concentrated on the general question. The importance of the specific never registered.

Marks gave the church a steeple. "Nevertheless, you doubt the wisdom of the transaction."

O'Malley shrugged. "As far as the boys are concerned, sure. It's obviously stupid for them to be collateralizing their stock. What happens when they can't make the payments? They'll lose everything."

Marks nodded. "I had not known that collateralization was to be a condition. Yet perhaps the boys will not default. Maybe they can afford it."

"Maybe someone can. They can't. The thirty-seven and a half million is amortized over five years at ten and a quarter percent interest."

"Not exactly usurious."

"No, the interest is fair. The purchase price is grossly un-

68

fair. I haven't figured it out exactly, but the boys will be responsible for payments of something like ten million dollars a year for the next five years. That's assuming Video Enterprises doesn't continue to lose money at its present glorious rate."

Marks shook his head. "It won't." He said it to himself, as if it were an angle of the deal he was a party to. Nevertheless, his face was still confused. "What is the present stockholder array at ACR?"

That was something O'Malley had thought of, too. "There are just over two million shares outstanding. Each of the boys owns one hundred thirty thousand, or about twelve and a half percent collectively. Klaus Rendt's company owns twelve and a half percent. The public owns one and a half million shares, or seventy-five percent, at a price of better than one hundred dollars per share. The public holdings are worth in excess of one hundred fifty million dollars."

"Who are the principal shareholders, aside from the original joint venture partners?"

"There's a pension fund in Chicago that holds twenty thousand shares, or almost one percent. After that it drops off dramatically. The next largest shareholder is a widow in Ocean Beach, Maryland, who owns seventy-five hundred shares, or about three-eighths of one percent. The median holding, excluding the joint venture partners, is one hundred thirty shares." O'Malley didn't have to do any calculations to find those numbers. There was a memo in the ACR file that laid it all out. Rendt had done his homework.

"How will the stockholder array be affected in the case of default?"

That was also in the memo. "If the boys default, their stock will revert to the corporation. Rendt will then hold almost fifteen percent of the one-point-eight million shares remaining." What wasn't in the memo was that Rendt wouldn't have a competitor in sight.

They didn't pay Marks a half million a year to overlook the obvious. "So in the event of default, Mr. Rendt will battle with his two hundred sixty thousand shares against the one percent holder from Chicago and the widow from Ocean City. The prize will be control of the corporation."

"That is correct."

"And who will win, Benjamin?"

"Mr. Rendt will win, sir."

He began nodding. They both knew that it didn't take 51 percent to exercise control. With the boys out of the way, Rendt could exercise absolute control with 10 percent or less. Then Marks did something very strange. He giggled. Right there in his gray suit behind his lucite desk. First a small snort. Then a horse laugh. Soon he was pounding his thigh and howling. O'Malley's unsmiling face only sent him to new heights of mirth. He buzzed for Mildred and tried to place an order, but the unknown humor kept distracting him. Mildred began laughing with him. Her sycophantic wheezing sickened O'Malley and quickly sobered Marks. He sent her shuffling for some China cups.

"I apologize, Benjamin."

"No problem, sir."

"It's just that—well, let's just say that I find the potential gain to Mr. Rendt amusing and unexpected."

O'Malley didn't, so he said nothing in response.

"Goodness." Marks wiped his eyes and took a deep breath. "Nevertheless, Benjamin, we have a job to do. Mr. Rendt is correct in observing that it is without our province to question the fairness of the transaction. The other parties are free to obtain advice if they wish. Since they do not . . ." He spread his hands and left the sentence unfinished.

"That seems to be the prevailing view."

Marks consulted his calendar, making little noises with his lips. "However, I do see that I have a problem with my other matters." He looked back at O'Malley. It was the sort of expression that made a smart man feel for his wallet. "Therefore, I'm afraid I must lateral this matter to you. You may assume you have primary responsibility. I'll draft a memo to the file to that effect."

O'Malley didn't realize that his wallet was now empty.

"All right."

"If you run into problems take advantage of Ms. Radnowski's experience. Has she been useful, by the way?"

A frog was camping in O'Malley's throat. "Yes. Ah . . . most . . . satisfying arrangement."

"Good." They both rose and shook hands. O'Malley neglected to count his fingers on the way out.

12

One of the marks of success and advancement at J & D was the ability to speak in sports metaphors. The female lawyers complained of what they saw as a disadvantage. But there really wasn't one. Many of the men knew nothing of the underlying games either. Nevertheless, effective communication was possible. If a lawyer were told, "The ball is in your court, now run with it," he knew exactly what was required, notwithstanding the concern such conduct would cause at Wimbledon. Litigators were continually bragging about throwing curves or high hard ones at opponents. Young associates were always being lateraled assignments or told to run interference for partners. Carrying the ball was good, dropping the ball was bad. A rising young buck couldn't wait to step up to the plate and serve an ace.

Therefore, when Marks made it clear, in classic jockese, that he was no longer to be involved with ACR, O'Malley knew exactly what he meant. But he was also surprised. Delegation of that sort was virtually unprecedented. Senior partners did not entrust multimillion dollar transactions to first-year associates unless there was a hell of a good reason. Unless there were special circumstances.

O'Malley employed an army of paralegals and secretaries to put the paperwork together but it still took a month to complete the twelve hundred pages of legalese. The paralegals organized documents, proofread, compiled appendices, and arranged the closing party. The secretaries pushed buttons and read printouts at computer terminals in the word processing center—known in simpler times as the steno pool—like engineers at Houston Control. The pages appeared as little green reproductions on seven of the thirty-two television screens over banks of input terminals, or typewriters as they are sometimes called. Draft after draft of the twelve hundred went down into the bowels to be resurrected clean at the touch of a button on a high-speed printer. A good-sized grove of trees went to its grave to support this effort.

The final twelve hundred comprised about fifteen separate agreements that nailed the deal down like a coffin. There was the basic sales agreement between ACR and an artificial entity named NEWCO; the promissory note from NEWCO to ACR; the escrow agreements; the collateral agreements; ACR board minutes; more collateral agreements; articles of incorporation for F&H Holding Company; assumption agreements whereby F&H took over all the assets and liabilities of NEWCO; F&H board minutes; and finally a secret management agreement that insured that the boys would never lift a finger for F&H, ACR, or anyone else. Added to that were a host of amendments, riders, letter agreements, and filings with the SEC, the FTC, Justice Antitrust, and the California Department of Corporations. At the end O'Malley was sure of two things. First, the deal was airtight. Second, the boys would lose everything.

O'Malley had the papers collated, bound, indexed, stamped "DRAFT" and sent to Marks, Rad, and everyone involved at ACR. Rad sent hers back with a sealed note that said, "I love it and I love you." Pisano sent over a memo saying, "It looks real nice." Marks just returned his draft; he had changed all the arabic numerals to Roman and vice versa. On the front was scribbled, "I assume you've talked all this over with the appropriate people." No one else responded.

The only duties left were to send the draft back to Houston Control to make Marks' sadistic changes and hold the closing party. A closing party is a time-honored tradition in deal law. After everybody justifies his fees by arguing about trivia for six months, there's an expensive catered affair at which corporate officials sign documents and pass out pens, everyone gets a transparent paperweight encasing a miniature reproduction of the front page of the agreement, and the businessmen get drunk and try to ball the paralegals. The lawyers get drunk, too, but they've already balled the paralegals so they usually leave early. It's all good fun and a reward to private enterprise for being more efficient than bloated government agencies.

This closing party established a new low for the genre. At Rendt's insistence the celebration was held in a conference room at ACR, with crackers, Velveeta, and jug wine for all. Rendt, Pisano, and the boys arrived on schedule and signed immediately, without ceremony. O'Malley wanted to wait for Marks but when it became clear that he wasn't coming went ahead and signed for J & D. Rad was there, looking as luscious as ever. Rendt seemed uncomfortable and kept holding his wine up to the light. After ten minutes of awkwardness Rendt discovered an emergency and left, the boys trailing alongside like the skirts of a sailboat.

O'Malley breathed easier with Rendt gone, hoping the uncomfortable affair could be wrapped up quickly. But there was still Pisano to consider, and Pisano had obviously started his own private party much earlier. Now he had Rad trapped in a corner, regaling her with a saga of the bad tip he had received from the feedbox at Hollywood Park. His hands were working like pistons driving the tale forward. Rad had a strained, set smile and her gaze passed over Pisano's shoulder, requesting help. O'Malley wandered over to save her.

"So you gotta understand what it was like," Pisano was saying. "This is her first time out and she thinks it's great, thinks the jocks are cute. But the numbers on the sheet are all Greek. I tell her, 'No need to look at the paper, that's for losers.' So we're sitting there, right. She's all excited and I'm just relaxing with a big cigar, holding twenty of these five-hundred-dollar tickets. And I say to her, 'Baby, hold these for luck.' So she takes them, and she's got them between her boobs with both hands like they're gold. And I say, 'Baby, you just relax. Frankie's got this covered.' The bell goes off and my guy breaks on top like he's Secretariat. She's jumping up and down with the tickets and I'm half-asleep like it's nine o'clock mass. They hit the backstretch and there's a football field between me and the rest of the pack. She thinks I'm God. My jock's got the whip in his back pocket and he's thinkin' about where he's gonna lay the log later. Then they hit the far turn and everything gets all bunched up. Can't see a thing. They head for home and it's like 'five' dropped in a hole. She's screaming, 'Where's five?' and I'm up lookin' for my ten grand. They all go under and about a half hour later 'five' comes limpin' along on three legs. I'm screaming, 'Shoot the bastard' and the cigar's burning a hole in my crotch. She's holdin' the tickets like she got a dead rat in her hands."

He shook his head sadly. Apparently such betrayal was unheard of at Aqueduct. Also apparent was Pisano's penchant for picking losers. But Rad and O'Malley remembered to laugh heartily, which cheered him.

"Hey, let's not talk about bad news. How about some vino, Benny?" O'Malley flinched at the name but dutifully held out his plastic glass, then slurped quickly to catch the overflow. Pisano turned drunkenly to Rad and grabbed O'Malley around the shoulders, causing wine to cascade down his pretty J & D pinstripes anyway. "You know, Benny here is from the old country. Newark, ain't it?"

O'Malley was wiping and squirming. "Bayonne."

"Yeah, that's right." His embrace got tighter and the words thicker. "I'm from Jersey City myself. Great town. Lots of action back there now, especially with the gambling down the shore. And right across the river is the greatest city in the world, ain't that right, Benny?"

O'Malley thought that was a reasonable proposition, so he clunked Pisano's plastic tumbler. The gesture didn't cause Pisano to loosen his grip. Instead he hugged O'Malley tighter and the words came faster.

"It's different back there. People back there got character. They care about important things, like the family." O'Malley hoped Pisano was speaking about his mother. "And it's great for kids. I just about lived in the city when I was seventeen because the drinking age was so low. We used to hang out at this Spanish place across from Saint Anthony's, I'll never remember the name. Nobody could speak the language in there so they could care less how old we were. A little rough getting back across the water, but that was half the fun. Great town for kids."

He looked at O'Malley, expecting a contribution. "I know what you mean," O'Malley said. "Out here they just put the kids in soccer leagues. What fun is that?" Pisano laughed in agreement, but his eyes narrowed a bit. "You ain't cracking the cubes, are you?"

"Hell, no." O'Malley said it quickly. To further demonstrate good faith, he told Pisano the name of his childhood bar. It was called El Cortijo and it was still where it had always been, a block off Bleecker, right across from Saint Anthony's, a quarter mile from NYU, still serving minors. Pisano roared and embraced O'Malley as if he were meeting his grandfather off the boat from Sardinia. Nevertheless, O'Malley decided to stow the quips for the evening.

There was enough jug wine for thirty so the three of them were well provisioned. After the first half-gallon was gone Frank and O'Malley were hugging like brothers, trading stories like seamen. Between each ribald tale they'd turn to Rad, becoming gushingly extravagant about her beauty, brains, taste, ancestry, and all-around wonderfulness. She loved the attention and tales and egged them on by begging for more. Pisano and O'Malley ran out of reality fairly early, but the apocryphal makes better stories anyway and there is a lot more of it. Nobody noticed the outer offices emptying or the sun sweeping past the San Diego Freeway and sizzling into the ocean off Santa Monica. It was late and dark when they finally quieted.

O'Malley was feeling mellow and friendly, all sheets definitely pointed windward. Pisano stretched and checked his watch. "Damn, I hate to break this up, but I'm supposed to meet some people for dinner soon." He looked crestfallen, then brightened. "Hey, why don't you guys come along? On ACR, of course."

O'Malley smiled inanely, ready to go any place with anybody. But Rad interceded. "No, I think it's time for this warrior to be put to bed." Her smile was a window into her thoughts. "And he needs to be rewarded for his wonderful work on this case."

Pisano howled and pummeled them both, swearing that even if they tortured his mother the secret would never pass his lips. They all drank a few more blatantly prurient toasts to Rad and then finally left. Rad took the keys and stormed down Sunset like a pro, the night air reviving the two of them with the smell of million-dollar flowers from the Beverly Hills lawns. At the canyon O'Malley took a cold shower and emerged refreshed, clad in a towel. They dined on fruit by candlelight for an hour and then they dined on each other in darkness for two. They lay in bed naked for half the night talking of their lives together.

O'Malley's legal career then had seven weeks to go.

13

The unraveling of his life actually started about three weeks before the denouement, such things as the destruction of a career taking a bit of time. But there were still twenty-eight glorious days between the sentimental journey with Pisano and the beginning of the end. Those days were new-penny bright and as tranquil as a dawn on the moors. The storied calm.

ACR was gone for all practical purposes. There were still the ministerial functions of transfer of paper and checks, but those tasks are handled by banks, not lawyers. O'Malley viewed ACR's departure with modest mixed feelings. It had been a bad case in a lot of ways and the principals were certainly bizarre. Nevertheless, it had given him Rad and a degree of responsibility over a complex matter that was surprisingly satisfying.

J & D had an innate sense of knowing when an employee was ready for more work. O'Malley had only begun boxing up the ACR documents for shipment to the file room when the calls came from the partners looking for an available body. O'Malley studied the names, breathed a sigh of relief that Marks' was not among them, and selected one with a reputation for fairness and minimal humanity.

It was a good choice. The partner was young, soft-spoken, and had pleasant manners, which he didn't reserve for superiors and clients. He also had a wife and three daughters and was as interested in spending time with them as he was with pursuing greatness. Even the case was attractive; a nice, juicy movie industry merger in which all the principals were what they seemed to be and didn't carry guns. O'Malley was informed somewhat apologetically that the case would likely take all his time for awhile but shouldn't involve nights and weekends. "Too bad," O'Malley replied.

It was an idyllic month. He slid in at nine and was out by six. When he wasn't working in the office he was working in the canyon, single-mindedly pursuing the goal of making Rad happy. Each evening he stopped at the market in Chinatown and stocked up on the freshest produce and seafood. When Rad returned to the canyon at 7:30 he greeted her apron-adorned with drink in hand like Donna Reed. O'Malley's culinary skills were more technical than imaginative, the theory being if it wasn't in the book it didn't go into the pot. Nevertheless, he labored over a new delicacy each night. Afterward he'd lead her to the couch. There they'd sip wine and watch the lights turn on, and while they chatted quietly, O'Malley would undress her and experiment some more.

Weekends were a continuation of the dream. The lovers would lie naked in bed with the paper and coffee until the sun was high, then yank on shorts and hop in the topless Healey for a run down the coast. They'd brunch somewhere on the water and spend the day on the sands with the gulls or in the shops with the people from Iowa, occasionally slipping away under a pier to sneak a joint with the surfers, giggling like high schoolers. When evening came the sun would douse itself with a flash in the water and they'd head back to the canyon, stopping along the way for an early dinner before the crowds came. There were hours saved for lovemaking and they were asleep by eleven. By the end of the month they were both ruddy from the wind and sun, trim from the good food and Rad's insistence that O'Malley travel gasping in her wake while she ran on the beach, and clear-eyed from the relaxation that came from making love.

It couldn't last. It didn't. The clouds rolled in on an ordinary Tuesday night. They were lying in bed. A television set was on without sound in the corner. Suddenly Rad jumped up and pointed. "Hey, look, there're the boys." O'Malley ran over and turned up the sound. Hardwick and Friedrich were walking down the steps of the Federal Courthouse surrounded by a pride of beefy white males carrying briefcases. A woman's voice overlay their progress.

"KNXL has learned today that a federal grand jury in Los Angeles is investigating financial irregularities in the affairs of Associated Computer Research, the California-based electronics firm.

Although grand jury proceedings are secret, KNXL has also learned from sources close to the investigation that subpoenas were sent to Allen Friedrich and James Hardwick, president and chairman of ACR. Friedrich and Hardwick are shown here emerging from a meeting with federal prosecutors earlier today.

In response to questions from KNXL reporters, Friedrich and Hardwick stated that they did not testify before the grand jury today. They declined to comment on the purpose of the meeting, based on the advice of counsel.

KNXL has learned, however, that the meeting today may have been designed to work out an immunity deal for the two executives in return for their testimony. Persons familiar with grand jury proceedings state that a private meeting with prosecutors virtually assures that an immunity deal is in the works.

Federal officials declined comment on the purpose of the meeting or on the subject of the grand jury's investigation. Back to you, Karen."

The camera switched to a painted talking head in the studio. She read the ACR copy with the same intensity she used for air disasters, freeway stranglers, and missing cats. "And

Fred [referring to her alcoholic co-anchorperson], we have more from New York on this fast-breaking story."

The camera switched again to a distinguished-looking gentleman standing in the aislelike streets beneath the Wall Street cathedral.

"News of the ACR investigation hit the tape twenty minutes before the bell and trading in the stock was frantic before the close.

ACR opened the day at one hundred four and five-eighths and inched up with the Dow to one hundred five and one-quarter before the news reached Wall Street. At the bell the Dow was up four and a half points on a moderate volume of thirty-six million shares. But the bottom fell out of ACR as the Los Angeles-based electronics firm lost twelve to finish at ninety-two and five-eighths.

Selling pressure on the stock is expected to be heavy tomorrow and analysts predict that the Exchange will suspend trading for a few days until more is known of the investigation.

Investors are understandably nervous about grand jury probes in light of several spectacular failures in recent years, involving such glamour stocks as Equity Funding Corporation, Mattel Corporation, and the entities controlled by fugitive financier Robert Vesco."

The camera went back to Karen in the studio, who squinted to read the prepared joke off the cue cards. "Well, Fred, I hope you didn't have your money in the stock market."

"No, Karen, my wife won't let me gamble." All the anchorpersons exploded in laughter.

"And when we return," Karen said, "Biff will have some blue news for Dodger blue."

There was a quick shot of Bill Russell fielding a two-hopper and throwing it, as always, into the Dodger dugout. O'Malley switched off the set with a curse. Rad was sitting cross-legged looking dazed.

"Holy shit." She said it long and soft.

"I didn't know you were such a fan." Neither of them laughed. Rad looked up at him.

"I don't believe it. No—take that back—I believe it. I should have known this was coming." She punched a pillow hard.

"Why?" When he didn't get an answer his voice got louder. "What the fuck's going on? Have you heard anything about a grand jury?"

She shook her head. "Let's call the office. Maybe Marks is still there." She called. He wasn't. Only a lot of overworked associates with a lot of questions, she said. O'Malley tried Marks at home and got a busy signal for thirty minutes, a reasonably sure sign the phone was off the hook. Then he tried ACR and got a recording saying that office hours were nine to six.

"Do you have any home numbers?" she asked.

He nodded. "They're all unlisted but I've got them written down."

"Where—at the office? We could have somebody get them."

"No, at home. Let's go over there and get them. We'll wake them all up if we have to."

She considered it and then relaxed with a defeated look. "No, let's forget it for tonight. I'm too tired to get dressed and too selfish to send you." She managed a weak smile. He didn't return it. For the first time in his memory his attention had shifted from her body.

"Let's walk through this," O'Malley said. "Do you know anything about grand juries?"

"No. Do you?"

"No." They both snickered briefly at their incompetence. The cop on the corner knew more about grand juries than these two lawyers.

"How about ACR? Do you know of anything that would cause the Justice Department to get interested?"

Rad snapped her answer at him. "If I did, don't you think I would have told you?" He saw she was getting anxious.

"O.K., don't get mad," he said soothingly. "But don't you have any guesses?"

She opened her hands. "It could be a deal I did. It could be something Marks worked on. It could be something J and D wasn't even involved in. How the fuck should I know?"

So it had to wait till morning. He decided to make peace. "Would it help if I helped myself to a snack?"

She grinned and her eyes lost their fire immediately. She stretched to full length, arms outstretched, toes extended. "Immensely."

At eight the next morning there were fourteen phone messages on his desk. Thirteen were from his fellow rookies searching for information. The fourteenth was from Armington Bishop. O'Malley called back and Bishop "asked" him to come up for coffee. O'Malley sprinted up the stairs, assuming he'd find a war conference already underway. He was surprised to see that the meeting involved only the two of them.

Bishop began talking about all sorts of nonsense; how was O'Malley liking the firm, how was he getting along with partners and clients, whether his workload was too burdensome. O'Malley answered quickly, then sat squirming in his chair waiting for Bishop to get to the point. Finally he did, but with the same exasperating circumlocution. When O'Malley had had enough he cut him off.

"Mr. Bishop, I'm . . ."

"Armington."

"O.K., Armington. Maybe I can speed this up. I'd really like to chat with you at any time about all of these matters but right now I'm tremendously concerned about the grand jury."

"So am I, Benjamin."

"So why don't we talk about that?"

"We are."

O'Malley stared dumbly. Then he got it. Bishop was conducting an elegant cross-examination, gently probing around the edges and working toward the middle the way a man eats an artichoke. The process was dangerous and insidious.

"Look, I'm willing to tell you anything you want to know," O'Malley said. "Just ask me straight out and I'll give you straight answers. I'm on your side, you know."

"Are you, Benjamin?"

O'Malley suddenly felt very cold. But also angry. "You're goddamn right I am. Whose side do *you* think I'm on?"

"I don't know, Benjamin. That's the purpose of our meeting—to find the truth and in the process to determine the nature of your involvement."

"My involvement with what?" He was shouting now.

"Your involvement with the embezzlement of fifty-three million dollars from the shareholders of ACR. More specifically, I suppose, your involvement with the efforts to cover up the embezzlement by the recent sale of an ACR subsidiary to a shell corporation. A sale that you engineered and signed off on."

O'Malley laughed at that and felt the last veneer of politeness fall from his words. "Look, pal, I don't know what horseshit you're selling. I'm the hired help here. If there was an embezzlement—which wouldn't surprise me in the least—it was your clients who did the embezzling. As a matter of fact I think I can tell you right where the money went. And if there was a coverup—which also wouldn't surprise me—it was the esteemed Mr. Randall Elliott Marks—*your* fucking partner—who did the covering up."

"You say you're not surprised to learn of the embezzlement. Where do you think the money went?" Bishop ignored the young man's rage. His questions remained cool and precise.

But O'Malley had now lost all judgment. He blundered on. "Fifty-three million dollars is precisely the sum that Video Enterprises lost in a three-year period. I don't think Pisano spent the money on movies at all. Or at least not much of it. I think it was an ingenious plot to siphon money from ACR. He makes all the movies for a song in Venezuela and launders the rest. It doesn't matter then whether the flicks live or die. He, the boys, and probably Rendt, too, just pocket the cash and write it all off at tax time."

"When did you form that theory, Benjamin?"

"Just now, when you mentioned fifty-three million dollars."

"That's quite remarkable. It's also a perfectly accurate, albeit inartfully stated, rendition of the United States attorney's theory. Are you sure you weren't told this earlier?"

"Quite sure." O'Malley was now feeling very, very sick.

"You also mentioned you weren't surprised at the involvement of the ACR principals?"

"That's right."

"Why?"

"Because they're crooks. I know it and you know it, too."

"I do indeed. The question is how—or more precisely when—you formed this judgment. Was it before or after you completed work on the file?"

"Before, long before." He sensed right away that the answer wasn't helpful.

"Did you communicate that judgment to the partner on the file?" Bishop asked.

"Marks, no. Well, sort of, but not really. It was only a guess. I . . . I didn't want to appear stupid."

"Did you tell anyone?"

"Baird. Jerome Baird in Litigation." He mentally kicked himself. Bishop knew who Baird was and also knew O'Malley was nervous. Bishop wrote the name down.

"Where and when did you speak to Mr. Baird?"

"A month ago. In his office. In a bar. Lots of times. Baird knows my feelings."

"Mr. Baird is a personal friend of yours, I take it?"

"My best fr— . . . yes, he is." Bishop smiled and scribbled some more.

84

"Did you tell Mr. Baird the details of the embezzlement as you have described it there?"

"No. Not the details. I didn't know them then." O'Malley stopped, then added hurriedly, "I mean, I still don't know any details." Bishop smiled again.

"Did you speak to anyone else?"

"Yes, Rad, uh, Ms. Radnowski in Corporate. She was on the file, too."

"Where and when did you speak with Ms. Radnowski."

"All along. In the office. Out of the office."

"On both business and social occasions."

O'Malley hesitated—a fatal hesitation, as is said in the books. "Yes."

"Do you see Ms. Radnowski often on social occasions?"

". . . Yes."

"Are you presently engaging in sexual relations with Ms. Radnowski?"

"How would you like to kiss my Irish ass, Bishop?" They stared. Bishop spoke again with his faint lisp.

"Not overly much, Mr. O'Malley." He wrote some more.

"Did you tell anyone else aside from Mr. Baird and Ms. Radnowski?"

"No."

"And did you tell Ms. Radnowski your theory of the case as you've described it here?"

"No."

Bishop nodded and began staring at the ceiling in approved senior partner fashion.

"Let's turn to your handling of the file. Who were you working with?"

"Marks and Rad."

"Did Mr. Marks have day-to-day contact with you or the client?"

"He knew the deal. He attended the meeting where it was all explained."

"You mean the first meeting, here at J and D?"

"Yes."

"Isn't it true that Mr. Marks left that meeting right after lunch? Before there was any discussion of this transaction?"

"Yes . . . I suppose so."

"Did he attend any meetings after that?"

O'Malley had to think about that. The answer was remarkable. "No."

"But you did."

"Yes."

"Did Ms. Radnowski?"

"No. Except for the closing."

"But you all attended the luncheon meeting at Genevieve's?"

"That's right.

"And Mr. Friedrich was called away by a frantic emergency by the comptroller of ACR, a Mr. Barrett. Do you know why?"

O'Malley had never before thought about it but now knew exactly why. "I can guess. It was somebody blowing the whistle. Barrett had to know what was going on—he handled all the receipts. He probably got scared, or someone working for him got scared."

"Remarkable, Mr. O'Malley, you're really quite good at this. Mr. Barrett's assistant was a Miss Kathleen Broder, now Mrs. Kathleen Weidman, a woman of high principle who was really never cut out for a life of crime. Just as you say, Mr. O'Malley, she got scared. Tell me, did you just happen upon that observation also?"

O'Malley ignored the question, now so intrigued with the tale that his own danger was secondary. "So why did they go through with the deal if Mrs. Weidman was going to blow the whistle?"

"Assuming you are not already in possession of that information, the answer is that Mr. Pisano had a conversation with her late one evening and convinced her that there was a great deal more to fear by speaking than by remaining silent."

O'Malley had absolutely no doubt that a threat from Frank Pisano would be an extraordinarily powerful inducement to silence.

"So if she didn't blow, who?"

"She ultimately did. You see, Mr. O'Malley, physical threats do not always breed long-term loyalty. They do, however, breed long-term anxiety. Last year Miss Broder married a serious young man by the name of Marc Weidman. Mr. Pisano even sent them a lovely and quite expensive present. Mr. Weidman was a student at the time. He is presently an assistant United States attorney. When Pisano threatened her she remained silent and anxious for a period of time. Then one evening she broke down weeping and told her husband. He knew how to respond."

O'Malley nodded and made the mistake of speaking his thoughts. "The one thing Pisano couldn't figure on."

"Yes, I understand you know Mr. Pisano quite well, don't you?"

"Hardly."

"You're about the same age?"

O'Malley laughed. "I'm about the same age as Maurice Lucas, too. Do you think he's involved?" Bishop wrote the name down.

"Is Maurice Lucas out of the French office?"

"Yes, then he went to the Portland office to play strong forward. Excellent ballplayer—really did as much as Walton for them. Now he's with the New Jersey office—I think Calvin Natt went the other way." Bishop looked at O'Malley as though he were insane but wrote it all down.

"Is that 'N-A-T'?" O'Malley ignored the question.

"Let's return to Mr. Pisano. You grew up together, didn't you?"

"No."

"You both grew up in northern New Jersey?"

"That's correct. To this day I have never set foot in Jersey City. I hope to die without doing so. I never laid eyes on Pisano before this case."

"But now he's a close friend." '

"No."

"You've had private meetings with him?"

"No."

Bishop consulted his notes. "On June 8, following the closing of the transaction, you and Ms. Radnowski met with Mr. Pisano for over five hours in the conference room of Associated Computer Research, did you not?"

So there it was. O'Malley didn't even have the energy to get angry or flippant anymore. "We sat there and reminisced about New Jersey."

"About the Jersey City you've never been to and about the past of a man you'd never seen before?"

"Actually it was about New York, not New Jersey."

"I see." Bishop screwed his gold pen shut and closed his yellow pad, then smiled amiably. O'Malley could feel the scarlet rise to his cheeks.

"Look, Bishop, this is getting us nowhere, although you may be having fun. If you've got some threats or accusations to make why don't you make them. Otherwise, I'm leaving."

"And as quickly as possible, sir. But I am a fair man, Mr. O'Malley, and before you leave I'll tell you precisely what I believe. And I'll be as brief as I can. As you say, the principals of ACR embezzled fifty-three million dollars from the shareholders of ACR. They even got a tax writeoff in the bargain. You came on the scene and based on a camaraderie with Mr. Pisano that may or may not have preceded your employment here—and I don't care which—you designed a plan to disguise the fraud by transferring the offending subsidiary to a fictitious third party, hoping, I suppose, that the embezzlement would simply be buried and forgotten once Video Enterprises was gone from the books of ACR. I assume that you received a piece of the action for your efforts, as they like to say in Mr. Pisano's world. You then deceived Mr. Marks about the nature of the transaction and sought to put the imprimatur of Jenkins and Dorman on the closing documents. You managed to keep Mr. Marks totally in the dark about the nature of the arrangements. Indeed, even at the very end he wrote you a memo stating that he assumed all the proper people had been consulted."

That he had. O'Malley had wondered why then but didn't wonder anymore.

"A nice theory. And you think you can prove it by the bullshit little questions you've been asking me here."

"Partly. But only as corroboration. The principal evidence against you, sir, is the grand jury testimony of Messrs. Hardwick and Friedrich, your partners in this criminal venture."

The statement hit O'Malley deep in the pit of the stomach. He felt like crying or throwing up. The boys had saved their ass by laying it off on a J & D lawyer. It was just as Baird had predicted: The one thing that would entice the U.S. attorney to bypass the heavies was the opportunity to nail someone from a big firm.

"Anything else?"

"Just the deposit on June 30 of one hundred thousand dollars into your checking account. I know we don't pay you that well. By chance have you been successful in pork bellies?"

"Would it matter to you if I said I don't know anything about that?"

Bishop simply smiled.

"O.K. Let's hear it all. Anything else."

"Just a couple of minor details. J and D will be representing the corporation in this matter. Obviously our interests and yours are wholly adverse. I suggest that you retain separate counsel. It is likely you will be indicted within a fortnight."

O'Malley was determined not to break down. He stared at the bridge of Bishop's nose like the sights of a rifle.

"And the other detail."

"Just this." Bishop pulled open his drawer and pressed a button. There was a loud click. He extracted a cassette tape. "I have taken the liberty of recording our conversation and I intend to turn it over to the federal prosecutor. You will likely hear many of the same questions when you testify before the grand jury. Therefore I suggest you give the same answers. It is a gross violation of California law to tape you without your permission, of course, but my position is that since this is a federal prosecution, California law is inapplicable. The position may be insupportable, but I'm sure your lawyer will have enough to do without litigating the question."

"You know you're a son of a bitch, don't you, Bishop?"

Bishop shrugged and affected an effeminate tone. "All males are sons of bitches, Mr. O'Malley."

O'Malley rose to leave but stopped at the door. "Oh, Bishop."

"Yes."

"Will this affect my progress at the firm?"

14

When he left the office he felt strangely calm, the anger Bishop created clearing his mind the way a storm blows away the smog. It was clear to him that a great number of very intelligent people were now frantically engaged in erecting complex legal machinery to destroy him slowly and unpleasantly. He had already been fired, he would soon be indicted by a federal grand jury, he would then be suspended immediately by the State Bar, and would ultimately be disbarred. Finally he might go to prison. Along the way he could count on spending every penny he had on legal fees. If anything was left it would go to pay the fines.

But O'Malley checked his arms and legs and found them all there and so far there was no physical pain. That was always his benchmark for differentiating real problems from paper problems. This was a paper problem. A very, very heavy paper problem.

So he went to see Baird, who was staring out the window as usual. The look on O'Malley's face surprised him.

"You look like a Moonie. Have you by chance found religion?"

"My tribulations are an Atlas rocket that have propelled me above the chaos of everyday life."

"That's very nice. Let me get a pen, I don't want to forget that."

"You scoff. But that's because you have not found peace."

"If you're planning on telling me about your love life—don't. I haven't slept with anything organic in about five years."

"No, I come not to torture you. I come to enlighten—to show you the peace that may also be yours for the small price of being fired."

Baird shrugged. "That's old news."

"Granted. But you must also be indicted and possibly convicted and disbarred."

"Explain."

"Before I begin you must pour a large amount of golden liquid into your hidden pewter chalices."

"O'Malley, it's eleven o'clock in the morning."

"What are you, Big Ben? This is peace I'm offering."

Baird poured. O'Malley talked. He told him everything, rehashing what he already knew and bringing him up to date on the grand jury and the morning coffee with Bishop. When he was finished it was close to twelve and the halls were empty. The streets thirty-six stories below were filled with small black shapes.

Baird refilled his own cup for the third time. His hands were calm but his face had an unprecedented animation. "That's quite a story, O'Malley. And to think I thought you were coming in here to bore me with another chapter from your tedious little life."

"Any ideas?"

"Yes, you need a lawyer."

"Who?"

He brightened even more. "Why me, of course."

"They'll never let you do it. You're a part of this firm, the firm that's going to represent the corporation. How many of those have you had, anyway?"

He shook his head. "The grand jury will go on for at least another month. Theoretically, that's a secret proceeding, so there's at least a chance that Bishop won't know who's representing you. That will enable me to remain here for awhile and see what I can find out. When you're indicted I'll have to come out of the closet, to use a phrase that is popular in my neighborhood. Then I will resign, a thought that is as attractive to me as a cool lagoon to a legionnaire. We will spend the next six months litigating your case in the courts and in the State Bar. You will pay me the full amount that you would pay a private lawyer, plus a slight premium for abandoning this illustrious institution."

It was quite an offer. Baird was proposing to throw away a shot at partnership in one of the most prestigious firms in the country in order to help. O'Malley could see he was deadly serious. He could also see that Baird would not stand for sentimental expressions of gratitude.

"Just one question. I don't mean to insult you, but do you know anything about criminal law?"

"Of course. I've never done a criminal case, but litigation is litigation. The rules are different and come out of different books, but essentially it's all the same. I work my ass off to develop every fact helpful to us and blunt every fact helpful to them. I'll have to do a little research, of course, but that will put me one up on the prosecutor."

O'Malley laughed. This was going to be great, the blind and the blind. He held out his hand and shook with Baird to consummate the deal. "O.K., counselor, where do we start? I assume we've got to have a chat with the boys?"

Baird waved the question away. "We'll talk about the boys tomorrow. The first thing I've got to do is hit the library and find out what the fuck a grand jury does."

Terrific.

O'Malley walked next door to sit and suffer in peace. He opened the office door and almost collided with a blue-shirted moving man, a very large blue-shirted moving man. The man had all the drawers open and files and personal papers alike piled on little red carts. It was clear that Bishop wasn't wasting time.

"May I ask what you're doing?"

The man wiped his face and pulled out a slip from a grubby shirt pocket. "Orders from Mr. Carey." Carey was the efficient and quite officious office manager. The man was squinting at the smudged, crumpled slip. "Says we supposed to be movin' all the files from this office up to Mr. Bishop's on forty-eight. Supposed to be done right away, too. Least I think that's what it says."

"Let me see that." O'Malley pretended to study it carefully.

"O.K. I see the problem. Isn't it always the case—they tell you guys half the story and expect you to do your jobs right." The man nodded and wiped like that sure was the truth.

"You see, I'm being promoted and moved up to Mr. Bishop's office."

The man looked around. "Yeah, I can see that. So you want me to take this stuff up now."

O'Malley shook his head. "No, Bishop's still there. You see, he's being promoted and made head of our Newport Beach office. So we have to get his stuff out before we can move mine in."

"I ain't got no slip for that."

"I know, I'll give you a slip." All J & D attorneys had

93

authority to order messengers and moving men about.

"So when you want him moved?"

"Well, he's up there now, so we have to wait till he gets done today. You know how these partners are." He sure did—half the problems in his life came from J & D partners.

"So here's the deal," O'Malley said. "Can you guys do some OT tonight?"

"Sure. But it's double time and a half."

"No problem." O'Malley wrote up a slip. "You gather up a crew and come on over tonight at ten o'clock. I want you to go up to Mr. Bishop's office and take out every file, every piece of furniture—desk included—everything from the walls, every piece of paper in the office, and load it on your truck and store it in your warehouse in Newport Beach until we call for it. Then it will be clean to move my stuff up. Think you can handle that?"

"Yeah, I guess so. We'll need about five guys. It'll take about two hours to get the stuff out and another hour to drive to Newport, but it shouldn't be a problem. What do I do, see the guard on forty-three when I come in?"

"No, no need for that." O'Malley gave him a card key, a means of entrance that he wouldn't need anymore. "You just come right to forty-eight and use this to get in. There's a freight elevator outside the door that runs direct to the basement. Just load the stuff on the elevator on forty-eight and transfer it to your truck in the basement. You can drive on out of here and never have to hassle with the guard."

"That's good. I don't get along with that guy. They gave him a uniform and now he thinks he's fucking Eliot Ness."

"Ain't it the truth?"

"What about the key?"

"Send it back to Mr. Bishop with the bill."

They shook and the man left. Maybe it would work and maybe it wouldn't. Nevertheless, O'Malley found himself whistling as he gathered up his belongings.

15

The boys were murdered in their large brass bed in Hancock Park on July 14, 1978. They were asleep when it happened and never saw the two intruders arrive.

The murderers placed pillows over the boys' heads and kept them there for at least ten minutes after their breathing stopped. Then they replaced the pillows under the lifeless skulls and put the boys in the same embrace in which they had found them. It was five days before the stench from the rotting corpses traveled over the acre of lawn and began to bother the neighbors.

O'Malley got real familiar with the scant known details of the crime during a series of pleasant chats with Detective Sergeant Robert McCabe at Parker Center, the headquarters of the LAPD. McCabe had asked him to come in voluntarily, just so he'd understand that this wasn't a "custodial interrogation" and there was really no need to get into all that Miranda nonsense. They talked about lots of things: O'Malley's job status (unemployed), his relationship with the boys, where he had been on the evening of July 14. They'd finish about four and O'Malley would go home and come back the next day. It was all very civilized. After three days of this Baird got to the point in his criminal law study that tells you not to talk to the cops, particularly in a potential death-penalty case.

Apparently there was very little to go on. The boys had gone to work that day at ACR like every other day. They attended meetings on financial matters in the morning and meetings on the grand jury probe in the afternoon. The guard's list showed them leaving at six. They dined at Port's on Santa Monica Boulevard at 6:45 and attended a play at the Pantages in Hollywood at 8:30. The play let out at 10:20 and they were seen at Musso & Frank's at 11:00 having coffee and pastries. They left at midnight and died that night. Friedrich's smashed watch had stopped at two.

The boys had occupied a sprawling brick colonial that backed up onto a golf course. The eight-foot-high ivy-encrusted stone wall that faced the street was riddled with security devices. On the side facing the golf course there were three wire strands fitted aesthetically between ancient oaks and overhanging a small brook. The wire was neither electrified nor barbed. All three strands had been snipped in the middle and there was no evidence the murderers had even gotten their feet wet.

Mrs. Pamela Redstone, wife of the famous psychiatrist, was nine and one-quarter months pregnant and occupied the estate abutting the golf course a quarter mile south of the boys. At 1:50 A.M. she woke up for the ninth time that night and dug her elbow into her husband's ribs. Her husband handed her a watch, told her to time her contractions and wake him if the water broke, then went back to sleep. Mrs. Redstone wasn't having contractions so she went out on the deck for a cigarette. At 2:12 by her watch she saw two men—one "kinda hippy-looking"—running across the twelfth green into the rough around the eighth fairway and on through a gate into the street beyond. She thought about calling the police but decided against it.

The physical evidence was virtually nonexistent, primarily because the boys' idea of defense and security was apparently copied from the French in World War I. From the front their domain was impenetrable. From the rear the killers gained entrance by snipping the three wires, strolling across the wide lawn (in formless rubber shoes), opening an unlocked screen door, using a credit card to flip a latch, and walking from there to the bedroom. There was some mud and grass on the tile floor, but these were spaced at such odd intervals that it was impossible to gauge the stride and hence the height of the intruders.

The marks on the bodies were ordinary and expected. Hardwick had a broken nose and various contusions around the mask. Friedrich had two broken fingers from slamming them against the wall in his final blind struggle and the same black and blue around the eyes and mouth. Friedrich also had a large oval contusion in the solar plexis, indicating his killer had driven the air out of his lungs with a fist to hasten the process of asphyxiation.

McCabe told O'Malley it would have taken a moderately strong man to do the job. It had also taken someone who knew how to kill. The killers had the advantage of surprise and probably got the pillow over the boys' faces easily enough. After that it was a death struggle, with the boys thrashing, kicking, and scratching in their final efforts to get precious air. Any break in the seal would begin the battle anew, so the murderers were likely astride the boys' heads, using knees, hands, and elbows to keep all passages closed. Friedrich probably broke free at some point, which accounted for the blow to the midsection. Amateur killers would have stopped and fled soon after the struggle ceased. These killers knew that repose meant only unconsciousness, that the body would automatically breathe again if given the chance. They knew that death requires a longer period of pressure with rebuffs to unconscious death spasms.

It didn't make a pretty picture. O'Malley found himself morbidly wondering if the killers spoke while they sat panting for ten minutes over the boys' quiet forms.

Having nothing physical to go on, the police looked around for people with motives. There were no wives and no butler.

The police then not unreasonably looked to see who the boys had accused in their conversations with the U.S. attorney. That's when McCabe invited O'Malley down to chat.

McCabe was not a stupid man. He used O'Malley as a resource, providing a certain amount of information in the hope that O'Malley would provide more in return. At the end of their talks McCabe patted him on the back, told him not to leave town, and volunteered the prediction, based on twenty years of police work, that the federal grand jury investigating ACR would clear his name. O'Malley went home and relaxed a bit for a week.

O'Malley was indicted by the federal grand jury for securities fraud on July 29, 1978, fifteen days after the boys' murder and seven days after McCabe's reassuring words. Three days later he was indicted by a state grand jury for being an accessory to an embezzlement. He asked Baird whether they could indict him twice for the same thing and Baird said he'd check on that but right now he was trying to figure out what happens at an arraignment. On August 8, 1978, seven days after the state indictment, the State Bar suspended his license to practice law pending an investigation "re disbarment." Suddenly the pretty distinction between real and paper problems vanished. For four days O'Malley drank Jack Daniels without such dilutions as ice, water, or a glass. It was on the morning of the fifth day that he found himself hanging half-dead on·the aforementioned plaster of paris dolphin.

16

O'Malley stared up through the blinding light and saw a lovely pair of tan legs clad in heeled sandals. They were familiar, pretty legs. A little paler than he recalled but life was tough all over.

She took off her shoes and dangled her feet in the water. "Hi." He raised an index finger feebly in response.

"I haven't seen you in awhile."

"I've been ill."

"Been feeling a little sorry for yourself, have you?"

"Don't be insensitive. At times like this it's very important to go out and cry in one's beer—or in my case, one's Jack Daniels." The sound of evil Jack's name made him almost lose control again. He grabbed the dolphin tighter and tried not to think of all those dead soldiers littering the battlefield of the house.

"Well, it's been five days now by my count and—"

"Four." The word came out hoarse, all moisture having long since been rubbed out of his throat. He cursed at the pain. "I must have smoked a fucking carton last night."

"O.K., four. Don't you think that's quite enough?"

O'Malley laughed and had an urge to respond as a child, to tell her to mind her own fucking business, that she didn't understand the pain and how any analgesic was acceptable, that he needed support, not nagging. But he didn't. For one thing, it seemed silly and melodramatic. More importantly, the notion of her standing up, putting on her shoes, and walking away was intolerable.

"I'll make a deal with you," he said. "If you agree that the last four days constituted perfectly acceptable and rational behavior under the circumstances, I will agree that it's gone on quite long enough."

Her smile flashed happy and warm. "It's a deal!" She jumped up. "Listen, O'Malley, I intend to stay here and mother you today. Is there anything special you'd like?" Hangovers always made him horny. He tried to leer but his face would only twitch. She put her hands on her hips. "There will be plenty of time for that. I was thinking more of putting food and coffee in your stomach."

"Tea and sympathy will be fine."

"Sorry, Mother knows best. Why don't you just stay in the water and try to recover until I call you." She went inside and he heard her gasp. He had a clear vision of the destruction that greeted her.

She was tough, though. She blasted the stereo to give her strength and went through the place like a whirlwind. She came out with box after box of empty bottles, cans, and debris for the garbage. Then she started on the full bottles, the full ashtrays, and the unsmoked cigarettes and they landed in the same place. That was O.K. with him.

The summer sun traveled high above the brown smog line and began again to bake the parched, poisoned hills. After a time, beads of sweat glistened on her arms as she lugged the boxes out. She stopped after one trip and eyed the pool. Then she squirmed out of her khaki walking shorts and blouse and dove into the pool naked. She cut the water like a fish and came up in front of him. Wordlessly she began inspecting him as if she were buying a horse, pulling down the skin over the cheekbones and checking the eyes, running her hand over his three-day stubble, massaging his filmed incisors with a forefinger. She seemed to make a decision. "You'll live—with a little work." He wasn't sure but decided to take her word for it.

She hopped out of the pool and into her shorts and went back to the fray. After a time she came back, bare-breasted with a towel around her neck and a makeshift scarf. "O.K., you're next."

He followed her to the bathroom, where the bath was drawn and clean towels laid out. On a table nearby was a razor, three Excedrins, three Alka's, and a glass of water. He downed everything quickly and slid into the hot water. Soon he smelled the cooking bacon.

When he was washed, shaved, drugged, and fed, and everything in the place neat as a pin, she sat him down at the large oak table in the den and brought in two legal pads and a pot of coffee. "How do you feel?"

"Fine."

"Are you ready to work?"

He nodded.

They began with the easy stuff—making lists and opening file folders. They analyzed each indictment: number of counts, operative statutes, dates, parties, co-conspirators, maximum penalties. The latter was a bit of a jolt. If convicted on all counts he faced eighty-six years in prison and a maximum fine of $6.3 million. O'Malley thought that was greedy, even for the government.

Then they made lists of dates—the date of the indictments; the dates of arraignment, motions, and trial; the dates of bail hearings; the dates of warrant and subpoena returns; even the dates of the crime itself—or at least as much as they could fathom from the intentionally conclusionary and vague language of the indictments.

Next they analyzed his economic situation. Rad was an absolutely first-rate lawyer and her questions on O'Malley's personal finances were direct and unembarrassed. He got into the rhythm and began responding with precise answers. Actually he was not badly off. In eighteen months the house J & D purchased for him had almost doubled in value in the tulip boom that once passed for the southern California housing market. With Rad's help and a little borrowing that money could sustain Baird and him for six months. Simple. They now had a war chest.

With the personal details out of the way Rad turned next to strategy. O'Malley was still in too much of a fog to think clearly and only half listened as Rad ticked off the problems and options. There were three problems, she said: the federal case, the state case, the disbarment proceedings. Of the three the only important one was the federal case. An acquital or good deal in federal court would virtually insure that the other two would wither and die. "Thus we tell Baird to have everything else put on ice pending the outcome of the federal proceedings." She looked at O'Malley for disagreement and when it didn't come wrote the instructions down. Then she dropped her pen and stared at him. Her voice was sharp.

"So what did you know about the embezzlement?"

O'Malley looked up, surprised. "I didn't even know there was one until I talked to Bishop. You know that. We watched the news reports together."

She nodded. "Don't get excited. I'm not accusing you of anything but I need to know what they might have against you and also what we might have to use against them." She paused. "So what did you know about the sale of Video Enterprises?"

He shrugged. "I suspected something. I always suspected something but I never knew enough to really figure it out." He tried to let his mind go back to the meeting in Rendt's office at ACR. "You see, at the beginning I couldn't understand why anyone would buy the company. Vid Ent was losing money—and had consistently lost money for almost seven years. At first it wasn't much. Then Pisano began making movies and the company lost over fifty-three million dollars in just over thirty-six months. The thing that I thought strange was not the money losses—anybody can lose money—it was the fact that the boys were putting up their own stock as security for the purchase of a loser at an outrageous price. You see, I thought that the deal was unfair to the boys, that they were being manipulated or forced into it. The purchase price was ridiculous."

"How much?"

"Thirty-seven and a half million."

"Did the company have any assets?"

"Nothing to justify that kind of price. A few leaseholds on bad parts of Sunset. Some equipment. Some cars for salesmen and Pisano, but even those were mostly leased. Little if any foreign assets, except for the films themselves. And the films were worthless, although they had a high, phony book value. All in all, maybe a quarter million in real assets, total. And no earnings, of course. But you probably know more about this than I do."

She shook her head. "No, I really don't. I knew ACR had a subsidiary named Vid Ent but that was all. I had never even met Pisano before the closing." She dropped her head to the notes. "So what do you think happened to the money, the fifty-three million dollars?"

He spread his hands. "All I know is what Bishop told me. The money went south and Pisano laundered it. I assume it's stashed in a bank in the Cayman Islands or someplace."

She nodded. "Any evidence of that?"

"I'm just guessing. Why?"

She shrugged. "It's a bargaining chip. Maybe we can convince them they've got problems. Tax problems. Violations of currency laws. I don't know. Have you heard anything about foreign banks?"

"No."

"Well, let's leave that for the moment. What do you know about the murders?"

"Lots." He told her about his ill-advised conversation with

Detective Sergeant McCabe and the information he had picked up. She listened intently, asked a lot of questions, and wrote it all down.

"What do you think of McCabe?"

"He's neither stupid nor insensitive. He regards me as someone with motive and no less opportunity than anyone else. But he doesn't think I'm a killer."

"Are you a suspect?"

"Technically, yes. But I honestly do not believe he suspects me."

"Whom does he suspect?"

"Everyone. And no one. He's smart but he really has very little to go on. He knows the murders were tied up somehow with the fraud. They had to be. Or if not the fraud itself, at least the grand jury investigation. But beyond that he doesn't have any more information than you or I that I know of."

"What about the FBI? Are they involved?"

"No. Murder is not a federal crime. Of course in this case the victims are witnesses in a federal prosecution so they could hang their hat on that if they wanted to. But so far it looks as if they're deferring to the jurisdiction of the LAPD."

"By the way, do you have an alibi?" For the first time her voice broke slightly. The only way he'd have had an alibi would be if he had been sleeping with someone else because on that night, for reasons he had long since forgotten, he had not slept with her. She seemed to want him to have an alibi and equally desperately want him to have been alone that night.

"No—sorry."

She grinned and wrote it down. "Too bad."

"O.K., let's turn to the evidence against you," she said. "I take it a lot of it is circumstantial." She was too good a lawyer to say "just circumstantial."

"Yes, and some of it's heavy. Like the deposit into my checking account of a hundred thousand dollars."

"Have you seen any of the documentation for that deposit?"

"No. And the government's already gotten an impounding order for the money."

"So we'll need to subpoena the bank records and just hope that whoever deposited the money used the bank's deposit form rather than one stolen from your checkbook. We can also hope that they didn't take the time to do a good job on the forgery." She was scribbling furiously. "Then we'll need a detective to interview the bank tellers—they should remember a deposit that large in cash—and a handwriting expert that we hire and is on our payroll. I'll take care of all that." More scribbling.

"Then, of course, there's the direct testimony," she said.

"You mean the boys?" She nodded.

"Well, again, all I know is what Bishop told me. The principal people in on the embezzlement were the boys, Pisano, and an accountant named Barrett. Barrett's assistant blew the whistle to the U.S. attorney. The boys had to name someone besides Pisano so they picked me. I guess that's when someone decided to substantiate the story by putting the money into my account. I can also guess that it's not very healthy to tell tales on Frank Pisano."

"So you think Pisano killed them?"

"I don't know. Sure. Why not?"

"Did anybody tell you that?"

"No."

"Not even McCabe?"

"No."

"Where's Pisano now?"

O'Malley shrugged. "Gone. He's been indicted, of course, just like Barrett and me, but he hasn't been seen since. I'll bet he's dining on fresh red snapper in Caracas at the moment. And no, I don't know why I think that."

"What about Rendt?"

"The facts or my opinion?"

"The facts. I know your opinion."

"Well, Rendt wasn't indicted so it's a sure bet the boys didn't talk about him to the Justice Department. Why, I don't know. But I can guess. You were there at Genevieve's and saw what happened."

She thought back. "Let's see. We were eating and Barrett came in all excited. Friedrich didn't want to miss lunch but Rendt made him go. So what?"

"That's all you remember?"

"Sure, what else was there?"

"For one thing, Rendt had a gun."

That surprised her. "No kidding. You saw a gun?"

"I didn't see it, but I saw where it was kept. They both have guns. Rendt carries his in a holder under his right lapel. Pisano's is on his hip, like a cop's."

"Really. Have you actually seen Pisano's gun or are you just guessing?"

The question exasperated him. "Rad, trust me on this. I'm a cop's kid. Until I was twelve I thought males were issued guns with their drivers' licenses. I've seen them in every conceivable location: in shoulder holsters, on hips, in pockets, strapped to legs. When a man is carrying a gun on his hip there's a whole series of unconscious gestures that go along with it. He'll favor the side that it's on. He'll pat it for reassurance, the way a man pats his wallet when he's walking through a crowd. He'll adjust it discreetly when the leather chafes. He'll do obvious things like avoid sitting on it. When Pisano sits in a chair he lists about twenty degrees to starboard. There's no doubt about it. The gun's on his left hip. For what it's worth that also means that Pisano's right-handed."

She shuddered. "Remarkable." Scribble, scribble. "But let's get back to Genevieve's. What happened there that has anything to do with whether the boys tell all they know about Rendt."

"The gun is the big thing. And Friedrich's attitude toward Rendt. Don't you remember how Rendt just ordered him around? The boys were terrified of him. I don't think they would have implicated Rendt. They were too frightened."

"But not too afraid of Pisano?"

"Apparently not. Big mistake."

She nodded. "Well, leaving that aside for the moment, at least we know that Rendt's in the clear for now. Is he still around?"

"Sure. Why would he leave? He's sitting pretty."

"Any idea where he is?"

"I assume in his bed at night and in his office during the day. Rendt's got no reason that I know of to deviate from SOP."

"All right. Is that all the players?"

"All but two—Bishop and Marks. I don't know what Bishop's story is. I can't believe he's stupid enough to be part of any of this. He's got a solid gold reputation to protect and all the money any sane person would need for a lifetime. He's an asshole, but I think he really believes that I'm a crook and is acting in good faith to protect the corporation and the firm. Marks is another story. I never trusted that son of a bitch from the beginning. He knows I was just following orders but apparently he's feeding damaging stories about me to Bishop and God knows who else. I think we have to assume he's doing it for a reason—probably because he's into it up to his pink, powdered neck. But you're still there. What have they been up to recently?"

She shook her head. "I haven't seen Marks for a couple of weeks, but he doesn't keep me apprised of his comings and goings, so that's not unusual. Bishop hasn't been around either but he's got his own problems."

"Like what?"

"There was some bizarre screwup with the moving people a couple of week ago. They completely stripped his office. Even took the drapes down. They took it all the way down to Newport and left it in a truck overnight. Then when the new people came on in the morning they got it confused with a shipment going back east. The furniture was shipped to Reserve, Louisiana, to some oil drilling contractor who likes the stuff and won't give it up without a fight. The files are scattered in dead file warehouses in Fontana and Carson. Bishop's been down there every day going through the warehouses looking for . . . What's so funny?"

"Nothing, I'm sorry."

They worked for hours. When they were through she took his hand and led him to the bedroom. He reached for the button on her shorts but she squirmed away smiling. She pushed him gently back onto the bed.

"I told you I'll take care of everything," she said. "In your weakened state you may have an aneurysm."

"Let's have mutual aneurysms," he suggested.

She found a tender spot and pinched, getting a howl in response. "That's for the joke." She found another tender spot and ran her hand over it softly. "That's what's coming if you lie back and relax."

"Whatever you say."

She smiled broadly and began fumbling with the buttons on his shirt. He tried to reach for her but she pulled away again.

"Isn't this a little strange?" he asked.

"Why strange?"

"I feel like a sixteen-year-old getting undressed at a drive-in."

"What's wrong with that?" She pushed his hands gently away again and began running her hands over his bare chest. "I am doing what in cruder circles is known as 'feeling you up,' O'Malley. Your job is to 'get felt.' "

He laughed. "And that's all?"

She nodded. "For now you are my object. Later on . . ." She smiled. "We'll see."

O'Malley relaxed with amused resignation. She leaned over him and kissed him, cradling his head in her right hand and running her left through the fine hairs of his chest. The small kisses grew longer and her cool, dry hand grew warm.

Beads of sweat began to form around his eyes. She was still fully dressed. Her mouth moved from his face to his neck.

"This isn't bad," he mumbled. Speech was becoming more difficult. Rad was covering his neck with warm kisses. "What's wrong with being an object?" he wondered aloud.

"You like it, huh?" she asked. "Good. You'll probably like this even better." She moved from his neck to his chest, running her lips around the now moist hairs. "Mmm. Salty."

He was starting to twitch a bit. She was now giving little bites to the nipples on his chest, bites that seemed to send electrical signals down the back of his legs someplace. He tried again to twist away. "Baby, wait . . . Rad . . . Christ that's weird . . . nice, though." Rad smiled and ran her hand across his chest. "What's weird?"

He was glad she had stopped. "I didn't know the nerves in the chest were connected to the hamstrings. Or maybe the Achilles tendon. Can I play now, too?"

"Not a chance," she said. He started to rise but she wouldn't allow it, quickly straddling his chest with her back to him. They were both giggling now, enjoying the match. "I'm pinned, shoulders to the mat," he said. "You're supposed to be gracious now and do something nice, like let me up, or at least let me fuck you."

"Sorry. To the victor goes the spoils. What would a Viking do in my place?" The question unanswered, she showed him, pulling aside the belt and buttons of his jeans and yanking them down without ceremony. Naked now, save for the material bundled at his ankles, he felt decidedly out of position. She made a point of inspecting him. "I see someone's enjoying this," she said. He didn't argue.

She leaned forward and began kissing again. If speech had been difficult for him before, now his sight seemed to fade. The world was a blur except for a crystal-clear perception of the marvelous things she was doing to him. He found himself humming torch songs from the '40s and wondering if time could be manipulated like light in a snapshot. This moment preserved, to stay in forever. He humming his little songs and she giving those marvelous kisses, first little, now longer . . .

He seemed to waken from a dream to find her smiling next to him. He thought about moving but her smile said it still wasn't necesssary. She undressed slowly for him. He watched languidly but with concentration, enjoying each gesture. When she was naked she leaned over him again, facing him this time, feeling him against her belly. When she was near his ears she bit softly and whispered, "Didn't someone promise to fuck me?"

They lay quietly for what seemed a long time. They stirred, entered a reverie, napped for ten minutes, and stirred again. He was lost in the feeling of warmth. After a time she rose to her knees. She looked at him intently. He looked back quizzically. Then she kissed him lightly on the lips. She sat, swung her tan legs over the side of the bed, and walked toward a chair on the opposite side of the room. Her clothes were piled in disarray on the chair.

He felt an odd elevator sensation. A quick chill replaced the warmth.

"Going somewhere?"

She picked up her outer clothes and tugged those on, then stuffed the rest in her purse. She turned to him, holding her purse and shoes. The face wasn't yet wet but the eyes were slightly puffy.

"Let me try that again. Going somewhere?"

She spoke into the floor. "I have to get up at five for that meeting with the Japanese. You know, I told you about it."

"That's pretty early, five A.M."

She nodded.

"And it's probably important for you to get a good night's sleep."

She nodded her head again.

"Maybe even in your own house. Just so you'll be close to your clothes and all."

"Yes, that's right."

"I'd offer to come over there, but I know we'd probably wind up staying up late. Then you'd be tired tomorrow." This time she turned away. "You know, it's remarkable how we've managed this long with all those early meetings you've had," he observed.

It was awhile before she spoke. "O'Malley?"

"Yes."

"You know it's not like we've talked this out or anything."

"I understand."

She turned quickly back to him. "And I'm willing to help. I really am. That's why I'm here today."

"You've been a great help. I'm tremendously grateful. I feel much better."

"But I . . . I don't think it's fair . . . I mean, there's no gain to anyone if . . . if . . ."

"If I drag you down into the mud with me."

"I didn't say that. I'm willing to take risks. I'm taking a risk just being here."

"It's only a risk if you plan on staying there."

"Is that what you think I should do? Leave?"

"Sure. It's as easy as pie. Just walk out the door. Leave your address with accounting and they'll mail you a check." He knew that procedure well.

She looked at him, then turned away again. "It's different for you."

"And why's that?"

She spread her hands. "I don't know. . . . Look . . ." She turned back to him. "Because you're a goddamn misfit, that's why. Look at you, for Christ's sake."

O'Malley looked down at his naked body. "What's wrong with that." He patted his stomach, pinching a bit of skin. "That's just the way I'm sitting. I'm going to start a running program on Tuesday, then you'll see. . . ."

"I'm not talking about that." She came over and kissed his belly. "That's cute." She picked up his mangled hand. "Look at that. What J and D lawyer has a hand like that?"

"I didn't get that as a J and D lawyer," he said evenly.

She waved her hand over his body. "It's the whole thing. You look like a stevedore. Your hands are like a stevedore. When you're not being careful you even talk like one." She was beginning to cry a little now. "I love it. I really do." Her eyes quickly blazed and she brought her fists down hard, twice, on his barrel chest. "But what the fuck are you doing in my life," she screamed.

He thought about it dispassionately, as if it were an academic question being posed. "I don't really know," he said. "I remember one day it was cold as hell, the way it gets in New York. And I thought, 'Why don't I go live someplace where it's warmer.' As for law school, that was the old man's idea. He said, 'There's two kinds of people in this world: lawyers and people getting screwed by lawyers.' He made that one up and thought it was a scream. Anyway, I just happened to be good at it, I guess. When the J and D people saw me on paper, they thought I was their boy. Me, I was just trying to get warm. Under ordinary circumstances . . ." He shrugged.

Rad looked at him with her mouth open for a full thirty seconds. Then she shook her head slowly. "Jesus Christ, O'Malley. Don't you know that's a weird story. People plan and scrape and connive all their lives to get to J and D. And when they get there they hang on like barnacles. It's like . . ." She began sputtering and gesturing, but no words were coming out. O'Malley was staring with interest. "Why am I trying to explain," she said. She held up her fingers, using one for each sentence. "You can't possibly understand what it means for me to be here because you've never even understood what it means for you to be here. Two, you're a fucking misfit, you don't even know what religion you are. Three—"

"Sure I do."

"Do what?"

"Know what religion I am," he said. "Patrick O'Malley married Ethel Silvers in 1947. A match made in heaven but celebrated in City Hall. Neither of them was what could be called observant, except when it came to showing up for labor meetings and Democratic Party fund raisers. At the beginning Ethel said the children of Jewish women are Jewish. Patrick said that was fine with him as long as nobody minded Jewish altar boys. They didn't discuss it after that except every December, when the old man told her if she lit any more candles the tree would catch fire."

Rad listened and nodded. "I rest my case."

"So what are you going to do?" She didn't answer. "Let me put it another way. When are you going to leave?"

She looked at him intently. "That's what it comes down to, doesn't it? In your mind, I mean?"

"That's right. Them or me. You can't have us both. If you walk out of here now, I'll know just where you stand," he said stupidly.

Rad's eyes flashed. "Well, let's not keep you in the dark."

She picked up her shoes and purse and headed for the bathroom. There was the sound of running water followed by the opening and closing of doors. Then her heels clattered down the forty steps to the street. Her car had needed a tuneup for months and he sat in the dim light listening to the grinding of the starter. Then there was a roar and a metallic grinding of gears. Soon there was no sound save the tinkling of the dolphin spitting into the pool.

In late July the sun takes a long time to leave. He lay quietly in bed watching the shadow of a windowframe move slowly from left to right across the wall. It moved about a foot every hour. After it moved three feet it dissolved and he fell asleep.

When he woke the only light in the room was the luminous dials of the clock, telling him it was eleven o'clock. That meant it was eight in Bayonne.

The phone rang for a long time before he answered. When he did his voice was thick and slow with sleep.

"Hi. What are you doing asleep at eight o'clock?"

There was a long groan. "Ben, you got the three hours right but it works the other way. It's two A.M. here."

Shit.

"Look, I'm sorry. You go back to sleep. This is a nothing call. I'll catch you at the station tomorrow."

"No. Don't be silly. Just give me a moment here." He could see the man at the other end rubbing his face. "Your mother's in there holding her chest. Let me just go tell her it's not the coroner calling about your crazy brother. Then I'll take it in the other room."

After awhile there was a series of clicks. He could picture him sitting in his chair with the cold coffee.

"O.K., pal, I know you called for a reason. Why don't you just take it from the top and tell me everything."

The dam broke and the words poured into the phone.

It was thirty minutes before he stopped talking. There had been no interruption. When the younger O'Malley stopped, the only sound was the buzzing of millions of transcontinental connectors. The only sound for quite awhile.

"Dad? You still there?" O'Malley felt strangely anxious at the silence.

"The sons of bitches." The cop spit the words into the phone.

"I know."

"What are you going to do about it?" he asked. The words were angry.

"I don't know. I guess just try to see what they have on me. If it's what Bishop says, then there's not much I can do. Work a good plea bargain, I suppose."

"The hell you will."

"What else can I do?"

"Fight them, goddamn it. You're a hardheaded kid. Show them they can't do this to you."

O'Malley shook his head as though his father were there to watch him. "Dad, you don't understand. This isn't a bunch of punks. I can't gather up some friends and solve the problem in a parking lot. These guys are influential people. The whole thing is just too complicated. There are special circumstances involved. I just can't—"

His father cut him off. "Ben, I don't want to be hard on you, but stop making excuses. It's not complicated at all. The white shirts had a scam going and when it fell apart they looked for someone to lay it off on. You were new and they figured you for an easy mark. What's so complicated about that?"

"Nothing. The complicated part is that they were right. In their world I am an easy mark."

"Maybe you once were. But no more."

"And why's that?"

"Because they killed someone," he said. "Ben, you've got to realize that these guys are not professionals—at least not at killing people. Right now they're scared to death. Start putting pressure on and there's going to be a crack someplace."

O'Malley had originally just wanted a backboard to talk at. Now he was listening intently. The cop on the other end of the line knew what he was about.

"What's the best way to put pressure on?"

The voice began to get excited. "Just start at the beginning," he said. "With the most obvious. Ask as many questions as you can to as many people as you can. See as many things as you can. When that dries up go to something else. Believe me—these guys are going to be watching your every move. Once they find out you're not laying down and dying they're going to get very, very nervous. And nervous people make mistakes."

"O.K., that's possible," O'Malley said slowly. "But my lawyer doesn't want me talking to anybody."

"You let your lawyer do the legal work and play with the papers. You just do like I told you."

O'Malley knew that Baird would have a heart attack if he heard this advice. But for the first time in a week he felt exhilarated. As if there was something he could do. "All right. I'll think about it. Anything else?"

"Just one thing and then I've got to get back to your mother. Remember always there's no disgrace in getting

115

framed like this. Try your best to beat them, but if you lose, just remember you got a family. And the family knows you didn't do it."

"I know that. But thanks anyway."

He wasn't finished, however. His voice was hard and serious. "So if you see you're gonna go down, and there's no way out, make sure you don't go alone. Take one of them with you. One way or the other. Legal or illegal. Try to get the biggest one." He paused. "You understand what I'm saying, Ben?"

"Yes."

"And look for the money. Find out who's tryin' to get the money and you'll know who did it. That's all these people care about. Then take him down."

"All right."

17

It was clear to O'Malley that the only nice thing about being a criminal defendant is that no one expects you to do anything except sit around the house contemplating suicide. At ten the next morning he jumped into the Healey and rolled down onto Hollywood Boulevard. The streets were filled with brown choking air and the remains of the previous night's action. The marquees over all the first-run houses were unlit. In the morning only the most basic wares are peddled on the Boulevard.

The corners were filled with little packets of dirty-faced sixteen-year-olds. They stood in groups of five or six and moved purposefully only when a black and white rolled near. Otherwise they moved as if they were walking under water. The faces changed constantly. Only the bad teeth, ratty hair, and the look of despair that follows filth and unchanged clothes remained the same. There were equal numbers of boys and girls, but they paid little attention to each other. Their focus was riveted on the river of the street and the competition to sell their skinny behinds to men in ties and large American cars.

He turned down Vine past the rotting art deco department stores that had once made the intersection the Rodeo Drive of Los Angeles. On the next block the porno shops were set between the glaring asphalt parking lots like raisins in a cake. When Vine crossed Sunset it passed through a phalanx of glistening new office buildings brought in by federal money and the Hollywood Revitalization Committee. The shiny towers added the same vitality to Hollywood as a new suit did to a corpse.

A mile further down, the street got wider, oak trees and lawns appeared, and Vine changed its name to Rossmore for the same reason unwelcome immigrants have always changed names. Hancock Park is a cornucopia of architectural pretension that appears unheralded at Hollywood's border. Gaping English Tudors sit side by side with Spanish haciendas like commuters on a subway. There are Victorians, New England colonials, Italian villas mistakenly decorated with Mexican tile, and airy Wright houses onto which subsequent owners have made leaden additions. The common denominator is sturdiness and thickness: solid brick, deep wood, and sturdy stucco, all to protect the inhabitants from the harshness of the LA winters.

The community makes certain that it will never be mistaken for Beverly Hills. In Hancock Park the residents wear dark suits, read books, and think the trades are winds. The husbands control downtown finance and corporate affairs and pay their five bucks for the movies like everyone else. If Beverly Hills is tinseltown, Hancock Park is Darien. There are thick trees, not a palm in sight, children and normal dogs, and discriminatory private clubs. When the pilgrims came west they brought a little corner of Connecticut with them.

O'Malley drove past the realty notice on the boys' house and parked a quarter mile south. The Redstones' house was an immense granite monstrosity. He had to reach up to pull the bell cord and the gong reverberated deep inside the stone walls. Mrs. Pamela Redstone came out looking wan and heavy. She looked him over the way ladies regard peasants.

"What can I do for you?" The voice was as thick as the eyes. She was still not past twenty-five, but the face had aged three years for every two on the calendar.

"My name is Ben O'Malley. If you have some time I'd like to talk to you about the murder up the street."

"If you're from the police your friends have already come and gone. If you're from the press, my husband won't let me talk to you." She checked him out again. "On the record, that is."

O'Malley crossed his fingers. "No, I'm a lawyer. I'm just trying to get some basic information."

She studied him and then shrugged. "All right, why not. I heard they had money and when there's money around there's lawyers around. My husband says lawyers are like the little white worms that eat the insides of dead things." She gave him a coquettish grimace. "Are you one of that kind?"

"I used to be. I'm reformed now."

She swayed. "Not too reformed, I hope. Well, come on in, lawyer. We'll have a drink and you can ask your questions."

He followed her into a room that looked as cheerful as a Gothic set. Everything was dark and heavy. Thick burgundy drapes blocked the light from intruding on the granite fireplace and the gloomy mahogany furniture. The walls were done in listless brown and punctuated by oppressive oils depicting scenes from nature. It was ninety-five degrees out so the air conditioning was going full blast to make up for the heat from the fireplace.

"Nice place you got here."

"I'll bet you like tombs, too."

"Well, maybe it could stand a little cheering up."

She cackled and poured something orange over ice from a crystal decanter. "Yeah, we all could."

O'Malley examined the roaring blaze with wonder. There was no sound of wood crackling. "Isn't it a little warm for a fire?"

She looked at it strangely, as though it were the first time she'd seen it. "Yeah, I suppose so. There's no wood in there, of course, just a gas fire with cement logs. My husband says it adds atmosphere to the place so he keeps it on night and day. The thing throws out a lot of heat, though. That's why we keep the air conditioning up so high." She shrugged. O'Malley tried not to think of the slobs in the gas lines.

She came over and handed him an orange drink. "Here, lawyer. To your health." He sipped and made a face at the concentration of vodka. She knocked off half her glass with one gulp and refilled it from the decanter. "Come on. We'll sit down and you can ask your questions." She sat an inch away from him and toasted the blaze.

"I understand you saw two men running over the golf course after the murders."

"That's right. Two black shapes running like they just killed somebody." She thought that was funny and gave a hoarse laugh that ended in a cough. She held up her cigarette for him to light.

"Could you determine anything about their features?"

"Just one guy. There was a moon out and clear as day on the course but they were dressed in black and pretty far away. But there was this one greasy-looking guy with all this hair. He had it part under a cap, part in and part out. He turned around. I could tell he was a young punk but that was about it. Kinda skinny and fat-assed if you know what I mean. Kept grabbing at his ass, too."

"Did they say anything?"

"When the hippy turned around his pal shouted at him to 'come on' but that was all."

"What happened then?"

"Nothing. They just kept going. The kid beat the old guy to the fence and hopped over, then his pal followed. They were blocked by the trees once they got past the fence."

O'Malley nodded. "Did you know the victims at all?"

"Sure I knew them. About as well as anyone knows their neighbors in this town. I went up and said hello when they moved in. I saw the walrus a few times at the market up in Larchmont. Then I said goodbye when they rolled them out under a white sheet. They weren't really my type, if you know what I mean."

"Did they live alone?"

She nodded. "Lived alone, kept quiet, and were in bed by eleven. Just like everybody else on this fucking street." Her voice was getting low and cracked. So she filled her glass again.

"Many visitors?" She didn't know.

He wanted to talk more but could see it wasn't going to work. Her eyes kept closing as she sipped at the vodka. He asked about her new baby. She waved at the window. "Park . . . maid." He thanked her and rose to leave.

"By the way, if you don't mind, I'd like to go out the back way and look at the golf course. Maybe walk the way the killers did?"

"Can't . . . fence out there . . . can't get back."

"That's all right. I'll just walk to the clubhouse."

She knew he was lying but didn't care. She waved him off and stared into the fire, rocking softly with the crystal canister nursing at her breast.

Instead of the boys' wire strands, the Redstones had a gate secured by a rusty latch. Apparently no one feared the golfers. He opened the gate and hopped across the two-foot moat into some fairway rough. He walked straight into the trees, feeling Pamela Redstone's head turn, her eyes burning holes in his back. When he was through the trees and out of her sight he turned right, heading north.

He kept close to the line of trees protecting the residents

from the missiles of the double-knits for the full quarter mile. He could feel the danger level increase as he got closer to the house and his body responded physically to the fear. He felt nauseated and dry-mouthed. Every instinct told him to go back.

He walked past the house twice before spotting the cut wire. He looked back once over the course and was disappointed to find no excuse there. The course was Monday morning quiet, none of the little red carts patrolling. The trees were dense and he selected one about twenty feet from the brook to lean against. The gnats came swarming at the sweat on his face.

Nothing moved in the house for a half hour. The only activity on the course was an elderly couple who hit the ball up the middle for a hundred yards and walked hand in hand up to their balls to do it again. Very efficient and very romantic, a breath of sanity that left when they did. He remained staring through the heat at the mausoleum, trying not to think of Mrs. Redstone's air-conditioned screwdrivers. When he was sure the place was empty he walked toward the broken wire.

The soft slushing of the mulchlike summer leaves was as loud to his ears as clattering pots and pans. At the broken fence he crouched and briefly entertained the delicious notion of leaving. When that urge passed he let his imagination re-create a moonlit July 14th evening.

The murderers had likely sat huddled there breathing hard, like GIs who reach a ditch after a sprint over a flat plain. They used the respite to watch the house and the course for signs of activity. When they were sure that everything was quiet and they were well rested, one likely turned to the other and nodded. Then came the snipping and the killing.

That raised the interesting question of where they came from. He sat with his back to the house and surveyed the course again. The Redstone house was due south of him and the killers had escaped in a southwest diagonal line. Thus it was a good bet they came in that way. But why? The eastern

121

and western borders of the course were buttressed by the forts of the Hancock Park residences, and if recent experience was any guide, it would have been virtually impossible for the killers to enter the grounds of those residences from the front. That left only due south and due north and the respective diagonals. Due north and south were probably out. The fairways were straight and long on this part of the course. There were adjoining par-fives facing in opposite directions separating him from the western boundary of houses. Each was over five hundred yards long and was followed by perfectly linear par-fours that were in excess of four hundred yards. At the northern and southern boundaries of this thousand-yard expanse were bridges enabling busy streets to pass over the cart paths. If the murderers had entered the course from the bridges there would have been an enormous chance of being seen from the street and a long journey over the moonlit course in the bargain. He could see why they chose the southwest fence over the bridges; what he couldn't fathom was why they didn't come from the northeast or southeast to begin with and simply stick to the line of trees. It was almost as though they thought the house was on the other side.

He turned and walked to the huge oaks that served as braces for the wire strands. The killers had no problem here. The strands had slack even when connected and now all six pieces dangled limply in the little brook. They hadn't even had to push them aside. He hopped over the brook and left the shade for the glare of the brown, sun-parched lawn.

The wide, treeless expanse of grass was empty save for a redwood table and a rusty barbecue. The boys had obviously not been into backyard entertaining. He crossed the lawn efficiently and nonchalantly, imagining that on the 14th the intruders came across low and fast like commandos, their rubber soles silent and impressionless. The screen door to the house was still unlocked. He opened it with his shirt and tested the back door with an elbow. It was locked, but not much.

The door was old, ill-fitting, and kept closed by a simple

latch lock. McCabe was right—opening this door was only slightly more difficult than turning the knob. As kids they had found that the little flat metal keys used by mechanics to adjust the timing on automobiles were best. At that time he knew a lot more people with timing keys than credit cards. Now that O'Malley was rich he had a credit card to use. The door swung open on the second try. He wondered cockily how many J & D lawyers possessed that little skill.

Before entering he picked up two rocks and made a fist over each. Then he closed the door with an elbow and stood breathing in the dark, deathlike stillness.

His fear was almost tangible now, fired by the taste and smell of death in the house. The disinfectant used to disguise the stench of the victims' decomposition was thick and only partially effective. After the boys' bodies and belongings had been taken away the house had been shut as tight as a tomb. Whatever items remained were covered with sheets as pale as burial shrouds.

He put the fist-enclosed rocks in his pocket to make sure he touched nothing, then began inching through the dimness. He had the advantage of the pale light that forced its way into the house from the noon sun outside. The killers had moved in blackness. Yet even with the light he walked heavily into unseen abutments and tripped once—in each case forcing his hands to remain wrapped around the rocks. If the killers had been this clumsy in a furniture-laden house they would have awakened the dead. As it was the dead had remained asleep until it was time for them to die. Maybe the murderers were simply more professional. Maybe they knew where they were going.

The bedroom was the farthest room from the door. He found it after a frustrating trip through a maze of anterooms. It wasn't the bare mattress that convinced him he was in the right place. It was the string tacked to the bed in the form of two human bodies.

There was nothing to do here except mourn the dead, which he did. What the police hadn't removed, the moving

123

men had. There was undoubtedly an estate sale someplace where the expensive worldly effects of the two little go-go engineers were being sold to the highest bidder. They had had quite a ride, these two, and had ended it by putting him in a concrete frame. But he couldn't be angry at them because they didn't deserve to be killed in their sleep.

Nevertheless, he suddenly wanted badly to get out of there and began feeling his way back with shoulders and elbows. Halfway to the door he heard soft scuffling and the fear came back with a rush. He relaxed only slightly at the sight of a six-inch tail scurrying across his line of vision. It was probably the only rat in Hancock Park and had been drawn like a shark to the boys' five-day stench. He watched it disappear into a hole past something glinty. He knelt down and stared at the glint for a long time before picking it up.

There was one more thing he could think to do. He put his hands in his pockets again and retraced his way out the door, across the lawn and brook and then south along the line of trees. When he reached the Redstones' he turned right and cut directly across the two fairways to the far fence. Nothing. Then he headed north again until he was directly across from the giant gnarled pine in front of the boys' house. The foliage on the western side was thick and thorny and he had to hack his way through until he came to the fences and ornamental bushes separating the western residences from the fairway. The first house had no wire and neither did the four to the north of it. He came back to the beginning and headed south. The first house he came to had the same wire barrier as the boys'. And the same cuts in the middle. Inside the yard a small girl talked to herself in a sandbox. He wondered if they would have killed her parents anyway.

Straight across the fairways to the gnarled tree was the path the killers took when they realized their mistake. There was a possibility they had dropped something on the way but all of a sudden he didn't care. The heated brown air was making him sick. The sight of the girl in the sandbox and the thought of the violence she had narrowly missed made him want to vomit. Tomorrow was time enough for nausea to become anger again. For now it was enough to hop the fence and make his way around the block to the Healey.

18

By the morning of the federal arraignment Baird was cooking, strutting and chatting excitedly. O'Malley sat tight-lipped in the cab next to him. This was to be his introduction to the federal criminal process and he was more than a little cowed. When the cab stopped and he saw the building he found himself staring open-mouthed at it. The federal courthouse in Los Angeles is a massive seventeen-story marble and stone edifice that was built in the '30s and looks as if it were designed by Albert Speer. The lower three stories have black marble faces and bars on the windows. The upper fourteen rise majestically over Spring Street like a linear colossus. The whole thing occupies a full city block. Inside, the corridors and courtrooms are opulent and windowless and bustle with security guards and FBI agents. Baird walked in as if he owned the place.

Baird led him up to the eleventh floor to the magistrate's chambers. Magistrate Reardon was a kindly looking gentleman who seemed happy to have exchanged the turmoil of private practice for black robes, a $45,000 per year salary, and an eleven to four job that required about one-third of his mental facility. For an hour Baird and O'Malley sat in the back of the courtroom with the ACR accountant and his lawyer, watching while a parade of Mexicans in dirty jeans and handcuffs were arraigned for crossing the border without a license.

O'Malley felt even weaker when the clerk intoned the case of, "CR-Number 78-1709—*United States of America versus Benjamin Aaron O'Malley, Bruce Edward Barrett, and Francis Xavier Pisano.*" They all rose and stood in a row before the magistrate.

All, that is, except Francis Xavier Pisano. Reardon looked around squinting, first at the row before him, then at the papers on his desk. After a time he seemed to realize there were only two defendants and two lawyers when the forms on his desk specifically said there should be three of each. As always when confused, he turned immediately to the assistant United States attorney. The assistant was a young guy fresh out of law school who had sat through fourteen arraignments that morning. He was hidden by two stacks of files and was furiously paging through them looking for Pisano. Everyone waited patiently while he rustled his papers. Finally he came to a decision.

"Your honor, the Government does not believe that Mr. Pisano is here today." Suddenly O'Malley felt much better about the whole affair.

The magistrate was a kindly and patient man. "Mr. Simpson, that much is obvious. The question is: Where is Mr. Pisano and why isn't he here?"

"Uh, yes, I see. Well . . ." More rustling. Suddenly he brightened. "Your honor, the United States believes that Mr. Pisano is a fugitive from justice." He looked very pleased with himself.

"Well, gentlemen," Reardon said, referring to the lawyers, "is there any reason we can't proceed today without Mr. Pisano?" Barrett's lawyer was playing with his calculator, probably trying to figure out the bill. He muttered, "No objection." Baird jumped on the question like a starved dog.

"Your honor, it seems to me that we must have Mr. Pisano here in order to have all the parties before the court who were charged in the indictment. Otherwise there will be needless delay and my client's right to a speedy trial will be adversely affected while we wait for Mr. Pisano to be found, arraigned, and given an adequate opportunity to prepare for trial. However I do have a suggestion that I'm sure the United States will agree to. We need only sever my client from Mr. Pisano and I'm sure we can proceed expeditiously." The young assistant's face went from yellow back to its normal shade. It sounded good to him.

"The Government has no objection, Your Honor."

O'Malley began chuckling inwardly at Baird's quiet coup. Most of the hard evidence was against Pisano and Barrett; now there was a good chance the prosecutors could introduce none of it against O'Malley. In addition, Pisano probably had a rap sheet a mile long that the jury would hold against all of the defendants. Now that was out of O'Malley's case also. Finally the Government now faced the prospect of two trials instead of one and would be much more eager to deal. The young assistant's boss was not going to be pleased.

"All right, that will be the order of the court. The next order of business is the pleas. Do the defendants waive the reading of the indictment?"

Everyone did; they all knew it far too well. Reardon read the rights, O'Malley and Barrett said they understood, and each croaked out "Not guilty" at the appropriate time.

"The third item is the conditions of bail. Have these defendants been bound over, Mr. Simpson?"

Baird jumped in quickly. "Your honor, Mr. Simpson did not conduct the grand jury investigation and is probably unaware of the arrangements that were made between the defense and U.S. Attorney's Office. Mr. O'Malley is hardly the type to flee the jurisdiction of the court. At the time of the events in question he was an attorney at the law firm of Jenkins and Dorman." Reardon stared at O'Malley over his glasses with something approaching awe. "We agreed at that time that Mr. O'Malley would not be arrested but rather the indictment would be served on me personally and I would represent that Mr. O'Malley would be present for all appearances. As the court can observe we have honored that pledge. Therefore I propose that we continue to honor the agreement between the parties and release Mr. O'Malley on a signature bond with no travel restrictions."

Barrett was staring at his lawyer with a "So why did I get arrested?" look. Simpson didn't know anything about a deal but knew he had to salvage something so he started screaming about Barrett. Reardon decided to split the baby—he released O'Malley on his signature and made Barrett put up a $50,000 bond, surrender his passport, and agree not to leave Los Angeles. Barrett began eyeing O'Malley with envy and Baird with lust.

"Now, the only item remaining, aside from the unpleasantness in the Marshall's Office, is the schedule for motions. Do you gentlemen anticipate filing any motions prior to the trial?"

Barrett's lawyer said he was sure the Government would be professional and cooperative and didn't see a need for a lot of cumbersome motion practice. Baird took a sheet of paper from his briefcase and rattled off twenty-three motions he intended to make: six different motions to dismiss the indictment; fourteen discovery motions for grand jury transcripts, bank records, interview memoranda with the boys, the letters of authority for the U.S. attorney to prosecute the case; and three motions in Latin that no one in the room understood. Reardon wrote them all down and set briefing, argument, and hearing dates for every one. O'Malley felt like dancing. Assistant U.S. attorneys have lots of cases and like to work nine to five. Baird was bent on making the prosecutor really sick of this case really fast.

"And now that we're through with business, it's time to select the winner. Linda, the envelope, please." Reardon undoubtedly used the same joke for every arraignment. His clerk reached into a bowl, selected a slip, and handed it up to him. "And the winner is . . . Judge Oliver Greenman. His courtroom is on the second floor. You have your appearance date, gentlemen."

The four of them were barely in the hall when Baird had Barrett and his lawyer against a wall, talking excitedly with his arm around the lawyer's shoulders. O'Malley stood back and let him do his thing.

He came over grinning. "This is great. Pisano's out of the case and Barrett's got a lazy lawyer. As long as I do the work this guy will tell me anything. I've already got an interview with his client scheduled."

O'Malley shook his hand. "Baird, you're doing a great job," he said. "There's only one thing that bothers me. Reardon said something about unpleasantness at the Marshall's Office. What's that all about?"

"Oh, yeah. I guess I didn't mention that to you." O'Malley's glee faded. "You see, Benny my boy, you have to get booked. You know—fingerprinted, photographed, that sort of thing."

"Oh, fuck."

"I know it's a nuisance but you have to do it. Go down to the first floor on the Main Street side. You'll see a room called 'Marshall's Lockup' and—"

"Called what!"

"Marshall's Lockup. Don't be an infant. Go down and get taken care of. I'm going up to seventeen to do some research. I'll be there for about twenty minutes. After you're done, meet me in the Attorneys' Lounge on the second floor. There's a lot to do."

The Marshall's Lockup was a combination of the J & D clerical well and a well-kept zoo. In the middle of the room sat twenty or so beefy males and females clicking away at manual typewriters. Along one wall the locked-up stared at them behind tastefully designed bars. O'Malley gave his name and was ushered by the upper arm past the hoots of the inmates, who loved his suit, to a room in the back. A very nice lady told him to take off his jacket, then placed a card with a metal chain around his neck. Then she slipped behind a tripod-based camera and put a cowl over her head. That done, she took each digit, rolled it across some black guck and rolled it again over a card. He signed about thirty forms and she smiled and thanked him as if they were at the check-out stand at Safeway.

"All set?" O'Malley nodded.

"O.K. I want to bring you up to date," Baird said. "I've left the firm. I was supposed to see Bishop before I left but he's someplace in Louisana with some oil people. Barton was filling in as head of the department so I had my chat with him. All very civilized. They think I'm crazy so they're dispensing with the going-away party.

"Second, you ought to know that your friend, Rendt, is making out like a bandit on this one. The boys' new corporation defaulted on the first payment on the note, as you predicted. The word at J and D is that ACR is going to start sending letters to the registered agent demanding payment. They'll make a record for six months and then try to foreclose on the boys' two hundred sixty thousand shares. Because the shares are security for the loan they may not even go into the probate estate. Even if they did it wouldn't matter. The boys died without a will and, of course, have no progeny. Friedrich is supposed to have a mother in East Germany but she's the only known heir. Maybe there's enough money at stake for some lawyer to come in and make a crazy claim for the stock, but no one's too worried about that. The State of California may get avaricious and try to claim it all, but they'd have to prove that the loan to the boys was a phony loan. Everybody knows it was phony but the problem is proving it. So the state will probably settle for five million dollars or so and go away, leaving Rendt with the stock."

"So Rendt will control ACR and pay five or six million to buy off the state and any other claimants who pop out of the woodwork?"

"That's about it. Plus another million or two for J and D's legal fees. That's eight million, which is not a bad price to pay for a company with a net worth of five hundred million and assets of four times that much." It certainly wasn't, O'Malley thought. A deal like that might even provide a motive for murder.

"I'm not surprised," O'Malley said. "I told Marks way back that Rendt would wind up with it all."

"The third item is not going to make you any happier. McCabe has been taken off the murder investigation. He's been replaced by a guy named Spiro Andersen, if you can believe that. Andersen's reputation is checkered at best. I talked to McCabe and he's pissed. He thinks that Andersen is going to kill the murder investigation because of pressure from ACR. Even now the murder investigation is no longer concerned with ACR financial irregularities. Now the official word is that the boys died during the course of an unsuccessful burglary attempt."

O'Malley laughed out loud, but not out of happiness. Maybe he should have been happy; at least he wasn't going to be accused of murder. But he knew it was no burglary. The snipped wire in front of the little girl's sandbox proved that the killers were looking for a very specific house.

"It's got to be impossible for the LAPD to ignore the financial irregularities," O'Malley said. "I've been indicted twice for those irregularities."

"That's where it gets even stranger. It's also where the good news starts. Bishop called me yesterday from Louisiana. He wants to meet. He wouldn't say why but did say it would be in my client's interest to meet with him. Bishop wouldn't touch me with a stick unless he wanted to make a deal. I think they're going to cooperate with us."

That blew O'Malley away. This thing was turning into Disneyland. "Why on earth would Bishop want to help me?"

"Figure it out for yourself. It makes sense in a warped sort of way. If there were financial irregularities and you and Barrett are convicted, it places a cloud over everything. The murder investigation then has to look at you and the ACR principals as possible suspects. The State of California then has an outside shot of proving that the loan was a phony loan, which means that because there was no will the State gets the boys' shares and becomes Rendt's partner."

"And if I'm acquitted or the charges are dropped?"

"Then things are a lot easier for them. Andersen writes the murder off as a bungled burglary. The State has to start from scratch to prove a fraud and phony loan and they don't have the horsepower to do that. So the State goes away for five million dollars. Everyone apologizes to you, you get your ticket back, and Rendt gets ACR."

"What's our play?"

"We have only one play and they know it. You and I know that Video Enterprises was a massive fraud. But if we prove that we put your head in a noose. A fraud makes you a suspect not only for the securities charges but for the murder as well. It is in our interest to prove that Vid Ent was clean. That puts our interests and Mr. Bishop's in perfect harmony. That's why he wants to meet."

The whole thing was shudderingly neat. In law, business, and foreign affairs there is no such thing as ideology or morality, simply interests in flux. Bishop, ACR, Rendt, and Marks were proposing to be friends again because all interests were becoming aligned. He couldn't get at them without cutting his own throat. A mutual balance of terror. The perfect frame had become the perfect box. Unfortunately he'd seen the girl in the sandbox and the bed where the boys had died. He decided to protest some more.

"It can't be that easy. How can they cover it up when the boys already spilled their guts to the grand jury?"

"I didn't say it would be easy. But it certainly can be done. For one thing the boys did not testify before the grand jury. They were interviewed by an assistant U.S. attorney and an FBI agent. The entire grand jury process probably took a half hour and the only witness was the FBI agent, who regurgitated everything the boys said. Remember, a grand jury is not a court of law. There is no judge, no defendant, no defense attorney, and no witness other than the person testifying. Moreover, none of the rules of evidence apply. That means hearsay, rumor, innuendo, or any other garbage can be brought in. There's no one to object because the only people in the room are the grand jurors and the prosecutor."

"There's no testimony from the boys?"

"That's right. The informal interviews with the prosecutors are classic hearsay. So is the FBI testimony."

"So we're home free?"

"Just about. The prosecutors have the whole story and could prove it independently of the boys' statements. But to do that they need ACR's cooperation and I don't think they're going to get that now."

O'Malley nodded, thought about dropping the subject, then realized the question had to be asked. "Don't you have a problem cooperating with people we know are crooks and might even be murderers?"

Baird looked at him as he would a child. His words were angry. "Ben, you are in deep shit and if you forget that, go down to the lockup again and take a long look at what's waiting for you. I'm your lawyer. My job is to keep you out of the jug. To get you they have to prove one, there was a fraud, and two, that you were involved. I intend to make them prove both. I could not care less what the facts are and I will take my help where I can get it."

He stared at O'Malley with his jaw set. There was no use arguing. They shook hands. Baird headed back to the library and O'Malley went down the escalator, down the august marble steps, and into the searing heat of Spring Street.

There was no question he was relieved. For the first time there was a way out, a way to clear himself of the charges and get his ticket back. But what would he do then? Get a job with another firm? Marry Rad? Move to Mendocino County and watch the redwoods grow? It would all be forgotten in a year and he'd again be free to stay up nights drafting more contracts, more debentures, preparing for more meetings with people like Marks. There was a time when he thought of high-powered dealmaking as moderately heady stuff. Those dreams were long since shattered by the smell and pain of the real thing. He didn't want to go back to any of it. He especially didn't want to go back to it knowing for the rest of his life that the price of tedious affluence had been cooperation with thieves and murderers. But that wasn't the question. The question was whether he was willing to risk prison in order to get Rendt.

The answer was obvious. And not very flattering.

The dung-colored air was sultry and he thought the light would never change. He felt a tug on his jacket and turned around and saw no one. Then he looked down and saw a little black face staring up from about three feet above the ground.

"Hi."

"You gotta dolla, mistah?"

"How about a dime?" He went fishing. The kid wasn't having any of it.

"Nope. That man said you gonna gimme a dolla."

"What man?" He pointed at a white Plymouth roaring away from the curb a block away.

"He said you give me a dolla and I give you this." He handed O'Malley a crumpled slip of paper. The writing was in pencil.

Benny. How's it hanging? I've got some information for you about our case. I'm at Bungalow 14–B
at the Beverly Hills Hotel. Come on over tonight
about ten. Don't bring anybody. Frank.

O'Malley read it over twice. So Pisano was in town. The kid started tugging again, a little nervous about letting his security go prior to payment. O'Malley gave him his buck and the kid gave a salute as a receipt. It would be crazy to go. Pisano was his prime candidate as one of the boys' murderers. Pisano was also a fugitive and meeting him alone would be stupid and dangerous. There was no possible information that Pisano could give that would improve O'Malley's position. O'Malley was virtually out of this mess and the only thing he could do now was fuck up a good thing. He rolled the paper into a ball and threw it in the street. For once he would play it smart.

19

The Beverly Hills Hotel is the home of the Polo Lounge and one of the storied hostelries of Los Angeles. During the 1930s its pool was Hollywood's business center. Now the center has shifted to paneled offices in glass and steel towers, where the new breed of magnates and mini-magnates meet with lawyers and accountants and wear vests instead of bathing suits.

But if a little magic has gone, the jaded pink hotel tries its best not to show it. The old lady still stands stately on Sunset Boulevard on one of the prime pieces of real estate in Los Angeles. The excellent restaurant and famed pool are still inside. The bungalows are still opulent and prohibitively expensive. And, on a few occasions, like an aging ballplayer coming up to the plate to do it one more time, a big deal is actually made in the Polo Lounge.

The slack in the movie crowd has been more than made up for by rich folks of all descriptions; industrialists from Europe and Japan, lawyers from New York on fat expense accounts, matronly widows from the Midwest traveling off a dead spouse's insurance. They all assume that everybody is in the business but them, an illusion that the management does absolutely nothing to dispel.

O'Malley arrived about nine-thirty and went to the hotel's smaller bar to drink and think in peace. Bungalow 14–B was back in the maze someplace and it was obvious he'd need a discreet guide to find it. The guide appeared in the form of a blond surfer-type named Barry wearing the standard maroon jacket with the hotel emblem. After some quiet negotiation O'Malley was $20 poorer and Barry was off to find out what he could about the resident of 14–B.

While Barry was gone O'Malley thought hard about how to approach Pisano safely. He didn't have a weapon yet, although that acquisition was now on his list. For a moment he considered taking the surfer in with him for protection but had to reject the idea; Barry hadn't bargained on potential death for his twenty. He decided on a more orthodox approach. He'd go in alone but have Barry call the room five minutes later. If O'Malley didn't come to the phone for any reason Barry would call in the troops.

Barry was back an hour later with the information: 14–B was occupied by a Mr. James Allen, who listed his occupation as real estate developer and his home as Chicago. All the hotel staff thought the guy was in the Mafia. He'd been in there for two weeks and as far as anyone knew he had never left the room. He took all his meals and drinks from room service and was running up huge bar tabs. He had given $1,000 in cash to the desk clerk when he checked in as an advance against the bill, so the management thought he was terrific. He also tipped big and was uniformly courteous to the staff. He had had a number of visitors—two, maybe three women in strange garb came late in the evening and stayed in the bungalow until early morning. Three men had been frequent visitors; sometimes two or three came together, sometimes only one.

O'Malley asked for descriptions of Mr. Allen and his guests. Allen was undoubtedly Pisano. The identity of the first male guest was also evident—Klaus Rendt himself. The second was more difficult to identify, but O'Malley was fairly sure it was Marks. The third was probably the ubiquitous pale man who followed Rendt around like a shadow. Barry said the women were hookers. There were one or two blondes and one brunette and they both wore beautiful Japanese kimonos. One chewed gum.

O'Malley asked who was back there now and Barry said no one except Allen. Late in the afternoon Rendt had visited and left quickly. Earlier the blond hooker, not the gum chewer, had stayed for an hour. Otherwise there had been no visitors, although it was possible someone had gone back without the staff's noticing. O'Malley nodded and asked for directions. Barry took him outside and walked him halfway to the bungalow, then pointed along a path that wound its way around a fish pond. At the end of the path a small white Spanish house was tucked under some gigantic palms. There was one pale light in the front room but otherwise the little hacienda was as black as the night around it. O'Malley made sure that Barry remembered his instructions and then told him to make it ten minutes instead of five, figuring that the first five minutes would be spent outside, in fear. Barry left and O'Malley stood in the dark quiet and stared.

He looked for shapes and shades in the pale light but nothing moved. His stomach fluttered and turned. He checked his watch and had to wipe off the sweat to read the dial. When the needle swept past the twelve he took a deep cleansing breath and walked toward the house.

Halfway there a door slammed and he almost jumped into the fish pond. A slightly inebriated young couple came giggling down the path, quickly sobering when they saw O'Malley standing wide-eyed in the dark. They eased around him as they would a dangerous animal, then ran laughing toward the light. When their voices faded behind the pool cabana door he continued forward to meet Frank Pisano.

He tried to peer inside the bungalow but the heavy drapes were pulled tight. The door was open enough to allow a stripe of vertical light the width of a string to escape. He rang the bell and waited.

At first he thought he heard rustling, but it was only nerves transporting the wind in the trees to the inside of the house. He waited tensely, imagining at any moment that a silenced bullet would rip through the wood and into his heart. James Allen could then slide away into the night and Detective Andersen would write it off as another burglary, or a Mafia vendetta if he had imagination. His feet started to get cold and his toes numb. He rang the bell again and stood while the muted tones melted into the stillness.

The string of light was an obvious solution. All he had to do was push. But he was sure that was what Pisano wanted. A murder on the steps might be seen, not so a bullet delivered inside. But why couldn't Pisano just open the door, shove a gun in his face, and order him in? The quiet answered the question: no reason at all.

He tried the bell a third time. When silence again followed the ring he pushed against the string of light and walked after the opening door into the room.

Frank was sitting staring at O'Malley in a high-backed comfortable chair. The gun in his fist was pointed straight at O'Malley's midsection. The right side of his face was contorted in a vicious leer. O'Malley walked over and looked him in the eye. He wasn't afraid of Frank any longer. The left side of Pisano's face was splattered over the full length of the white stucco wall.

The desert night was cool but that didn't account for O'Malley's shivering. The shudders built on themselves like a child's swinging, each adding force to the spasm that followed. The ten seconds he stared at Pisano seemed like a week. Finally he had to turn away and bend over to ease the cramps. That didn't slow the violent shaking or the sudden sweating.

The ten seconds burned a photograph in O'Malley's mind that would never go away. He saw the small, neat hole in Frank's right temple that didn't even muss the glossy black hair. When the steel jacket came out the other side it had taken everything with it: hair, skin, bone, brain, and blood. It had left a man with half his head attached to his shoulder and the other half lying on the floor. The demarcation line between head and air was ragged with hanging red skin and provided a window to the interior of the skull. When the spasms refused to stop O'Malley fell involuntarily to his knees and simultaneously wept and retched on Pisano's freshly shined shoes.

When it was all over he sat on the floor and took deep breaths. He tried not to think of anything until the ringing phone interrupted the reverie. It was Barry, right on schedule.

"Is Ben O'Malley there?"

"Yeah, this is me." O'Malley's voice was hoarse and cracked but more or less under control. The kid wasn't satisfied.

"O.K., so let me talk to Mr. Allen." Smart.

"Mr. Allen is indisposed at the moment. He's resting."

"Yeah, that's what I thought. Look, if I don't hear another voice I'm calling the cops."

A good idea, as long as he called the right cop. "Barry, this is Ben O'Malley. I'm the guy who gave you the twenty. But there's been an accident here. That's why Allen can't talk."

"What kind of accident?" Barry's voice was wary.

"A bad one. Here's what I want you to do. Call Parker Center—that's the LAPD—and ask to speak to Detective Sergeant McCabe. You got that? Robert McCabe and only Robert McCabe. When you get him tell him to come over here right away."

Barry had his mind on all the problems this could cause him. "So what if he won't come?"

"If he asks any questions tell him . . . tell him that Ben

O'Malley says that Pisano went out with the boys tonight."

"That's it?"

"That's it. And give him Allen's room number. Tell him I'll be waiting here. Tell him to come straight to the room."

The whole thing sounded fishy to Barry. "Look, if there's been any trouble I gotta tell my boss. I can't just bring the cops out here without telling anybody."

The last thing O'Malley needed was an officious hotel manager buzzing around Frank's remains. "Barry, do it like I say and there's another twenty in it for you. Make the call and then come on over here. Alone." He glanced back at Pisano, who was still staring out the wide door. O'Malley kicked it shut. "And filch a pint of Jack Daniels before you come. I'll give you twenty for that, too." He would have given a hundred. Apparently O'Malley was appealing to Barry on the right level. Barry also wanted to see.

"O.K. I'll do it. But if you see my boss you don't know me."

"Fair enough."

O'Malley was used to Pisano's face now, or at least enough to look at it. He felt strangely calm again, calm enough to want to open some drawers before the crowds arrived.

O'Malley could see the old man on the roof, talking about being the first cop on the scene of a murder, which in Bayonne was virtually a nightly event. Nothing complicated about it, he'd say, just use your common sense. Walk around slowly. Don't hurry. Look at all the obvious things and draw all the obvious conclusions.

First he put his hands into his pocket and sniffed at the gun, still in Pisano's fist. The acrid stench of the murder weapon was strong. The killers obviously had a weird sense of humor. They had put the boys back in their embrace, lying on the pillows that had killed them. Here they put Pisano in his favorite chair and gave him the murder weapon to point at the cops. Maybe Rendt had a kinky sense of humor. But it sure as hell didn't sound like Marks.

O'Malley walked through the house quickly and didn't find any more of Pisano lying around, a reasonably sure sign

140

that Pisano had died in his chair. He came back and walked over to Frank's right, the side of the entry wound. He sighted across the top of Pisano's head. There was a bare wall about six feet away that had caught the blood. In the middle of the splayed scarlet design there was another design, this one of cracked plaster. O'Malley went over and stared hard at it. In the middle of the plaster design there was a small hole. He couldn't see anything in the hole but he was sure McCabe would be able to find a flat piece of metal in there, flat because the nose of the bullet had probably been deliberately weakened by two intersecting cuts. Only a dum-dum bullet could have gone in so easily and come out so flat, and with such horrible consequences to the body through which it had passed. O'Malley had learned a bit about dum-dums in Bayonne, but much more from the *Los Angeles Times,* which editorialized monthly against their widespread use by the LA Sheriff's Office. The sheriff said dum-dums cut down on injuries to innocent bystanders.

He next wandered around the living room. It hadn't been cleaned recently and was a bit unkempt, although not unusually so. The ashtray on the coffee table was full. All the cigarettes were the same brand and smoked to the nub, except for two, which were only half consumed and capped by a dark stain at the end of the white filter. Next to the ashtray was a room service tray with plates for one and an empty champagne bottle. Its twin was in the waste basket nearby. There were no glasses in the living room. O'Malley found out why in the bathroom. The basin was half-filled with cool water, its porcelain bottom covered with numerous glass shards—but only two more or less intact champagne glass bases.

The bedroom was in moderate disarray, a few articles of male clothing strewn on a rumpled bed, more cigarette leavings in an ashtray on the bedside nightstand, and a round water mark sitting high on the waxen wood. Save for two uncorked champagne bottles in the refrigerator the kitchen was clean and unused.

One proposition O'Malley would bet his life on was that the Beverly Hills Hotel provided morning maid service.

O'Malley was back examining the living room wall when there was a soft knock on the door. He went out and pushed Barry back, closing the door behind him. Barry was wide-eyed and exhilarated. O'Malley took the bottle from him.

"Have you ever seen a dead man before?" O'Malley asked.

"Sure, lots of them." Barry was lying and wanted in. O'Malley needed him there when McCabe came but also needed him conscious.

"O.K., we'll go on. But you've got to be ready for it. A man's been murdered and there's lots of blood. Think you can handle it?" Barry nodded excitedly. This would provide stories on the beach for months.

O'Malley stood aside and let him go through. Barry stood with his jaw on his chest staring. "Holy shit. They blew his fucking head off." That they had. O'Malley took a long swig of evil Jack and shook a little as the brown liquid went down and did its job. Barry grabbed the bottle back without taking his eyes off Pisano.

"Did you get hold of McCabe?" O'Malley had to ask twice before Barry returned to earth.

"Yeah, he was there. He asked a lot of questions but I told him just what you said. He said he'll be right out and not to touch anything. Goddamn, look at that fucking blood! What's that white gook on the floor?"

"Don't be ghoulish. And keep your hands in your pockets when you don't have them wrapped around the bottle." Barry did as O'Malley told him without thinking. Otherwise he stared at Pisano. When he'd seen enough, O'Malley took him by the arm and walked him backward to the door. "I'll wait for the cops here. You go out to the front of the hotel and try to bring them back quietly. That way we won't have the whole hotel trying to sneak a look." What O'Malley wanted to do was cover Frank up, give him some privacy against the indignity of prying eyes like Barry's. But that privacy would be a while yet.

McCabe came striding purposefully down the path at the head of an army. Behind him were cops in business suits, cops in blue uniforms, cops with cameras, and half the guests in the hotel. Barry was being dragged along by a little bald man who was alternately shouting at him and trying to get the guests to believe there was nothing to see. So much for Frank's privacy.

McCabe didn't shake hands. "Hello, Ben. He in there?" O'Malley nodded. McCabe pushed open the door and waved his people through. The ones in business suits went in, snapping pictures, measuring, and opening drawers. The uniformed cops turned to face the crowd and keep them back. The scene was chaotic. There was a steady babble of voices as people traded rumors. Barry was trying to surrender his hotel jacket to the bald man but the man kept cuffing him. O'Malley still had the Jack Daniels in his hand and he made good use of it.

McCabe went through the bungalow quickly and came out satisfied. "O.K., Ben, come on in. We can talk there." Inside there was only slightly less commotion. Frank was the most dignified man in the hotel.

"I don't want to make you nervous but I have got to read you your rights."

"You mean I'm in custody?"

"Let's just say you're free to leave. Unless you try to leave." O'Malley nodded. He wasn't particularly concerned. He still respected McCabe's intelligence and wanted to talk to him even if Baird would disapprove. McCabe reached into his pocket and brought out the card containing the language from the seminal Warren Court opinion that had dragged American criminal procedure out of the dark ages.

"You don't have to do that. I got an 'A' in criminal procedure." McCabe put the card away.

"O.K., what happened?" O'Malley told him of the cryptic note from Pisano and the means by which he had found the bungalow. McCabe listened intently, then was quiet for a moment.

"So after the kid showed you the house he left. You were then here for ten minutes by yourself. Did you shoot him, Ben?"

He had to ask the question. That didn't mean it had to be taken seriously. "I hoped you wouldn't ask me that," O'Malley said. "You're right. After the kid left I came in. Pisano was sitting in the chair alive as you and me. I asked to borrow his gun. Then I asked him to turn his head a little to the side so I could shoot him. After he was dead I turned a sunlamp on the blood so it would dry quickly. Then I was unexpectedly overcome by guilt and remorse so I threw up on Pisano's shoes and called you." He held out his hands for the cuffs.

McCabe made a face. "Don't be a wise ass." He looked back at Frank. "Well, at least I know this one wasn't a burglary."

The legions of business suits had already found the cracked plaster containing the bullet. They had finished photographing the wall and one was extracting the bullet with the care of a surgeon. It came out flat and coppery. The surgeon handed it to McCabe.

"We'll check it out, but I doubt if this will tell us anything. You say the gun had been fired?"

"It smelled funny. I assume that means it's been fired. Can't your ballistics people tell you if the bullet came from the gun?"

"I don't know. Ballistics simply matches markings. With one of these bullets it's hard. It's so chewed up when it comes out there's nothing left to match." He suddenly realized he was talking to someone outside the fraternity. "But that's not your problem. What you can do is tell me why Pisano wanted to see you."

O'Malley didn't know and told him so. "The message just said he wanted to give me some information about the case." The conclusion was inescapable, at least in O'Malley's mind, that someone didn't want that information divulged.

McCabe may have thought so, too, but if he did he

wouldn't admit it. "Maybe, maybe not. We'll see. What else do you know—or think you know?"

O'Malley ignored the remark and began talking fast, bringing McCabe up to date on Barry's information. Then he took the now surprised McCabe by the arm and led him through the house, showing him the two glass bases in the washbasin, the cigarette leavings, the full and empty champagne bottles, the condition of the bedroom. When he was through McCabe couldn't hide a smile.

"Stop down at the office tomorrow. I'll have you fill out an application for the LAPD so you can get paid for all this effort."

"I'm serious, McCabe. This is like a map."

"Really? And why's that?"

"You have to assume that the hotel had this place as neat as a pin this morning. So what was he doing in bed this afternoon? And who was he drinking champagne with? And why was the person so nervous about fingerprints that the glasses got smashed in the washbasin? Find yourself a non-smoking hooker—remember all those butts are the same brand and only a couple have lipstick on them—and you'll find the person who was here when he got it. Or at least someone who knows a great deal about how he spent his afternoon."

"Maybe the hooker killed him. Maybe he didn't pay her or something."

O'Malley shook his head vigorously. "The hooker didn't get him. It was the same guy with the same warped sense of humor who got the boys. Christ, you're as bad as Andersen. Next thing you'll be telling me is that it was a bungled burglary."

McCabe laughed at that. "No I won't." He ran his hands through his hair. "O.K., maybe you're right. We'll check it out. Anything else?" O'Malley shook his head.

"All right, you can take off. I've got a lot to do here. Talk to your lawyer and if it is all right come in and see me in the

145

morning. I have a feeling I'm going to be back on this case."

That was good news. The bad news was that McCabe's face said the cop found it strange that people connected with O'Malley kept turning up dead.

20

It was close to 1 A.M. when O'Malley took the Healey east on Sunset back to Hollywood. The Strip was only moderately active since this was a school night. At Hollywood and Vine that wouldn't matter at all.

When he got down around the Cinerama Dome he turned left. The hills and home were straight ahead but instead he turned left again on Hollywood Boulevard. The street was still congested. It was easy to cruise slowly and watch the action. A block west of Vine a horde of black and whites were investigating a burglary. As sheep dogs they drove the herd of waifs-for-sale west toward Cahuenga and Highland.

At Las Palmas he pulled into a red zone and waited. The pedestrian traffic passed eight abreast in both directions, only slightly slower than the meandering vehicles. A few of the kids walked over to check out O'Malley and his car, but when he didn't respond headed back to the corner. Finally a skinny dirty face with yellow teeth and a grimy T-shirt decided to try her luck. Maybe she was sixteen, but he doubted it.

"Nice car." She said "car" with an "h" sound in the middle. She was a long way from her Boston high school.

"Thanks." The word was noncommittal. He was not interested in leading her down that road unless she was already
there.

"Whattaya doing here? Ya waitin' for someone?"

"Maybe. Maybe just waiting."

She tried to flash a sensual smile but it came out jaundiced.
She was obviously shooting. He hoped she wasn't making
enough money to make the trend irreversible. "So howdja like
a girl while you're waitin'? If you want, I gotta brother who's
gay." She pointed to a kid even skinnier than herself, a feat
that didn't seem possible. Her "brother" smiled and waved.

"What's your name?" O'Malley asked.

"Lola." Fat chance. "And that's Tab." They were probably
Ellen and Harry. "What's yours?"

"Warren Burger."

"O.K., Warren. So what's the story? You want to take a
ride, maybe? Tab gives real good head. Me, too. If you want a
blow job it'll cost you twenty-five dollars and we can just ride
up by the parking lot to the Hollywood Bowl. If you want to
fuck it'll cost—"

O'Malley cut her off before she ran through the whole
menu. "All right, Lola. I want both of you."

"Yeah. Far out. Well that's O.K., too. It'll cost you extra
and no heavy S and M."

"Lola, get your pal. I'll give you thirty bucks to split between you. You won't have to do anything for it but come up
to my house in the hills, drink a cup of coffee, and give me
some information."

Her eyes got narrow and her voice came out flat. Lola had
heard this tune before and she didn't like the beat. "You're a
PI, right? You're lookin' for runaways. Well, I ain't turning in
no runaways." How sweet, O'Malley thought, honor among
urchins. He checked out the street behind him. If he got
caught doing this he wouldn't have to worry about the
federal case. But the cops were still milling around the burglary site. He pulled out two twenties and waved them in
Lola's face, causing passersby to shake their heads at the lack

of subtlety. "O.K., let's keep it simple. This is for the two of you. We'll go back to my home and I'll, uh, take pictures." Lola brightened. That she understood.

"Why didn't you say so? I'll get Dick—I mean Tab." She waved to her pal and the two of them squeezed into the passenger seat without a problem. O'Malley inched into the traffic and roared up the first side street away from the envious gaze of the remaining waifs.

When they got to the house the kids ran around looking at everything while O'Malley kept his eyes on the silverware. Compared with the back seats of cars this was really big time. Tab was especially impressed.

"Man, do you *live* here?"

"Yes, it was sort of given to me about a year or so ago." That really blew Tab away.

"You mean you *own* this place? Even the pool?"

"Actually the bank owns it. I just take care of things for them."

"Goddamn. This'll be a ball. We'll even give you some extra time, won't we, Lola?" She nodded agreement. What a wonderful deal. They'd stay for a week if O'Malley let them.

"I appreciate that, Tab. Look, how about if I get you some coffee."

"Nah, I don't want no coffee. I'll take a beer if you got it, though."

O'Malley considered it. The two of them were between fifteen and sixteen. They were incipient addicts, maybe more than that. They spent their days getting taken care of and their nights on their knees in parking lots getting the dollars to do it all some more. A beer would probably be the healthiest thing they'd had all day. He got out three Budweisers.

Lola was stretching on the couch. "So what's the story, Warren? Where's the camera? You want me and Tab to get it on for you?" Her pose made O'Malley shudder involuntarily.

"Well, as it happens, my tastes are sort of unusual."

They both looked wary. Lola spoke first. "I told you we're not into heavy S and M. We'll listen but if it's real kinky, it's extra."

O'Malley put the two twenties in the middle of the table and set his beer on top of them. The sight of the green raised their acceptable kink level.

"I'm into soap." They stared at each other.

"What kind of soap, man, and what do we hafta do?" Tab was visibly concerned.

"Regular, ordinary, everyday Palmolive. And all you have to do is wash each other. From head to toe. Every inch. Hair with shampoo. Teeth with toothpaste. Behind the ears. Under the arms. Back and front. I don't get off unless it's squeaky clean. So you have to do the whole thing at least three times. And you have to scrub with a washcloth and a brush. And if the person getting washed starts complaining, you have to scrub harder."

They looked at each other again. "Whattaya think?"

Lola shrugged. Tab turned back to O'Malley. "And that's it? You get off just by watching us?" O'Malley nodded. Tab seemed confused, lost in something approaching thought "Wait. I get it. After you watch us take this bath I come out and give you head, right?"

O'Malley tried not to gag. "No. Please. Don't worry about me. I'll get off just watching." He tried to make it sound more normal for them. "Like I told Lola, maybe I'll take some pictures." He affected an embarrassed, perverse smile.

Tab started laughing. "Man, it takes all kinds. O.K., what do we do first?"

"Take off your clothes, both of you. Then take them through that door and into the next room—it's known as the laundry room—and put them into the blue machine—that's known as the washing machine. While you're doing that I'll try to stay upwind and draw a bath." They did as he asked, giggling at the strange request. O'Malley went into the bathroom and filled the tub with hot water. Then he laid out as many instruments of ablution as he could find, essentially as many as he owned. This was going to take awhile.

They came back looking like two pallid scarecrows. "You're first, Lola. And remember, Tab, if she starts complaining, just scrub harder. Three times each. I'll stick my head in from time to time. Let's go." He heard Lola shriek like the witch in the Wizard of Oz when she hit the water. Tab solemnly informed her that that meant extra scrubbing.

O'Malley returned to the kitchen feeling like a saint. He dragged out some cold roast beef, bread, and a block of cheddar. When the soup was simmering, the laundry churning, and anguished splashes coming from the tub, he sat back with the Bud to figure out where to go next.

Forty-five minutes later Tab was going in for his third immersion and Lola was repaying him for previous indignities with relish. There was a brown ring around the tub a quarter inch thick, but the kids looked like new people. He gave them each a bathrobe while the clothes finished drying and then brought them out to the food. They attacked it ravenously. When they were done they looked clean, relaxed, and sated, exactly like underweight high schoolers in Des Moines. He gave them back their clothes and reached for the bills.

"O.K. guys, here's your twenties. It's probably the easiest twenty you'll ever make." They didn't disagree. "Now, here's the deal. There's a lot more where that came from. All you have to do is provide me with a little information."

Lola started whining about squealing on runaways but Tab shut her up. He hadn't felt this good in months and had gotten twenty bucks besides. Anything this guy wanted to talk about, Tab wanted to hear.

"I'm not interested in finding runaways," O'Malley said. "I'm interested in finding the names of two or three hookers, old ones, like twenty-five or so. They visited a friend of mine at the Beverly Hills Hotel a number of times in the past two weeks. One was blond. At least one, maybe two, were brunette." He couldn't think of much else to tell them. "If we need to I can tell you the room number and my friend's name. Right now I just want you to tell me how we can find the business ladies."

"Are you heat?"

"Do I look like the fucking heat, Tab?"

Tab grinned. His smile was actually dirty white, once the yellow was brushed off. His eyes were alert, too. Lola was a stone stupe, but O'Malley had a feeling there was a glimmer of intelligence in Tab.

"What did they look like?"

"Like geisha girls out of a war movie." The two kids stared at each other blankly. "You know, Japanese, long beautiful kimonos, but obviously hookers." O'Malley had wondered all the way back from the hotel why Pisano would go for that type of lady and now, because he had no answer, he was past wondering.

"And you say there was two or three of them at the Beverly Hills Hotel?" O'Malley nodded. Tab wrinkled his brow for a moment.

"I once did a job out there and the manager just about threw me into the street. That's a class place. There's always a lady or two in the bar, but they don't look like Lola here."

"Fuck you."

Tab ignored her. "They don't look like they're working either. They look like guests—or starlets. They dress up and sit alone at the bar, that's how you know. But they sure don't look like what you're talking about."

"So what does that mean?"

"It means they came from the outside and didn't know the rules. Your friend either picked them up on the street or they're outcall."

"What's outcall?"

"Outcall. You know—you call a number and a guy answers. You tell him your room number and he calls you back. If it sounds legit he sends someone over. Sometimes all the girls from one organization dress like slants. That sounds like what your friend was into."

That sounded right. O'Malley knew Pisano hadn't been

151

out on the street. "Let's assume you're right. How do we find the right place?"

"I don't know. There's a lot of them. This is LA, you know. Every third person is working."

"But they can't all be working through these outcall places."

"That's right. Maybe I can do a little checking and find out the big outfits and who's into slants this year. One problem is everybody wants to work the Beverly."

O'Malley's offer was only an offer, as Professor Adams used to say in his contracts class. It needed an acceptance. And valuable consideration. O'Malley peeled off another twenty and made a mental note to begin keeping track of the cash flow. "Here. This is seed money to get you interested. You can take it and split if you want. Or you can come back with some information." He wrote down his phone number and handed it to Tab. "This twenty has a lot of friends if you take care of me. You could do a lot worse."

Tab could—and had. "You got a deal."

It was after four when O'Malley dropped them back among the living dead on Las Palmas. The competition stared at their clean clothes and clear eyes with the look of the betrayed. Lola wasn't out of the car fifteen seconds when a black dude showed her something in a baggie. They walked up an alley. Tab watched from the car.

"She's gone, man."

"I know."

He turned to O'Malley. "But I'm not. I'll try to do this thing for you. But either way I appreciate it. That bath shit was hilarious. Lola thinks its legit kink. But I know what you were trying to do."

The gratitude was genuine and O'Malley was warmed by it. For too long he had been thinking about the effluent of treachery and cruelty. Little girls in sandboxes and strings on beds and glinty things in ratholes and brains on the floor. Compared with all that the dirty faces on the street corner were small time. When they were fed and washed they approached innocence.

"You're not a stupid kid, Tab. Try to take care of me. After that we'll talk."

He grinned. "You mean you'll try to get me into a good college?" His laugh became a hack in the night air. He returned to the corner. O'Malley pulled out fast.

21

He knew sleep was impossible so he drove down to the Pantry to look at the paper and get a quick fix of muddy coffee and undiluted carbohydrates. Gossage was still hurt and the Yanks were down by a hundred or so to the Birds. The Frogs were up two on the Pirates. The only good news was that the Dodgers were still playing .300 ball and Garvey had had some sort of hair puller with Sutton in the clubhouse. They were probably fighting over Billy Russell.

He turned to the financial section, which, following the natural order of things, comes at the back of the *Times'* sports section. There was the usual piece on the shell game of movie accounting practices, which was always good for a filler. The Fed was raising the prime again in order to curb inflation—a move once again guaranteed to do just the opposite. O'Malley hadn't attended the University of Chicago and still didn't appreciate the beneficial, tempering effects of putting people out of work. He still had the simplistic view that raising the cost of money made everything more expensive and transformed taxpayers into benefit collectors. Maybe he was missing something.

He turned to the charts to see how ACR was doing and got a rude surprise. Somebody must have put the word to Wall Street that there was nothing to worry about. At the beginning of the investigation the SEC had suspended trading for three days. When it took off the lid there was a lot of backed-up selling pressures, which pushed the price into the low 70s. But that was weeks ago. The price had stabilized and even begun inching back. It would be a long while before it saw 104 again but it was already back to 83 1/8, unchanged from the day before but sporting a volume of a quarter million shares, plenty of action for a moderately held stock. There were undoubtedly still a lot of sellers who had purchased at the bottom of the slide and were now cashing in. For every one of those sellers there was a buyer. In short, someone with a lot of money was now betting on the come.

Tucked in the corner on the back page was a small article about ACR by a *Times* staff writer. O'Malley tried to read it and at the same time get down some of the molasses-thick coffee.

ACR CLEARED FOR SALE OF SUBSIDIARY
Los Angeles—Associated Computer Research announced today that the waiting period under the federal Hart–Scott–Rodino Act had expired without action by the Justice Department or the Federal Trade Commission. This clears the way for completion of the sale of Video Enterprises, Inc., an ACR subsidiary, to F&H Holding Company, Inc., a California corporation. The price of the sale is $37.5 million.

ACR further announced, however, that initial payments due under the sale agreement had not been received. In the event the divestiture falls through, ACR stated that it would take all appropriate legal action to proceed against the security interests that F&H had pledged to guarantee completion of the transaction.

ACR has generated considerable controversy in recent weeks, growing out of a grand jury probe into its affairs. Two of its officers—its comptroller and the president of its Video Enterprises subsidiary—have been indicted, as has its outside attorney, Benjamin O'Malley. In addition, ACR has been stunned by the deaths of its president and chairman, killed in the course of an unsuccessful burglary attempt.

However, Mr. Klaus Rendt, new Board chairman of ACR, said today that the company had completed its internal audit and had found "no irregularities in the conduct of the affairs of Video Enterprises." He further stated that while the deaths of two key officers was "a major blow" to ACR, he fully expected the company to "perform as our stockholders anticipate."

Mr. Armington Bishop, counsel for ACR, said that he anticipated "a brief period of mourning and retrenchment." But he expressed "serene confidence" that the officers and former attorney for ACR "would be fully absolved of all wrongdoing."

It was just as Baird had predicted: the boys defaulting, Rendt taking over, Bishop in O'Malley's corner. But that was yesterday, and yesterday they didn't have to explain Pisano. The morning *Times* was silent on Pisano, but the afternoon papers would undoubtedly have lurid headlines about the hotel murder. So should the morning electronic media. He wondered how Rendt was going to squirm out of this one.

He forced down a few pounds of steak, eggs, and french

fries and waddled out to the car as the sun was breaking over the smog line. O'Malley was coming onto twenty-four hours without sleep but his body felt as if it had been injected with methedrine. The freeway was empty as he went back to the house to clean up for McCabe.

At 7:20 came the local break in the national news action. Nothing. Not a word about Pisano. A minute and a half on a third-stage smog alert in San Gabriel. Two minutes on an RTD strike. Another two minutes on LA's generous plan to make up for Proposition 13 by cutting old-age homes. A minute on the baseball scores and the Garvey fight. Then a bunch of commercials and it was back to Jane Pauley in New York. O'Malley couldn't believe it. The LA press loved its murders and had a steady stream of five a day to talk about. And this one had everything—gore and glamour in the Beverly Hills Hotel. As he walked to the shower O'Malley had an unsettling feeling that someone was getting to the zebras.

He came out of the shower to find Baird drinking his coffee and reading his paper.

"Isn't that cold?"

"Also not very well made. How long has this been sitting here?"

"Since last night. Which is how long I've been going."

"How are you feeling?"

"Like shit."

Baird nodded. "Understandable. But you actually look quite well. Invigorated. Are you sure you don't have a picture stashed away?"

"Huh?"

"You know." He waved an arm and a British accent appeared.

"Ah! in what a monstrous moment of pride and passion he prayed that the portrait should bear the burden of his days, and he keep the unsullied splendour of eternal youth! All his failure had been due to that. Better for him that each sin of his life had brought its sure, swift penalty along with it. There was purification in punishment. Not 'Forgive us our sins' but 'Smite us for our iniquities' should be the prayer of man to a most just God."

"That's very nice. Can you do the one about the spider and the rain spout?"

"Pearls before swine. That's Wilde, O'Malley, as in Oscar."

"I think it's wild, too. Are you trying to tell me I'm in trouble again?"

Baird shook his head. "No, I would never convey important information to you in any form other than declarative sentences. Six words or fewer."

O'Malley went over and regained his coffee, dripping a bit on the paper in Baird's hand. "Did anything happen yesterday?"

Baird shrugged and turned a page. "Not really. Bishop called again. Another lovely chat. No new information, but at least I know he's back in town. We'll meet the day after tomorrow and I'll get the details."

"What about the accountant?"

"I talked to his lawyer again. It's a strange story, although the lawyer hasn't invested the time to really know what he's talking about yet. But from what I can gather, Barrett knows everything. Not only knows everything but knows where the documents are to prove it. Barrett wasn't getting much more than a pat on the head for his efforts so he's not loyal to Rendt."

"What good does it do us to prove the fraud? I thought you said we wanted to do the opposite."

Baird gazed over the paper out the door. "Right. We get them to drop the case because there's no proof of the fraud. They do that because ACR puts pressure on them and refuses to cooperate. ACR does that because I demonstrate to Bishop I can prove the fraud. Get it?"

O'Malley didn't. "No. But don't tell me any more. It will only confuse me. Is that it?"

"All but one thing."

"What's that?"

"You said you were up as long as the coffee. Where?"

O'Malley considered it. Baird should be informed of Pisano, but was now the time? He'd undoubtedly hear it on the news soon anyway. If O'Malley told him now, Baird would want to know details, including why O'Malley was at the Beverly Hills and where else he was planning to go. Nevertheless, Baird was his lawyer and friend. It wasn't right to keep him in the dark.

"All right," O'Malley said, "but it will injure the reputation of a fine lady."

Baird nodded and rose to leave. "Please preserve the good woman's name." When he got to the door he turned. "And silly stories aside, will you please also give consideration to telling me the truth about your whereabouts last night?"

"Yes."

At 9:30 he was back at Parker Center to see McCabe. The detective looked old and gray and the light was gone from his puffy eyes. His desk was stained with coffee rings and his ashtray full of cigarette leavings. He'd undoubtedly had a hard night. But work hadn't done this to his face. He motioned O'Malley to a chair with a yellow and brown finger and shut the door. He began without pleasantries.

"I've been in meetings for the past three hours with Andersen and the captain. Apparently I exceeded my jurisdiction by going out there last night. The word is that if Pisano is tied up with the boys, then it's Andersen's case. If not, then it's a case for the Beverly Hills PD. Either way, I'm out." The words came out sad and slow, as if he were watching the destruction of an ideal he believed in very strongly.

"They can't do that. You're the only one who's always known the murders are tied up with the fraud. They can't ignore that now. Didn't you tell them about Pisano's involvement?"

McCabe laughed with his mouth. The eyes stayed dull. "Sure I told them about Pisano. I told them everything I knew." He was having difficulty breathing and obviously didn't want to talk anymore. Especially to someone who could do nothing to help. He sighed and tried to get it all out in one breath. "At two this morning I got the captain out of bed. At two forty-five your friend Bishop was in a meeting with him. At three-thirty Andersen and me were called down to meet with the captain. We met from four-thirty till seven-thirty."

"Was Bishop there?"

He shook his head. "No. Bishop did what he had to do earlier. It was all finished by the time I got downtown. The official word is there's still no evidence of fraud or siphoning. Bishop claims they've completed an internal investigation and everything's clean. He's afraid that if we stir up a lot of talk about fraud we'll undo all the good work that they've done. His request was actually a modest one. He says we should proceed with the investigation and should look under every rock. He's promised the full cooperation of ACR. He only asks that we don't involve the corporation in any formal way until we get some hard evidence."

"And the captain bought that?"

"Sure he did. You think it's everyday we get Armington Bishop strolling in here? And Bishop didn't ask us to do anything improper. Just make sure we had the facts before we move."

That may have been the request but the effect would be devastating. The investigation would be buried as deeply as Pisano himself. Andersen would shuffle papers for six months and the whole thing would be forgotten.

"What does Andersen think happened?"

"He's not making any predictions yet. But he's already making noises about Pisano's so-called criminal past. He's apparently got a record. Also there's a notion around that he was involved with the families back East."

"What do you mean, 'involved'?"

"He supposedly had had long associations with known family members. Both past and present associations."

O'Malley made a sour face. "McCabe," he began patronizingly, "Pisano was a nice Italian boy from Jersey City. A crook, I'll grant you, but only a sole practitioner. He probably grew up with tons of 'family members,' whatever that means. So did I. That doesn't mean we're in the Mafia."

McCabe shrugged. He wasn't interested in arguing. "Tell it to Andersen. Only don't tell him about who you grew up with unless you want to become a suspect."

O'Malley spoke to himself. "I can't be a suspect. I'm part of the fraud." He tried to calm down and think clearly. "All right. Let's assume Pisano is a card-carrying member of organized crime. Doesn't it seem odd to Andersen that ACR would choose to place such a man in an important executive position? Doesn't that prove that ACR was crooked, too?"

McCabe took a sip of cold coffee. "Bishop's got an answer for that, too. He says Pisano had blue chip credentials. Went to fine schools and had significant managerial experience. He says Pisano was brought to ACR by a reputable executive headhunter, one of the biggest in the country, as a matter of fact. The pitch is that ACR is now shocked by the revelations of Pisano's quote previous associations end quote. Nevertheless, their audit shows that Pisano was clean at ACR, he says. He certainly believes it unfortunate that the man's past resulted in violence. Nevertheless, while he chastises ACR for poor judgment in hiring, he sees no reason to associate the corporation with the death of its employee. That's a quote." O'Malley nodded at him dumbly. The web was seamless. He was starting to understand McCabe's despair.

"Have they muzzled the press, too? I didn't see anything on it this morning."

"That's SOP for a Beverly Hills murder. Think about it.

When's the last time you heard a big story about murder in Beverly Hills? But believe me, they happen. The press can only write about crime if the police give them information. The BHPD is famous for its tight lips."

"I thought the LAPD had the case."

"It's now a joint investigation. It's Andersen's case but all the press goes out through the BHPD. If Parker Center gets an inquiry we refer them out there. That's where they get their 'No comment.'"

"Let me guess. That procedure was set up about three forty-five this morning." McCabe didn't argue.

O'Malley stood up to leave. The detective behind the desk was tired and embarrassed and wanted to be left alone. "I'm sorry this happened to you, McCabe, I really am. You're a good man and would have done a good job." McCabe shrugged and lit a new cigarette from one that was still burning. O'Malley stopped at the door. "I've actually got some things to tell you—things that would support your view of the murders. But I think it's best now to keep them to myself. And certainly to keep them from Andersen." McCabe stared back through half-closed eyes, the old butt still burning in his fingers.

"Don't tell me you're trying to play policeman, Ben?"

"To the contrary. I'm trying to find out who did it."

McCabe still had enough humor and energy left to laugh.

O'Malley drove around aimlessly for an hour while the heat and traffic fumes conspired to do him in. Maybe if he knew what he was doing he might have thought of something clever. As it was, all he could think of was to follow the old man's advice. When in doubt do the obvious.

He entered the familiar basement garage and parked among the familiar Mercedes. He punched the familiar elevator button for forty-eight. The receptionist was new and didn't flinch when he asked to see Bishop.

Bishop's secretary came scurrying out and peeked around a

corner to make sure it was true. Then she was gone. She returned with a dignified air as if the previous display had never occurred. "Mr. Bishop will see you now."

Bishop was sitting at a makeshift desk. Nothing in the office matched. The walls were bare and the drapes were plastic and discolored. He spoke with his back to O'Malley.

"I'm not going to stand or offer you coffee nor am I going to shake hands or engage in any other pleasantry. I am, of course, fascinated to learn what possessed you to come here. But my curiosity does not exceed my desire to see you leave quickly."

O'Malley sat down anyway. He had no hope of outsmarting a man like Bishop. His only hope was that Bishop was as honest as his reputation said he was, as O'Malley thought he was. "This shouldn't take too long, Armington. I just thought it was time for us to chat about a few things."

"As far as I'm concerned we have nothing to talk about."

"How about murder? I know three we could talk about."

"Is that supposed to be funny?"

"Which—the pillows over the nose or the metal through the brain?"

Bishop smirked and shook his head. "I see. You're feeling hurt and this is a little bravado. Well, get through with it and then get out. As I say, I have nothing to talk to you about."

"You weren't so closemouthed this morning. About three A.M. down at Parker Center."

"I see you've been speaking to Detective McCabe. I assume he's still upset over being removed. No doubt he's making accusations."

"Not him—me. You went down to the LAPD in the middle of the night and put the brakes on a murder investigation. I say you did it because Rendt and Marks are implicated."

That angered Bishop and he turned quickly to face O'Malley. "All right, young man, let's make this as short as possible. Your tale is absurd. But even if what you say is true, why should I waste my time speaking with you? In short, what are you going to do about it?"

O'Malley smiled and played the only card he had. "Hold a press conference. Make accusations. Create a little sensationalism. The usual thing."

That brought him up short. "You can't possibly. Why, you'd be cutting your own throat. A press conference about J and D! Why, I've never heard anything so outrageous. No one would pay the slightest attention to such wild accusations."

"I think you're wrong about that, Bishop. As a matter of fact, I think I'd make great copy." O'Malley spread his hands toward the imaginary headline. " 'Lawyer Implicates Jenkins Firm in Murder Case.' Why, the DA would have an orgasm. The *Times* would hound him to death if he didn't follow up. I'd be a hero. I'd probably work a quick immunity deal and spend the next two years happily working my ass off for your destruction."

It was all bluff, but at least Bishop was paying attention. Bishop, however, was not a man who took threats well. "You are truly slime. Go ahead and make your accusations. If I can't defend them I don't deserve to be practicing law." He reached for the phone. There was a red button to the security desk.

O'Malley spoke quickly. "Oh, you'd be just a footnote. Before you make your call, don't you want to hear about Marks?"

"You're bluffing. You know nothing that would implicate Randall Marks." He didn't push the button.

"Am I?" O'Malley began talking rapidly, dredging up all the dirt on Marks he could think of. It was the first time Bishop had heard O'Malley's side of the story and his eyes shifted slowly from anger to concentration as the tale unfolded. O'Malley tried to make him see the pattern, beginning with Marks' first association with the boys, through the stolen BEF files, to the present fraud. He tried to convince Bishop that the indictment was a setup, that Marks had intentionally disassociated himself from the deal so that he'd be safe in the event of a blowup. The plea was both analytical and emotional. O'Malley knew he'd have no second chance.

It was a solid hour before O'Malley stopped talking. Bishop had not interrupted once.

Bishop was not stupid. When O'Malley finished talking Bishop's hands were in front of him. Folded. Far away from the red button. But he wasn't convinced either. "What you've told me is a . . . a possible . . . a possible scenario. It is not evidence. You have yet to tell me anything that directly connects Randall Marks with any of this."

"Fair enough. What if I told you that Marks knew that Pisano was staying at the Beverly Hills? Before Pisano died, of course."

"You're lying."

"I'm not lying. Not only did Marks know he was there, he visited him. As a matter of fact, so did Rendt."

"That's a lie. McCabe never mentioned any such contact."

"You didn't give him a chance. He would've gotten around to it if you'd let him. Of course, it will never be known if Andersen runs the case. But I know about it. I spread a little green around the grounds."

Bishop was quiet. When he spoke again the voice was soft. "What do you want?"

"Where's Marks?"

"Why?"

"I'm not going to hurt him, if that's what you're afraid of. I want to talk to him, just like I'm talking to you. If you let me do that, and don't call and warn him, then I don't go public with what I know."

Bishop looked intently at O'Malley, then looked away. He didn't speak again for a long time and O'Malley could feel the conflict churning within him. The threats, even the evidence, would mean nothing to a man like Bishop. Unless he believed the tale O'Malley was telling. Believed it so deep inside that Marks' treachery created a moral imperative that transcended his duty to his client. Even his duty to his friend. And if he believed it at that level then even O'Malley's flimsy evidence would be enough. O'Malley's throat was dry as he waited for Bishop to speak again. When he did O'Malley had to strain to hear because the lips barely moved.

"Randall Marks is at the Stanford Court. Room six-eighty-four. He'll be there through this evening."

"Thanks." O'Malley got up and left. Bishop was still staring at the wall, his face not unlike that of Detective McCabe.

22

O'Malley drove straight to LAX and booked the first PSA to San Francisco. There was a forty-five minute wait. He went into a booth and dialed Rad at work.

"I'm surprised to hear from you," she said.

"I know. And I also know I was stupid. I'd like you to forget what I said if that's possible."

"It's easily possible. Where are you now?"

"LAX. I'm on my way to San Francisco."

"O.K. Why don't you drop the other shoe."

"To see Marks."

Silence.

"You want to run that by me again, please?"

"I'm going to see Marks. I can't explain it all to you now. It's very complicated. But I'm on to something and I have to go."

"Is he expecting you?"

"No."

"Don't go, O'Malley. I know you're frustrated and feel you have to do something. But this is not smart."

"Look, they just announced final boarding," he lied. "I've got to run. I'll tell you all about it when I get back."

"O'Malley, listen to me—" He broke the connection.

He next called Baird to make sure he wasn't breaking any laws by leaving LA. "No problem," Baird said, "but why are you going to San Francisco?"

"I'll get back to you," O'Malley answered.

The big airship thundered over the bay and came in low over the peninsula airstrip. San Francisco's airport juts into the sparkling water in a futile attempt to escape from Daly City, the home of the perfectly rectangular condominium. To reach that most glorious of American cities requires a forty-five-minute cab ride on an unadorned highway through tedious little towns. The city's glamorous reputation seems a lie until the roadway dips and rises to open onto the splendid red span slicing through the fog to Marin.

This time the cab turned to the right, passing along the bay on the way to the financial district. As always, he felt a sense of peace in this city. All cities in the world were originally designed to end up like San Francisco. But other great cities have untold millions of teeming residents whose waste and efforts have fouled them. San Francisco still has fewer than a million occupants, about the same number as a street corner in the South Bronx on a good night. They hang on the hills in their beautiful Victorians and watch the glittering bay, and there just aren't enough of them to cause much of a problem.

The cab let him off at the Embarcadero Hyatt, a truly grotesque structure designed by the same madman who did the Bonaventure. But what fits well in LA is an insult to San Francisco. One simply does not wear plaid pants to formal affairs.

But the Hyatt does draw every conventioneer in northern California and thus was a perfect place to clean up and buy a new shirt and tie, necessities if he hoped to get to the Stanford Court elevator unmolested by the front desk.

He went out the back door onto California Street and caught the cablecar rising to Nob Hill. The Stanford Court was originally the townhouse of Leland Stanford, the ancient curmudgeon who funded Stanford University, Herbert Hoover, and much of what is elegant and reactionary in California. It sits a bit to the side of the true nob of Nob Hill, ruling the city with its fellow emperors: the Mark Hopkins, the Fairmont, the Huntington, and an embittered, old, and quite discriminatory private club. Together they provide comfort to the rich, who have the option of remaining in opulent rooms with incomparable service or strolling downstairs to sample the fare of Fournous' Ovens, L'Etoile, Alexis, or Canlis'. Marks' hideaway was perfectly in character.

O'Malley was familiar with the decadent pleasures of Nob Hill from his J&D expense account days, and he knew that here there would be no bribing of bellboys. He also knew there was an excellent chance he'd never get to Marks' room. The Stanford is small enough to more or less know its guests and perceptive enough to know its guests don't like surprises.

The lobby of the Stanford Court also serves as the most comfortable bar in the western United States. O'Malley settled down in one of the cushy easy chairs with a view of the front desk and ordered a plain tonic, recognizing this might be a long siege. He was lucky. An hour and three tonics later the guard changed. When the new clerk was simultaneously engrossed in counting receipts and answering telephones O'Malley approached and began ostentatiously examining the pigeonholes.

"Yes, sir, may I help you?"

"Yes. My eyes are bad. You haven't gotten any calls for four-twelve in the past hour, have you?"

He looked at the empty box. "No sir, no calls."

"Damn!" The clerk waited inquisitively.

O'Malley clicked his teeth. "We're waiting for a jury verdict." The clerk said "Ah" sympathetically.

"Look, I wonder if you'd do me a favor."

"Of course, sir."

"I'll be sitting over there for the next fifteen minutes." He indicated the obviously used chair. "If you should get a call for four-twelve, or for a Mr. Chancellor Dandridge, Mr. Evansworth Erving, Mr. Crossan Belding, Mr. Armand Diatovitch, or a Mrs. Jamieson Edwards, would you have a phone brought over. Otherwise I'll take it in the room."

The clerk never even blinked. "Is that Erving with an 'I'?"

"No, an 'E.' "

"Very good, sir."

O'Malley sat back down with another tonic and a copy of *Fortune*. It was a calculated risk. As long as 412 didn't arrive or get a call in the next fifteen minutes he was home free. When fifteen finally dragged by, O'Malley paid the bill in cash, went back to the desk, and began squinting at the wooden honeycomb.

"Nothing yet, sir."

They clicked their tongues in tandem and O'Malley walked slowly to the elevator shaking his head. He waited till he was inside and the door had shut.

"Sixth floor, please."

A moment later the door shut behind him again and the noise of the lobby and city were gone. Muted yellow light from well-spaced chandeliers fell softly past mahogany flower tables and gilded mirrors onto the long, Persian rug, set like a jewel in the oak floor. The ceilings were intricately carved. The walls were clean and white, setting off in bold relief the polished brass fittings and dark mahogany doors. He walked in perfect silence down the corridor, concentrating on the ascension of even numbers.

When the numbers reached 684 he stopped and tried to let his ears penetrate the thick wood, but the exercise was futile. He wasn't surprised to feel the sweat forming again or the beginnings of fear and déjà vu. This was his third unannounced visit. The first two were visits to graves, one expected and one not. He prayed that Mr. Randall Elliott Marks was alive and well behind the brown, solid door.

He knocked twice softly, like a hotel employee. The door sprang open as if he'd tripped an electric eye. Marks was dressed in a soggy T-shirt and rumpled pants, looking sad and fat. But the man still commanded respect. The square, black automatic weapon in his right hand more than made up for his jailhouse pallor and bloodshot eyes. Yet O'Malley wasn't particularly concerned about getting shot. The tremors in Marks' hand caused the gun to describe a wide arc like a searchlight. It only passed by O'Malley once in every sweep.

"All right, don't move." Marks was trying hard to imitate a movie gangster.

"O.K."

"Just don't move one inch."

"All right."

He suddenly seemed to remember something from his childhood. "Raise your hands."

"Is this really necessary?"

"Just do as I say." Marks tried to brandish the weapon, but his shaking made the effort a redundancy.

"You got it. How's this?"

Marks pushed past O'Malley and began staring up and down the corridor. He had his back completely turned and his pink, powdered neck was an unprotected six inches from O'Malley's raised hand. One quick blow and the affair would be over. O'Malley needed no more proof that Marks was not the cold, sinister killer of Frank Pisano.

"Boo!" O'Malley said.

Marks flinched and twisted spasmodically, suddenly realizing he was vulnerable. As he spun O'Malley simply reached out and plucked away the gun as neatly as Franco taking a handoff. Marks' eyes got wide and fevered and he attacked like an animal fighting its way out of a corner. He was surprisingly strong for a man who had spent the last twenty years with soft chairs and soft food. In the first flourish he knocked the gun away; it went twirling like an ice dancer across the gleaming parquet floor and landed safely under the

169

sofa. O'Malley tried to say something soothing but Marks came at him like a Sumo wrestler, lifted him off the ground, and began running across the room. O'Malley began laughing as the two danced across the hotel floor. At the far wall Marks collapsed exhausted, falling panting and sweating against O'Malley with a sickly sweet old-man odor. O'Malley used the respite to grab Marks' right nostril between thumb and forefinger and twist upward. Marks screamed and flailed but otherwise followed O'Malley to an easy chair. O'Malley pushed him into it.

"Why don't you relax? You're going to be grabbing your chest soon if you're not careful."

Marks was wheezing heavily and his white T-shirt clung wetly to his flabby frame. The face was red and pale at the same time; blotchy, in a word. The once artfully disheveled white hair was plastered to his scalp. O'Malley was concerned and decided to lower the tension level. He shut the door, pulled up a chair in front of Marks, and lit a cigarette. He spied a near-empty bottle of brandy on the desk.

"Looks like you've been doing a little solitary drinking. You know that's one of the warning signs of alcoholism."

"What do you want?" Marks could barely get the words out.

"I want to talk. To ask you some questions and to have you respond truthfully. Maybe we can even be civilized if all goes well." That left open the threat that things could also not go well.

"Look," O'Malley offered, as calmly as he could, "why don't I pour us both a small brandy and you can relax." Marks began breathing easier and his eyes lost some of their fire. They became narrow and wary, fixed on O'Malley's face. When he didn't respond O'Malley poured two snifters and put one in front of Marks. Marks tried to ignore it but finally picked it up with both hands and downed it at a gulp.

"There's the boy. I bet that makes you feel better." O'Malley emptied the bottle into his glass.

"What sort of questions?" Marks demanded.

"The obvious ones. Who's been killing people? Why did you set me up? Why did you go to see Pisano before he died? Why are you holed up here? Why did you greet me with a gun? What are you afraid of? How much of the action are you in for? Why is Bishop stonewalling the murder investigation? Where were you on the night of July 14? Things like that. Let's just make believe it's a deposition."

"I don't have to say a thing to you. Who do you think you are? You can't barge in here." He suddenly seemed to realize the incongruity of the situation. "I don't care who you're working for or with. You're a fucking lousy wet nose, for Christ's sake."

"That's true. And you've made sure that I will never become a mature, sophisticated attorney like you. Nevertheless, Randall, honey, you must understand that things have changed. You see, you've put me in a position where I have nothing to lose. So here we sit in this little soundproof chamber. If you cooperate we'll discuss the whole problem like gentlemen. Otherwise—well, you remember that little trick with the nose? Don't make me do it again, because next time I'm going to keep pulling till I'm holding the fucking thing in my hand."

Marks glared at O'Malley with hate, but also to find out if the threat was serious. The threat was deadly serious and O'Malley's face conveyed that message unequivocally.

Marks seemed to collapse. "All right. I'm sure you know everything anyway. Go ahead. One at a time."

"Who killed the boys?"

He seemed surprised at the question. "I don't know." The asshole. O'Malley started to get up.

"No, I'm serious," Marks said quickly. "I really don't know. That was as much a shock to me as anyone. Sure I knew about the siphoning. I even knew that they were planning to implicate you when it became clear that Mrs. Weidman was going to the authorities. But there was no reason for me to kill them. They were the ones who would testify against you and absolve me. Surely you're aware of that."

"You lousy fucker. You were the one who advised them to frame me."

He shrugged. "Of course, it was my only option under the circumstances." O'Malley began to give serious thought to violence whether the man talked or not.

"What circumstances?"

"Special ones. Caused by the disintegration of my arrangement with the boys. You see, in the beginning it was designed to go on forever. Pisano would travel around the world making horrible films for one hundred fifty thousand dollars apiece. We—actually ACR—would provide him with millions for each of the films. Barrett and Pisano would maintain two sets of books and all the cash over the true negative cost of the films would be ours to divide. Pisano was in charge of safely disposing of the excess funds. I believe 'laundering' is the popular term."

"So what happened?"

"A number of things. Corporate profits on the computer end of the business began leveling off, which made it harder to justify infusions of large amounts of cash into Video Enterprises. The investment community, and particularly the lenders, were starting to ask questions. We decided to taper off. Then before we could pull out effectively, Mrs. Weidman went to the authorities."

"How were you going to pull out?"

"By disposing of Video Enterprises entirely. At first the divestiture was to be straightforward. The assets would be sold piecemeal in the United States and an unfortunate fire would dispose of the inventory in Venezuela. Then Mr. Rendt became foolishly greedy. He saw the transaction as a means by which he could compel Messrs. Hardwick and Friedrich to transfer legal control of ACR to him."

"Why? Why would they do that?"

"A number of reasons. They had never really been in control. Their only contribution was the original stolen BEF drawings and their only interest was money. They were already millionaires many times over, of course, partly from their legitimate ACR holdings and partly because they received a percentage of the money that Pisano was stealing. In addition, Rendt had a great deal of leverage over them. First, they feared him and always had. Second, he threatened to return to Germany and leave them to answer to the authorities alone. If they cooperated, Rendt promised they would receive five million dollars in cash—I believe under the table is the way it's usually described—and they would be free of worry on the fraud charge because Video Enterprises would be gone and forgotten. Remember, this was all prior to Mrs. Weidman's denunciations. But none of the rest of us knew that Rendt was forcing them to give up their shares. I myself hadn't been informed that the boys were going to lose their ACR holdings until you gave me your report." O'Malley remembered Marks' hilarity at hearing the details.

"So when did you advise them to frame me?"

"Later. After Mrs. Weidman went to the authorities. At that point the boys stood to lose all their ACR holdings *and* go to prison. They came to me for advice. I advised them to seek immunity and to implicate Messrs. Rendt, Barrett, and Pisano. They were most reluctant to take any action that would displease Mr. Rendt. I then suggested that they place the blame on you, which they did."

"Who put the hundred thousand in my account?"

"I did, or rather I arranged it."

"Why? I mean, I know why, but didn't you have enough already?"

"Not really. Or at least not enough for Armington Bishop. I have—or had—a great deal of credibility with Armington based on a long friendship. But Armington refused to take action against you solely on the basis of the boys' word, which he rightly distrusted. The money convinced him that it was you, in conjunction with Mr. Pisano, Mr. Barrett, and Messrs. Friedrich and Hardwick, who was to blame."

"Does he still believe that?"

"Let us say less so with each passing day."

But Bishop still believed it enough to use his weight to slow down the murder investigation. Nevertheless, O'Malley remembered the man's despair at the end of their morning interview. Bishop might yet wear white, or at least penitent purple, before this was over.

"O.K. No surprises there. Let's move on. Who killed Pisano?"

"I assume Mr. Rendt."

"Why? Pisano wanted to talk to me last night. Was he killed to prevent that?"

Marks considered the question. "No, I don't believe so. I think Mr. Pisano was killed for money. You see, the money is now located in a large number of accounts in various countries, principally Switzerland, Lichtenstein, Panama, and the Cayman Islands. We three—Pisano, Rendt, and me—are joint holders of the accounts, each of us with a number known as an account access code. None of us knows the others' numbers. The codes were sent to each of us independently by the banks and all three codes are necessary in order to make withdrawals. Pisano was threatening to attempt to travel to the less scrupulous banks and bribe the access codes from the banking authorities. That was a great risk. It was also barely possible that Mr. Pisano, because he arranged for the accounts, had already bribed the authorities and was already in possession of at least some of the codes. I went to the Beverly Hills and attempted to dissuade him from this foolish course. So did Mr. Rendt. Mr. Pisano was adamant." He shrugged.

"So now there're only two holders and Pisano is no longer in a position to liquidate, having himself been liquidated."

"That's correct." It made sense. O'Malley looked at Marks. Suddenly the reason for his fear was obvious.

"And you're next. Rendt can't do a thing without your number."

The statement stunned Marks even though he had obviously been thinking of nothing else since he heard of Pisano's death. He began embracing his chest and abdomen, as though the room had become chilled, and rocking slightly as if he were seeking peace in a fetal memory. He didn't respond to the observation.

"Well, Rendt will truly be in a fat position if he can snuff you, Marks. Then he's got all of ACR and all of the buried treasure, too. But your murder might be a bit much even for Armington to rationalize. And for Detective Andersen to ignore."

He seemed to recover slightly. "I hope you're right. I think you are, although I could imagine several scenarios in which Mr. Rendt would find it in his interest to take action against me. But even if he does nothing violent, he now has the option of intimidating me into providing him with the final number."

"Is that what's making you sick, Marks, the loss of your stolen money?"

"No, it's the threat of death. It's simply that the loss of a fortune doesn't seem a very attractive fallback position."

"How long have you been holed up here?"

"Just since this morning. When I heard the news of Pisano's death from Armington I had an irrational fear that I would be killed on the same night. Perhaps it was a ludicrous concern. Perhaps Rendt wouldn't be that stupid. But nonetheless I was afraid. I came here on a business pretext and I communicate with Armington by phone, ostensibly to determine whether there are developments that will be injurious to the interests of the corporation."

"Don't you think Rendt killed the boys, too?"

He looked quizzical again, as he had the last time the question was asked. "As I say, I honestly don't know. Rendt is certainly capable of it, but the motive would be most unclear."

"Where were you on the night of July 14?"

He smiled. "I was delivering a speech in Monterey, California, to four hundred members of the American Society of Securities Brokers."

"What time?"

"The speech followed dinner. I would guess I spoke from nine to nine-thirty and answered questions until ten-fifteen. Then I retired."

Monterey was about three hundred miles north of LA. If he had a pilot waiting with a small twin he could have landed at Burbank by 12:45. The boys were murdered at two.

"It's barely possible that you could have made it back in time."

He shrugged. "Perhaps, but I doubt it. In any event, I didn't do it."

"Or you could have had someone do it for you, which is more likely anyway."

"I didn't do that either. And to save you some questions, I was dining at La Scala with Armington and his wife last evening from seven-thirty to ten. We shared a brandy at the Beverly Wilshire at ten forty-five and separated at eleven-thirty. Prior to meeting Mr. Bishop I was in business conferences at the firm from three P.M. to five P.M. and then returned home to dress for dinner." He thought about the question for a moment like a lawyer. "I suppose it's theoretically possible that I stopped on the way home and disposed of Mr. Pisano. It's also possible that I hired someone. Again, neither of those events occurred."

O'Malley nodded, thought for a moment, then stared at Marks.

"Tell me something. Why would a man in your position get involved in a cheap embezzlement?"

Marks laughed with real amusement this time. "It was hardly a cheap embezzlement."

That was certainly true. O'Malley decided that a question like that was a sure sign of fatigue. It was now over thirty hours since he had slept. He rose to leave Marks alone with his empty brandy and wet underwear. Suddenly he realized what had been nagging at him from the time he first came into the room.

"You knew I was coming, didn't you?"

"No—no, I didn't."

"Sure you did. You were waiting with a gun in your hand behind the door."

"No, I really didn't know." Marks was licking his lips again. O'Malley took a step toward him.

"Bishop called you and told you to be waiting for me, didn't he?"

Marks looked at O'Malley, then lowered his face. "O.K., you're right. Yes, he did."

As they used to say in Bayonne, the lie was all over his face like ugly on an ape.

23

O'Malley made his way back the way he had come and the feeling was not unlike descending from Olympus. Nob Hill, San Francisco proper, 101 South, Daly City, each providing a good bit less than the level before. By the time he reached the block-long queue that signaled the beginning of another bout with PSA's infamous service, he thought he had passed to the innermost of the nine circles.

He slept fitfully between rude coffee offers and woke only when the stretch-727 began decelerating over the desert east of Santa Barbara. Five minutes later and there was no doubt this was LA: The brown, parched summit of the San Gabriel

Mountains barely managed to peek over the haze. Up was a white-blue cloudless sky, down was a chocolate steam room.

It took him almost as long to get out of the airport as it had to fly from San Francisco. He finally sped out of the airport between dying palms and ran smack into the rush hour on the San Diego Freeway. He settled into one of the ten lanes and pointed north.

At Westwood he got off and began inching down Wilshire. The streets were crowded with white-collars returning home, UCLA students milling, and folks from San Bernardino in to ogle coeds. When he passed the bottleneck at Westwood, it was more or less moderate sailing into Beverly Hills.

By the time O'Malley got to the bank building where ACR was housed it was after six and the front doors had a dead bolt through them. There was a white button at eye level that would buzz the black guard and cause him to stop staring suspiciously and open the door. If O'Malley pushed the button the guard would then come to the door and ask embarrassing questions, like the nature of O'Malley's business. O'Malley would then be forced to try a tired story and the guard wouldn't buy any of it. O'Malley decided he was far too weary to think of anything clever. He waved at the black man's unmoving face and went to pay the ransom for ten minutes of parking for the Healey.

It cost another fortune to get the valet at Trader Vic's to take custody of it, as long as O'Malley understood, according to the express wording of the ticket, that no bailment was created and if the car was gone when O'Malley got back, well, that was life. The only thing the Beverly Hills Vic's shared with its counterpart on Central Park South was the spelling and the laughable prices. Maybe the bad food, too. But it did have a quiet bar and drinks that O'Malley thought might have healthy ingredients. For the price of two of them he could have gotten a large steak someplace else.

The bartender looked vaguely humiliated in his mauve flower shirt but, yes, he did have a phone book. It was about the thickness of a magazine and contained the numbers of the teeming hundreds of Beverly Hills residents willing to go public. O'Malley knew it was a useless exercise but turned to the "R's" anyway. K. Rendt was right there between Elliott Rendrick and Michael Rene and lived on something called Point View Terrace. It couldn't possibly be the same one.

A soft male voice answered the phone. It wasn't K. Rendt. O'Malley spoke hoarsely.

"Hello. This is Michael Baker of the *Times* business section. I'd like to get a comment from Klaus Rendt on the Justice Department action concerning ACR. Is he available?"

"Mr. Rendt is on the other line and will have to return your call. Mr. Baker, did you say?"

"Yes. From the *Times*. I'm in a booth, though, so I'll have to call back. Will he be available for the remainder of the evening?"

"Mr. Rendt has a heavy appointment schedule this evening. Can it possibly wait until morning?"

"Of course." O'Malley rattled off the first seven digits that popped into his head. "Just have him call me at the office. This is *Klaus* Rendt's home, is it not? Of ACR?" It was.

The bartender had a good map and a magnifying glass and after a bit of squinting O'Malley was able to locate Point View Terrace. The street was a little squiggle tucked well into the hills, surrounded by a host of other squiggles. There looked to be one way in and one way out.

There were a few things to do before he'd be ready to see Rendt. One was to find out if he'd bought anything for his twenty. The second was to become armed, which would cost him much more than twenty. For each of those tasks he needed to find Tab.

The action had shifted back to Hollywood and Vine, the traditional marketplace. The night crawlers were out in force, squinting against the slanted evening rays like newborns. The mosaic of the traffic flow was the same, housewives and homecoming workers competing with the customers for an inside lane. Tab was bent up against a Howard Johnson's, making sure that the building didn't slide into the Boulevard.

He recognized the car and came immediately. O'Malley cruised around the corner to the relative peace of Yucca.

"How's it going?"

"Not bad, bath man." Tab's voice was no longer clear and the skin was gray. The eyes were like gun slits, narrow yellow openings pinched shut at the corners by dried mucous.

"Glad to see you're taking care of yourself."

He shrugged. His clothes were the same as the last time they'd seen each other.

"At the moment I don't care," O'Malley said. "Just tell me if you've been taking care of *me?*"

"Don't get righteous, friend. A good thing came along and I took a piece. But I haven't lost you. Matter of fact, I know who visited your friend."

"Who?"

"It's gonna cost. A hundred for me and a hundred for her."

"Bullshit."

Tab grinned. "Well, maybe fifty for each of us will get you to the same place."

"Tell me what you know and how you found it. Then I'll decide if it's worth it."

The information sounded legitimate. Tab had called around to every outcall operation in town claiming to pimp for a resident at the Beverly Hills. The pitch was that he was looking for a repeat. Every place he called said they knew the girl he was talking about and would send her over. The twelfth place was able to accurately describe her uniform.

"So who is she?"

Tab raised his shoulders and dropped them. "Who knows. But I can have her come wherever you want."

O'Malley thought about it. He had to see her tonight but the question was timing. The sun was already dipping behind the hills and would soon leave Hollywood, saving exclusive rights to the glorious departure for the beach community. It all had to be done very fast.

"O.K. Have her pick you up at the Howard Johnson's and bring her up to my house in an hour." O'Malley gave Tab another twenty. "Balance on delivery. And one thing more. Can you get me a gun?"

Tab's eyes got wide. "Heat? You fixin' to hurt this lady?"

"No. I'm fixin' to protect myself against a man. But that's not going to happen until later. Can you do it?"

Tab was shaking his head. "Man, you look like a stiff but you are one heavy creature." But he could do it. Any preferences? Yes, a police .38, but O'Malley would take anything and pay extra for a .32 or up. O'Malley dropped him back on Vine and told him there was a bonus for promptness. He must have hit the right buttons; Tab's feet were running when they hit the pavement.

O'Malley went back to the homestead for a shower, shave, clean clothes, an apple, and a small evil Jack over ice. The whole thing was fitting together like the logs in a pioneer farmhouse. The answers were making him sicker than ever but the exhilaration of the chase was taking over. He was energized by a developing faith that when all the pieces were assembled and presented, neither Armington Bishop nor Detective Spiro Andersen nor anyone else would be able to deny the truth.

He used the forty minutes before his appointment with Tab to drive over to Rad's. She was out and the house was dark and cold. He let himself in with his silver key and found what he needed in a matter of minutes. When he got back to the house Tab was sitting on the curb next to a car with a woman in it. As O'Malley talked to her the woman lit new cigarettes with the burning ends of the old.

She said her name was Melissa and she worked for an organization called Executive Massage. She was soft-spoken, kindly, and intelligent and was obviously chagrined by her Oriental getup. O'Malley gave her fifty dollars for her time and Tab the thirty due, with an offer to Melissa for fifty more if she'd talk about Frank Pisano. She didn't hesitate. They spoke for an hour and her answers were sure and true. Tab had done his work well.

O'Malley sent her away so he could finish up with Tab. There was no need to tell her not to speak of their conversation. If asked and paid she would tell everything honestly regardless of what she promised. But O'Malley was sure she wouldn't be asked.

Tab had a baby-faced .32 with eleven bullets, the sort of weapon that is the final argument in many domestic disputes. It was once shiny-plated, but use, or perhaps only handling, had dulled the gloss. What remained was comfortable and useful. It would kill if pointed down a man's throat, but would frighten and protect at much larger distances. Tab wanted $200 for it. They settled on $135 after O'Malley fired it once into the dirt in the back yard.

O'Malley gave Tab a beer and let him watch television while he prepared. He put on his baggiest J&D pinstripe and taped the weapon under the voluminous folds of material enveloping the upper thigh and groin. Then he wrote two letters, a long one to Robert McCabe and a shorter one to Armington Bishop. When all was in readiness he had another evil Jack for courage, drove Tab back to his street corner, gave him detailed instructions and the letters for posting, and went west again to Beverly Hills.

24

The light had gone to the other side of the world and it was hard to find his way to Point View Terrace. The map showed it as an exitless cul-de-sac; it was, instead, south facing and terraced, looking at the city lights from a bend in the road. Point View Terrace had six houses, each beginning on an upper level of hill and proceeding down five or six level plateaus to the street below. The bend allowed him a look at Rendt's terraces: first, a Japanese garden; second, a small, well-kept row of citrus trees, third and fourth, the ubiquitous Jacuzzi and pool; then a redwood deck with a view of Catalina; and finally a concrete something or other that might have been a primitive moat.

The Beverly Hills parking rules are simple: Cars on the street without a permit are towed away. He found a party nearby and stowed the Healey with the Mercedes of the celebrants, then clattered back up the hill in his new shoes and three-piece suit. The house was protected by a ten-foot-high black wrought iron fence topped by ornamental spikes resembling a row of Roman spears. O'Malley could see that the gate opened electronically, either from the house or a car, and was probably connected by intercom to the main building. On the far side of the gate a curving, tree-lined driveway led to a marvelous Spanish entrance. Then house and grounds toppled over the side of the hill.

The decision to dress up for the burglary was premised on the notion that he'd look as if he belonged, thus avoiding early arrest by the ever-vigilant BHPD. That was before he knew he'd be climbing fences.

But as it turned out, it was fairly easy to get over the fence. Rendt's western neighbor shielded his domain with a high, ivy-splashed stone wall. The stone was old and deep and was all handholds and footholds. The new shoes slipped a few times, but basically the wall was a stepladder. At the junction of the neighbor's wall and Rendt's fence O'Malley was actually higher than the spikes. He jumped down about eleven feet, landing harshly in the soft earth behind a conveniently placed palm.

The grounds were well lit, but there was an excellent circle of darkness south of his landing provided by the gently curving west side of the house and a palm the size of a redwood. He scrambled low along the neighboring wall to the black haven. From behind the palm he had an excellent view of the front and west side of the house and half the southern terraces.

He didn't have long to wait before things got interesting. A half hour later, 10:05 by the indestructible Timex, a late model dark blue Mercedes slowed at the bend and poked its nose into the fence. There was a loud click as the locking gears disengaged and the gate swung magically inward. The car doused its lights and maneuvered the curved driveway by the beam from the house. At the entrance, Rendt's friend, the pale man, got out, clad in a chauffeur's cap and jacket, and looked straight at O'Malley's head. Then he surveyed the street and visibly relaxed. When he was satisfied he was alone he opened the trunk of the Mercedes and began grunting and heaving at a heavy load. It slipped out of his hands a time or two but he finally got a good grip and hauled Randall Elliott Marks onto the illuminated asphalt.

O'Malley thought Marks was corpse number four until he saw him move with distress on the concrete. The pale man ignored Marks' pain and again surveyed the street. Then he picked up Marks under the armpits and walked backward toward the house, Marks' two hundred dollar heels describing faint tracks in the entranceway. He held Marks with one hand and opened the door. Then they were gone.

O'Malley's breaths were coming in shallow bursts. He felt for the gun. It was still there, safety on and taped by the barrel to the inside thigh, the butt unimpeded by tape, the barrel pointed down, all chambers full save one.

The gun felt good. The sight of Marks being dragged across the driveway didn't. It brought all the fear and nausea back with a rush. But O'Malley's early thoughts of flight were quickly dispelled by the reality of the cage he had created. On this side the neighbor's stone wall was at least twelve feet high and smooth, containing none of the handholds of the front. A climb over the spears was also out of the question unless he wanted to be impaled.

That left asking to be buzzed out and the south terraces, the latter an entire hillside of brightly lit levels traversed by a steep and windy brick walkway. He'd probably be shot eight times before he reached the pool. Even if he could get to the bottom, there was still the strange-looking moat, a moat obviously installed there for security purposes. It looked like the barriers put around the polar bear at the zoo. Rendt probably had it stocked with piranha and water moccasins.

So the options were remaining under the tree and starving to death or going inside and creating some commotion. Such is the stuff of courage.

O'Malley was saved the immediate moral question of whether to go in at once and maybe save Marks by the re-emergence of the thin pale man. He came out and began fumbling again in the trunk of the Mercedes, this time emerging with a brown leather bag. There was more fumbling and his hand came out of the bag holding something shiny and sharp. He then began circumnavigating the house in a clock-wise direction.

O'Malley's father had talked to his sons at length about knives. Knives are like snakes, he'd say: Everyone fears them too much. They're primitive and deadly but only if fear prevents a defense. Most men don't even know how to hold a knife, he'd explain. They hold it in their fist with the blade pointed down, which allows a thrust in only one direction and exposes the body as well. Therefore, a knife wielder is at a disadvantage to an unarmed man, he'd say.

It was one of his less convincing theories.

In this case the question was academic. O'Malley could see the pale man clearly as he came to the northwest corner of the terraces in the noonlike glare of the house lights. The man began down the brick path, walking serenely and confidently, his head moving like a beacon. He checked around and under bushes and trees, using his free hand to move the branches. There was no doubt that O'Malley's hiding place would be discovered once he finished the terraces.

But the truly frightening part was the way the pale man held his knife: left hand palm up, right hand casually stiff, handle and blade across the open left hand at a slight diagonal, like a golf club. The knife rested flat and loose, bouncing slightly as the man walked. The blade was available for thrusts up or down, slashes right or left. There would be no exposing of the body and the stiff right hand would be there to help.

That brought to mind a corollary to the old man's knife theory: A killer who preferred a blade and knew how to use one was the most dangerous professional of all.

O'Malley didn't want to meet the pale man, even with the party favor .32. The man walked down to the fourth level, blinking on and off the pool light. It would take only minutes for him to check the moat, climb the terraces, and begin the inspection of O'Malley's tree.

O'Malley had only one play. He waited till the man began

another descent and then sprinted to the house, cursing as the leather heels clattered on the concrete. He ducked under the windows and went low and fast around the front to the east side of the property. On the far side of the house a narrow dirt path led down to the terraces. The path was darkened by the angle of the house. The dirt shut off the machine-gun clatter of running feet on concrete. He felt safe again, for about a minute.

The plan was simply to go where the pale man had already gone. It wasn't much of a plan. O'Malley shuffled quietly down to the bottom of the dirt path and peeked around the house. The pale man was leaning against the wall waiting, the shiny metal bobbing gently in his hand like a buoy in a quiet harbor.

O'Malley walked into the light. He could feel his eyes grow wide and frantic; the pale man's stayed relaxed and searching. Up and down, side to side, like a man looking at a new suit on a mannequin, like a killer looking competently for the easiest place to slide it in. O'Malley was confident that stories would not be useful. He spread his arms wide.

"As you can see, I'm unarmed. If you use that you'll have to explain another murder. As well as clean up your lovely garden."

Up close the pale man was even more frightening. And entirely without humor. His light eyes never stopped their calculated examination. His blade never stopped undulating. The body was wire lean and small, the skin on the face pulled as taut as a nylon mask over a skeleton. The bones protruded, trying to break through the skin; the cheeks had a deep, disturbed furrow. The hair was nordic and the lips full and red. He looked like a man who took great pleasure from his work.

"Why are you here?" The voice was high-pitched, hoarse, and so soft it would be hard to hear were it not for the careful, learned diction. A foreign voice. A voice from beyond the grave.

O'Malley licked his lips nervously. He needed time to

think. "The better question is why you're here. And what have you and Rendt done to Marks?"

"Why are you here?" The knife had stopped moving.

"To see Klaus Rendt," O'Malley answered quickly.

"Did Klaus Rendt send for you? Do you work for Klaus Rendt?" There it was. The question that supplied all the answers. Now O'Malley could answer confidently, sure that he was safe from the pale man's blade.

"Yes, I do. I know the number."

The man nodded and relaxed, which meant that the unthinkable was true.

"Come with me."

"No."

"Come with me." O'Malley's eyes were burning with sweat. The man wasn't going to say it a third time.

"Let's stop kidding each other. I know you can't use the knife." At least not yet. They were standing very close, the knife was loosely held and still. The man had the capacity to kill in an instant, but O'Malley knew that was out of the question. O'Malley blew out easily, trying to slowly relax, then jerked his hand violently upward, fingers outstretched, palm open. The goal was to slam the heel of the hand up under the pale man's nose, driving the nasal bones back into the brain. He was ninety percent there and exhilarated when the man moved his head, a quick, almost imperceptible flick to the right. O'Malley's arm shot past and he stumbled forward. The pale man shifted the knife out of the way and brought the stiff right hand down hard. Suddenly O'Malley's world was made of bright colors, which were quite enjoyable until the ground flew up and hit him in the face. O'Malley was on his hands and knees when the metal-tipped shoe came up hard into his ribs. He heard a sound like crackling firewood and the air rushed from his throat, replaced by blood and mucous. The pain was unbelievable. O'Malley's scream sounded as if it came from far away. He looked up once and saw the horrible expression on the pale man's face, horrible because it remained serene and examining. Then all he saw was the metal boot again, expanding toward his face in slow motion. Then the world exploded into a darkness of ruptured blood vessels and broken teeth.

25

O'Malley woke like a child, sniveling and making little animal sounds. At first he was happy to be alive. Then the pain came with every breath; terrible, wrenching pain like that of a woman in labor. The sharp point of a broken rib was digging into the muscle wall. O'Malley could virtually feel the internal seeping and welling of blood. When the sudden pain passed he was able to concentrate on the pulpy mess that had once anchored seven teeth.

Rising was an enormous effort, and O'Malley almost vomited trying it. But he got to his hands and knees and pressed his legs together. He felt for the cold metal and wasn't surprised when it wasn't there. Then he noticed he wasn't alone.

Marks was unconscious, sitting slumped in a chair, the unflattering pose emphasizing the folds of skin in his face and gut. The pale man was standing with his legs parted and hands behind his back, watching O'Malley with that same analytical eye. O'Malley looked around for Rendt, although he was sure Rendt would be long dead by now. But Rendt was there, sitting naked in a chair, with the same look of undiluted hatred O'Malley had last seen on Frank Pisano's face.

But Pisano had been leeringly dead and Rendt was not. The pale man had made sure of that. But Rendt would have given his fortune for the blessed release of death if only the pale man had permitted it. Instead Rendt sat trussed up and naked in his straight-backed mahogany chair, and there didn't seem to be an inch of bare flesh—save for the areas covered by the ropes—that had not felt the flaying edge of the pale man's knife.

The first gut-wrenching minutes passed and O'Malley was able to concentrate on his own pain—and thereby localize and categorize it—and on the pale man's handiwork. He was sorry for Rendt. He now knew Rendt hadn't killed anyone. But Rendt was the architect and had approved the boys' death. Rendt had simply miscalculated the capacity of the others for greed and betrayal.

Now Rendt was paying the price of that miscalculation. He was more or less awake and staring out like a man on a cross. He was also dying slowly. It would take hours yet, but even if the pale man did nothing more, Rendt would stop breathing. Quietly.

But O'Malley had his own problems. The pale man would ultimately kill O'Malley and Marks. The most they could hope for was that the sadistic urges had been sated on Rendt, allowing the killing to be done quickly. At the moment O'Malley was alive because of a lie. Nevertheless, it was a lie that would only give him life until the pale man's partner returned. O'Malley had to get the gun back before that happened.

"Are you awake?"

"No, I'm walking in my sleep."

"Are you prepared to talk?"

"Certainly, what do you wish to talk about?"

"What is the number?"

"Seventeen."

"What is the number?"

"Twenty-three point eight."

"Why did you come here tonight?"

"I'm from American Casualty. We're investigating burglaries in the neighborhood, and I've been assigned to do a survey."

The man grabbed O'Malley's ear in his fist and pulled. O'Malley screamed at the unbelievable pain. The man pulled him forward and put his face an inch away from Rendt's chest.

"Look at this man." O'Malley couldn't do anything else. Up close the blood was still liquid and flowing. The sight drove bile past his throat to join the pieces of teeth. What O'Malley wanted to avoid at all costs was seeing what the man had done to Rendt's face.

"Do you wish to look like this man?" No. No.

"No."

"Why did you come here tonight?"

O'Malley took a long breath and let it out. Why, indeed. Marks began gurgling, coughing blood, and starting to awaken. The pale man saw it, too. O'Malley's little gun was in the pale man's belt. O'Malley began talking rapidly. "You win. I will tell you everything I know. But you have hurt me badly. I think there is internal bleeding. Permit me to rise and use the bathroom to clean my face and see if there's blood in my urine. Then I'll answer all your questions. You won't have to use your knife or the gun. I will tell you what you want to hear in return for my life."

The man considered it. There was no risk in agreeing. The killing would come later. He looked over at Marks, who was only very slowly returning to the world.

"That is acceptable. See to your bleeding. You may take four minutes and the door must remain open."

"Fine." O'Malley staggered to his feet. He tried not to look at Marks but prayed Marks would hurry and awaken. The pain was unbearable and he almost collapsed. But he got to the bathroom and spent half his four minutes washing teeth and blood out of his mouth. The pale man stood in the doorway watching. O'Malley straddled the toilet with his back to the door and pretended to undo the belt and zipper. His fear was making him shake involuntarily. "Hurry up," his brain screamed silently at Marks. As a blessed reward he heard the whine from the other room. "Where am I? Where is this place?"

"You have seventy-five seconds remaining."

He turned his head. "Fine." The pale man was watching both of them now but Marks still hadn't moved. He just sat in the chair rocking, making little complaining sounds. The gun stayed tucked in the man's belt. He still had one free hand.

"Ten seconds." O'Malley decided he had to try it anyway. It would be all over very quickly.

Then Marks stood up.

The pale man backed away from the door, barking an order to Marks to sit down. Marks stared dumbly at him, still dazed. He didn't follow the order, or even comprehend it. Incredibly he even took a step forward.

The pale man reached in his belt and pulled out the gun. A vase next to Marks exploded, jolting the fat man to wide-eyed consciousness.

O'Malley charged screaming as soon as the pale man had the gun in his hand. A gun in one hand and a knife in the other, a total disadvantage if the holder can't use either. The chat about the numbers convinced O'Malley that his life was sacred, $53 million sacred, so sacred that the pale man's full hands were O'Malley's greatest weapon.

O'Malley was at least twice the size of the pale man. He came at him low and hard, driving the shoulder toward the man's belt. Every linebacker knows a runner can fake with his head and his feet, but not with his belt. Drive the shoulder into the belly, hands around the back, churn hard with the legs driving forward. Then Jimmy the Blade comes in blind from weak safety and takes his head off. Teach those fuckers to try to run reverses.

The pale man wasn't impressed, although a little surprised.

In a move that would have had them on their feet in the Playa De Toros he spun, swept the knife aside like a *muleta*, and, when O'Malley charged past, brought the butt of the gun down hard on the back of his neck with a flourish like the placing of the *banderillas*. El Cordobes would have been proud. So was the pale man and a faint contemptuous smile played across his lips.

O'Malley fell hard and cursed. Then he stood and faced the pale man's smile. The man gestured a command with the pointed gun. O'Malley punched him in the face.

He fell like a stone. The punch had been hard and straight. But except for bleeding the pale man was not affected. Importantly, the weapons never left his hands. He seemed proud of that. He rose and gestured with the gun again. O'Malley flew at him, landing clumsily, grabbing the man's hair and hitting out frantically. Most of the blows missed but not all. The ones that landed had well over two hundred pounds of enraged Irish beef behind them. The pale man was no longer pale. Fresh blood and blotches followed O'Malley's meaty fists. He was also no longer smiling.

Still he would not or could not drop the weapons. He spun and twisted, faster than O'Malley by far, for the most part avoiding the smashes. He responded by quick hits with the butt of the gun and the butt of the knife, virtually all of which landed. These blows were effective, but not nearly as effective as the man's bare hands would be. Without the impediment of useless weapons the fight would be over in seconds. Yet out of instinct or training the man would not drop the gun.

Slowly, inexorably, the battle shifted. O'Malley had him close, ripping at his face, pounding with loud fists against the man's head and chest. Half the blows missed but at least half landed flush. The pale man was tiring and less able to duck and weave. His smashes in return were landing on nerve endings enervated by O'Malley's previous pain. The pale man began to entertain the horrible thought he would lose. If he lost, he knew he would die.

He tossed both weapons away and spun easily out of O'Malley's grasp.

They stood facing each other. The pale man breathed easily and bled profusely. O'Malley was just as shattered and his chest heaved with the effort of sucking in breath. Each inhalation caused a high-pitched rasping sound. To exhale was torture.

It wasn't going to take very long anyway. O'Malley walked forward. He had his large fists at the ready. The pale man's hands were draped loosely at his side. O'Malley faked going to the body and came hard at the head, hoping for a one-shot finish. He got it. The man's wooden hand came up and down. O'Malley's ear split like a melon and he fell straight to the wooden floor.

He lay quietly. He had taken his shot and that was that. Dying would be so nice. All these hurts would go away.

"All right, don't move."

It wasn't the pale man talking.

"Don't think I don't know how to use one of these. I've been well trained." O'Malley looked up to see his .32 moving in wide arcs. Marks was walking backward with the gun, which was exactly the right thing.

The pale man stood quietly, not yet aware what a fool was holding the gun. O'Malley stood up and smashed him in the head with an andiron.

For a time he just stood and breathed heavily, staring at the quiet form on the floor. Marks had the gun more or less pointed in his direction. This irritated O'Malley.

"Give me that."

"Why should I?"

"Two reasons. One, you don't know how to use it. Two, if you don't give it to me I'm going to come over there and shove this down your fucking throat." He held up the stained andiron for Marks to look at. "And there's a third reason. Do you have any idea what this fellow's going to do to you when he wakes up?"

Marks hesitated. He wanted O'Malley to nave the gun but was afraid. "Why don't we just shoot him in the head while he's unconscious?" Nothing but class, O'Malley thought. He walked over to Marks and held out his hand. Marks put the gun in it.

O'Malley assumed the respite would be brief. The first task was the knife, the surgery-sharp knife. O'Malley barely touched it and a faint red line appeared immediately. He didn't make the mistake of keeping the knife as a weapon. While the pale man slept O'Malley sank it deep past the hilt into the loam of a potted ficus.

Next was security. O'Malley spread the pale man face down on the floor and spent a long time going over his body. There was another knife and a small two-shot pistol. But O'Malley still wasn't satisfied. He stripped the man naked and threw his clothes in a corner. He then draped one of Rendt's robes over him and left him face down on the wooden floor.

Then there was Rendt and the job of seeing if anything could be done for him. He was still conscious, his breath coming in labored, inconsistent bursts. O'Malley had to look at his face. The great oak head had been carved with the surgical scalpel and there wasn't a part of it that was recognizable. Rendt's sightless eyes were fixed on the wall.

"Rendt, this is O'Malley. Is there anything I can do?" Rendt answered in a cracked, dry whisper. It was precisely what O'Malley would have wanted in his place.

"Do you have any drugs—Demoral, Percodan, any pain killers or sleeping pills?" O'Malley asked. Rendt did and O'Malley gave him a lot, though not enough to kill. If Rendt was put over the top accidentally, well, that was still different than what he asked. The water was blessed for him, and the half-lids that were left blinked in gratitude. Then he was asleep. O'Malley left him tied. At least that was a hell he knew.

Marks was in pretty good shape and didn't need attention. He sat bolt upright in a chair staring at the man prone on the floor.

"O'Malley, look."

The pale man was moving. He gained consciousness easily and quickly. He stared quietly at Marks, then at the gun in O'Malley's hand.

"Please move," O'Malley told him. "Please try something. Please don't get face down on the floor. It would give me great pleasure to shoot you." He lowered the gun. "In the belly to begin with." The pale man disappointed him. He didn't do a thing O'Malley asked. Without conversation or ceremony he sat up, put on Rendt's robe, and lay face down on the floor again.

O'Malley walked toward him. "He brought you here," O'Malley told Marks. Then he pointed at Rendt. "He might have done that to you. More likely, he would have just taken the account access code from you and killed you quickly, unless he wanted to amuse himself, that is." Marks was covering his face at the sight of Rendt and moaning softly.

"Isn't that right, sport?" O'Malley asked. The man on the floor didn't answer, which gave O'Malley an excellent excuse to drive his heel into his back, right over the kidney. The man lurched with the pain.

"I said, isn't that right?"

"Yes."

"Good boy. You see, Randall, darling, this gentleman is seeking sole possession of all three access codes. You have one and would have given it to him quickly, of course. Rendt had the second number and probably held out for a while, but I doubt he stayed silent for too long after the cutting started. Am I right so far, sport?"

The man didn't want the heel to come down again.

"Yes."

"So that leaves the third number, which Pisano has, or had. Everybody thinks Rendt killed Pisano, so it stands to reason Rendt also got the number from Pisano. That was clearly this fellow's impression. But no matter how politely he asked, Rendt would not give it to him."

Marks shook his head. "Rendt is a fool. What good is money to him now?"

"Rendt's no fool. He would have given his mother to stop the pain. But he couldn't stop it. Because he didn't know the number. Because he didn't kill Pisano. Our friend here probably even realized that at some point in the torture process, but he was having too much fun to stop."

"Who is he?"

"Good question. Let's find out. What's your name, champ?" He was slow in responding. O'Malley was delighted to remind him that speed was important.

The man grunted from the kick and spat out the answer. "Manuel Enrille."

"Nationality?"

"Argentine."

"German parents?"

"Yes." With long associations with Rendt's company, no doubt.

"You see, Marks," O'Malley explained, "Manuel here works for Rendt, or used to. But he decided—or rather was convinced—to go for all the gold. I used to think it was all Rendt and a partner. Eventually I suspected Rendt didn't kill anybody, but I still thought he was in charge. However, when Manuel and I met outside, Manuel thought I was working for Rendt. That made it clear Manuel was working with someone else.

"So who did kill Pisano? It wasn't Rendt and it wasn't this fellow. Who's left? Who's his partner?"

"Isn't it obvious? Maybe not. I had to do a bit of digging before I found out." O'Malley was very pleased with himself. So pleased, he never heard the door open or the footsteps in the hall.

"Shut up, O'Malley. Don't say another word or I swear I'll use this." Marks' jaw was on his chest and his eyes were the size of saucers. O'Malley knew that Marks was looking at a weapon much larger than the .32. He didn't need to turn to see who was holding it.

"Hello, sweetheart. Come-in and join the party."

26

Rad looked at Rendt with disgust. Enrille was already up and had the .32.

"Did you have to do that to him?"

"You said to do whatever was necessary to get the numbers. He wouldn't give me Pisano's." He shrugged, somewhat chastened. Then he brightened. "I did get Rendt's." He handed her a slip of paper, waiting for approval like a dog with a stick. He tucked the .32 into his belt and took the .45 from her to train on O'Malley.

"Good work. Well, Rendt is a tough bastard. We'll have to think up another way. What about him?" She pointed to Marks.

"I haven't got to him yet." Marks looked yellow. She turned to him sweetly.

"Mr. Marks, would you please hand your account access code to Mr. Enrille?" Marks hesitated. Even at this stage he couldn't bear the thought of giving up his money. O'Malley decided to save his life.

"Randall, I think you ought to do what she says right away." Marks fumbled in his wallet and handed over a card. Enrille gave it to Rad.

"Good. Now we have Rendt's and Marks'. All we need is the third one." Manuel nodded eagerly.

O'Malley was laughing so hard that his side was splitting from the broken rib. "Goddamn, they grow them dumb in Argentina."

"O'Malley, shut up," Rad ordered.

"You stupid Kraut. She's got all three numbers now. You're out in the cold, which will probably be how you'll end up, that and stiff. She killed Pisano, you ignorant fucker."

"Shut up," Rad said. "You're lying."

"Try to use your pea brain for a minute, Adolph. Why would Rendt give you one number and not the other?"

"O'Malley, this is the last time I'm going to tell you." But it was too late. There was a little kindling of awareness in Enrille's eyes. Rad stared at O'Malley with helpless hate, no doubt cursing the loss of the .45. O'Malley smiled at her, then turned to Enrille.

"Let's take it from the top. I'll go slow so you can follow. I realize you two are lovers and you're planning on a wonderful life together. But before you there was Pisano. Before Pisano there was me, as much as I hate to kiss and tell." O'Malley looked over at Marks. It was barely possible that before O'Malley there was Marks, which would account for how she got her information in the first place. But why interrupt the tale with irrelevancies.

"Rad suspected there was money to be made all along, maybe Marks even told her—it isn't important. When she realized there was fifty-three million dollars at stake, she glommed onto Pisano like a bad cold. The first problem she faced was Pisano's desire for revenge against the boys. She probably tried to talk him out of it but ultimately realized that even though there was no immediate gain, she'd go along for the ride, knowing at least she'd have something to blackmail him with later. That was her first murder—she got Hardwick, by the way."

"That's unadulterated bullshit. I don't even know where they live."

"Well, that's sort of true. But you *thought* you knew where they lived. You were there once, with Marks here, a year or so before the murder. You told me yourself. You got a tour of the house and property and remembered the back was protected by only three wires and faced on a golf course. So you planned to come in from the rear. Only you wound up on the wrong side. You snipped the three wires all right, but then saw a child's sandbox, the last thing the boys would have had in their yard. That's when you realized your mistake and went across to the other side. Tell me—because I've thought about it—if the sandbox hadn't been there, and you broke into the wrong house and were discovered, would you have killed anyway?"

Her face never moved. Nevertheless, she didn't deny it.

"Anyway, after you found the right house you went in and killed. It was dark and unfamiliar. You ripped your jeans and a piece came off, designer medallion and all. When you left, you were spotted by one of the neighbors, who described you as a fat-assed hippy. From a distance, that's what you'd be, but really you're just a long-haired woman with a lovely rounded derriere. Mrs. Redstone—that's the neighbor—also said you were grabbing your buns, wanting to go back. That's when you realized you had lost your little nether medallion. I went in afterward. The medallion was in a rat hole. Here it is." O'Malley reached in his wallet and pulled it out like a magician.

"I went over to your house tonight." He held up her house key for Enrille to see. Undoubtedly he had one just like it. "The ripped jeans were there, together with that crazy kimono, right behind the false panel in the closet that you're so proud of. You know, you really should have burned that stuff." O'Malley stared into her face. The pale man was starting to get very interested in the story.

He turned to Enrille. "But all that's ancient history—old murders. The clock ticks forward. Marks had arranged for me to be accused of the fraud. Rad was my lover and knew everything, everything I did, everything I found out from the police. By then she was also Pisano's lover, of course, but they had a very open relationship. Pisano was very pleased to have an inside track to the workings of the police." O'Malley slowed the story and looked at her again. "Also he, like me, like you, was in love with her and was prepared to do anything she asked.

"But events began taking control, and even she couldn't stop that. Pisano was in hiding. The triumvirate was disintegrating. Rad realized she could no longer rely on Pisano for a share of the money. Pisano was scared and threatening to leave the country. At first Rad just wanted to get Pisano's number to prevent him from leaving and cutting her out. Then she realized there was a way to get it all. But to do that she needed a partner, a partner strong enough to take what she needed from Rendt and Marks. That's when she decided on you. My guess is that you two fell in love about ten days ago."

The guess must have hit right on the mark. Enrille stared at Rad with his light blue eyes. She was getting nervous but still maintained an outward composure.

"Manny, don't believe him. Can't you see he's trying to drive wedges? He wants to save his life and get it all for himself."

Enrille turned back to O'Malley. "Continue please."

"My pleasure. So what have you got? Pisano's holed up in a hotel and scared, about to leave the country. But before he leaves he wants revenge. How? By driving down to federal court where he and I were scheduled to be arraigned, where he knows he'll find me. He passes me a note, saying he wants to see me. He intends to tell me everything before he leaves.

"Rad saw all this coming and had been preparing. The problem was Pisano didn't trust anyone anymore, his lover included. So Rad had been working up an elaborate erotic game to get his confidence back. She used a hooker by the name of Melissa, whom I've talked to at length. She sent Melissa to Pisano with a cute little love-banner around her chest. The banner said, 'To Frank. A little present from a lover. If you like my present, use it and there's more ahead. I love you.' Frank was fundamentally a crude bastard, a nice guy in a warped way but definitely not one to turn his back on a free piece of ass, as he might put it. He used the present and thereby set up an entré for Rad. She let Melissa go twice, and Frank got warm, responsive, and sentimental. Then Rad appeared—the brunette hooker noticed by the staff. She wore the same absurd garb and talked the same hooker cant as her agent. Frank thought it was hilarious, the one person who was not trying to take his precious number, the one person he could always count on, even confide in. So he welcomed her in warmly. They made love together and drank champagne together. And, as always after making love, she smoked a couple of her lover's cigarettes. They talked about leaving together. When he told her where his number was—right there in his wallet and they'd have to kill him to get it—he signed his death warrant. She went behind him and told him how brilliant he was and how much she loved him. Maybe she massaged his throbbing neck muscles to relax him, maybe put him to sleep. Then she reached under her kimono, pulled out her gun, and blew his brains all over the wall with a cross-cut dum-dum."

There were more than a few rhetorical embellishments in that story but it *might* have happened just like that. Anyway, O'Malley knew the bottom line was true. The pale man was staring at his shoes, the .45 hanging limply in his fist. Rad's face was still without fear. But the lips were contorted with rage.

"Manny, you're a fool if you believe that. I have never wanted any part of this. You remember. You had to force me." She cast her eyes down coyly. "You remember. It was that night you forced me to do those . . . those other things."

What a performance. Enrille looked uncertain for a moment. To believe O'Malley might mean he was less a man. O'Malley spoke quickly.

"Well, there's one bit of corroborating evidence that I'm sure is true. Parker Center put the Pisano murder at seven-thirty P.M. Let's give her an hour on either side. I'll bet she wasn't snuggling with you between six-thirty and eight-thirty last night."

Enrille's head snapped around to Rad, his hand tightening on the gun. She began backing up, almost landing in Rendt's burgundy lap. Now the voice was slightly entreating. "Manny, you know I was in the office. I told you that. I even called you from there."

"You called at ten P.M. I called you at eight-fifteen and there was no answer. I had thought you were simply temporarily indisposed." He kept his eyes fixed and his hand tight around the black handle. When he spoke he didn't move his head. "Tell me what else you know."

"Glad to. I know this is hard to believe—it's been hard for me, too. I was the last person to suspect her." O'Malley looked at his drawn, intent face. "Make that next to the last. Anyway, until this afternoon I was sure Marks had a bigger part of it than he did. Then I went to see him in San Francisco. He was waiting for me, scared and with a gun in his hand. There were only three people who knew I'd be going there: my lawyer, Marks' partner—who told me where he was to begin with—and her. My guess is she called Marks and told him something that scared the shit out of him. But why hypothesize?" O'Malley turned to Marks. His face was the color of refined sugar, but he found enough flowing blood to speak.

"She called me at three this afternoon. She said O'Malley had murdered her lover Pisano—we all knew about their romantic involvement, of course—and was now working for Rendt. She said O'Malley was coming for me to get the last of the three numbers. She also told me the police were on to O'Malley and he had to get out of the country fast. If I were courageous enough to kill him, the police would believe it was self-defense and I'd have nothing more to fear."

That explained Marks' terror at O'Malley's knock. O'Malley turned back to Enrille. "So you see, Pedro, it was perfect. I get snuffed by Marks and stop my amateur investigating, which had been bothering Rad for some time. Marks is a murderer and she can blackmail the number from him. She already has the number from Pisano and you can get the number from Rendt. The only problem was, I didn't get killed, and she then had no easy way to get the number from Marks. I'll bet that pissed her off, didn't it, Marks?"

Marks nodded excitedly, eager to help convince Enrille. "She telephoned a half hour after you left my hotel room. When I told her of our conversation she was livid. She called me a fool and said my life was in danger. She told me to get the first plane out and meet her in one of the satellite parking lots at LAX. When I got there she was nowhere in sight. This gentleman"—he indicated Enrille—"appeared to drive me to her. When I entered the car, he struck my head. I was in this room when I regained consciousness."

Until this afternoon her timing had been precise. But O'Malley's unanticipated continued life had thrown things off. "I hope you're following all this, Heinrich, because there's going to be a short quiz later." He was. His lips had lost their full effete red and now were narrow and blue, held tightly together by the muscles from his clenched teeth.

"You see," O'Malley continued, "as of this morning she had the crucial number—Pisano's. I'm sure that's when she told you to come over here and begin putting the screws to Rendt." Enrille's head went slowly down onto his chest and rose again—once—in affirmation. "But when I didn't die and Marks couldn't be quietly blackmailed, the plan had to be changed. So she interrupted you in mid-slice and told you to pick up Marks at the airport."

He nodded. "And what is the plan now?"

"Now she's back on schedule. She would like for you to give her Marks' and Rendt's numbers, as you have already. She would then tell you to go out and find the third number, just as she started to earlier. Her instructions could be anything; the only crucial ingredient is that the two of you go in separate directions. You go one way and she goes straight to LAX with the three numbers and the airplane ticket, which she now has in her purse." O'Malley thought for a second. "There's probably another variation of that plan, of course. One in which you don't go anyplace." Enrille nodded.

O'Malley was through talking. That was all he knew, all there was to know. The room got very quiet; the only sounds were the ticking of a large clock and Rendt's slow tortured breathing through the drugs. Rad was staring at the pale man with red, enraged eyes. He was gazing into space, lost in some murderous erotic reverie that probably involved Rad and his little surgical blade. It seemed as if it stayed like that for a long time before she spoke. O'Malley was stunned. The voice was still icy cold and calm. Direct. Not a quiver or a shake.

"Manny, it doesn't matter anymore. I've got all three numbers now. We can remain business partners. There's no need for us to be enemies, Manny. Nobody gains that way."

He wasn't impressed. There was more than money involved now. Now there was a little matter of Latin honor. He studied the .45 and manipulated it. When it clicked shut it was the same sound for Rad as the release of the catch on the gallows floor.

O'Malley felt the click deep inside. He thought that he was past caring, certainly past protecting. But Enrille's calculated movements and slow, executioner-style procedures were affecting him at an elemental level. Rad was standing quietly now, awaiting a certain, violently shuddering death. O'Malley couldn't take it. It wasn't erotic memories, old time's sake, or sentimentality. Or at least he didn't think it was. But he didn't think he could just stand there and see a beautiful, healthy woman ripped apart by high-powered, steel-jacketed slugs.

"Don't do it, Enrille."

Enrille didn't even hear O'Malley, his glazed eyes fixed on Rad. He raised the .45 and O'Malley charged again. Enrille's grip was loose and his mind far away. O'Malley hit him hard, dead center, and the gun flew away in a lazy arc, exploding

205

meaninglessly as it went. Enrille seemed surprised and woke up enough to chop O'Malley to the floor again. O'Malley was getting very sick of the repetition.

"Don't do it, Manny."

This time the voice was high and soft. Enrille turned to her. She was getting up from the floor. She had the .45 in two hands, like a cop. He shrugged and pulled the .32 from his belt. He began laughing while he moved the empty hole over.

She cursed at him and moved away, almost falling over Rendt. Suddenly all hell broke loose. She fired blindly, wildly. O'Malley dug his face into the floor as mirrors and bric-a-brac shattered all over the room. She was shouting, Marks was crying, and O'Malley was trying to climb into the oak floor with his fingernails. The room quickly filled with a cordite stench. The echo of the reports was deep and long. When O'Malley heard only clicking and sobbing he raised his head. The little .32 was lying on the floor at Enrille's feet. Enrille stood staring at Rad with a surprised, embarrassed look. Then his face contorted and he fell, trying to reach around and grab the part of his back the cross-cut .45 slug had taken with it on the way out. His trunk and legs were held together by a few hardy ligaments and that was all. He began the screams that would probably continue for the ten minutes he had left.

Marks fainted. Enrille was howling. Rad and O'Malley were both shellshocked and spent. Rendt was the only one in the house maintaining his stoic decorum. But O'Malley was sure he saw a smile fight through the coma and land peacefully on Rendt's purple, shredded lips. He didn't seem to mind the hole in his robe at all.

27

As far as O'Malley was concerned, it was all over. The minuet might go on and on, probably would, but they'd be dancing without him. He sat on his haunches and reviewed the carnage, trying to block out the sounds of the dying. There was still Marks to think about. O'Malley bent over the slumping form to make sure that Marks hadn't swallowed his tongue. He made sure he grabbed the .32 first.

Marks was in good shape, a little shaken and probably a candidate for a coronary, but as yet nothing vital had been destroyed. When he was awake O'Malley patted him on the back and turned to Rad.

"You better split, baby."

She thought about it, then stared straight ahead. O'Malley couldn't believe it. The gray eyes were still straight and true. "I can't. You'll call the police. I'll never make it to the airport."

"You can't do anything else." O'Malley looked around. "The best I can do is take my time. You get out and I won't hurry to make the call." Why? For old time's sake and to avoid complicating matters. She wouldn't get far anyway. She knew that.

She nodded. But she was not through yet. "Look, Benjamin, we don't have to be enemies. I have all three slips."

O'Malley laughed. "You mean we could run away together. Maybe fall in love?"

She smiled weakly. "It's not as crazy as it sounds. We've had great times together. We talked about going away. You even said . . . said you loved me."

"You must have thought there was an echo in the room when I said that."

"I know. I've made mistakes. But I never loved those others. I just did it for the money. You were the one I always loved. And now we can be together forever. With over fifty million dollars to split."

"What about him? How would we prevent Mr. Marks from tattling on us?" O'Malley felt like a cat playing with a wounded bird.

She shrugged and looked away, embarrassed at the obvious. "We'd . . . we'd have to . . . we couldn't let him tell."

Poor Marks thought he was back in the cooking oil. His head jerked back and forth between the two of them.

"And once we leave and get the money, how long would I stay alive?"

"No! I would never do anything like that. I know it's hard for you to believe. But it's true. I love you." O'Malley looked around at the people dying. No, she'd never do anything like that.

"Tell me one thing because I'm interested. Why? Why would a woman with everything need more? Need it enough to kill"—he had to stop and count—"three people. Five in about an hour. Was it all for a little money?"

Her look was again embarrassed. Then she shrugged. "I could tell you about the past." She looked at Marks. "About . . . about demands he's made in the past. But that's . . . that's not the reason." She looked up at O'Malley for help. "It's a *great deal of money* we're talking about, O'Malley." He nodded. And resolved to stop asking stupid questions. He glanced over at Marks, not at all curious about the demands he had made. The question was rhetorical.

"Isn't it ironic? He's the cause of all this and will be one of the few to walk out alive."

"The night is young," Rad said.

O'Malley patted Marks' arm for reassurance. "No, it's not. It's old and dead. And I'm real tired and I want to end this and go to the hospital where I belong." With the excitement gone, the cracked rib was starting to ache again. "But I'm glad we had this little chat. I'm glad to see you're ready to kill again, in cold blood, with a man staring you in the face. It'll make it a lot easier on me if they dress you in a hospital gown and drop the pills."

Her face contorted with rage. "You're a fool, O'Malley. I'm offering you a chance for a life most people can't imagine. Your every whim will be satisfied immediately. You can live in luxury any place in the world. Every women will be yours for the asking." So much for true love, O'Malley thought. "Think of it. Fifty-three million dollars. Greenback dollars. Don't you underst—" She stopped.

They heard it simultaneously, low and far away, then high-pitched and pulsating. It didn't go away. It got loudest at the outside gate and stayed there. Then others joined it, lots of others. O'Malley looked at the .32 in his hand and threw it away. It clattered to the ground. Of all the killing weapons it had stayed virgin pure. She remained erect. With dignity. Her only reaction was the blood draining from her face.

The intercom clattered like a burst of gunfire.

"This is the police. Open this gate immediately."

O'Malley checked his watch. A little late but close enough. Maybe he'd try to get Tab into a good college after all. Rendt was dead by the time he got to the button to buzz McCabe in.

28

It was more than six months before the midnight calls from the press stopped, a blessed event that coincided, not unexpectedly, with the entry of pleas by Rad and Marks. He knew it would be much longer before he'd stop sitting silently at night, sometimes all night, staring and thinking. Usually staring more than thinking.

Things went well for Rad, all things considered. She didn't die at the hands of the state and was not even condemned to die, which was something, anyway. McCabe was actually courtly when he arrested her, entering the room like a gentleman arriving for dinner, ignoring the carnage, picking up the gun at her feet with a handkerchief, gently taking her by the arm, asking no questions. A police matron was at his side, a tribute to McCabe's abilities as a detective.

But all the gentle treatment in the world couldn't have soothed her jangled psyche. Rad's blood-drained face at McCabe's entrance was a prelude to the breakdown that had been a long time coming. A month in a psychiatric ward was necessary before she could talk coherently with her lawyer.

The authorities could not have cared less about Rad's mental unraveling. This was a big case and the district attorney, not without reason, saw it as his ticket to the governor's mansion in Sacramento. At the first press conference, held the morning after the arrests, the DA announced that Rad would be charged with five counts of first-degree murder, each with an allegation of special circumstances, the death-penalty allegation. The press conference was followed by speeches about the importance of the case as a demonstration of the commitment of the DA to seek the ultimate penalty against all who deserve it—rich or poor, black or white, man or woman. He assigned a special flack to brief the press daily on the progress of the prosecution, which the DA was handling personally.

That was Rad's first big break, the DA being something less than a first-rate trial lawyer. The second was the state of the evidence against her. All of the witnesses except for Marks and O'Malley were in refrigerated drawers in the coroner's office awaiting autopsies, autopsies that revealed nothing more than that Rendt had died of knife wounds and Enrille of a large bullet. Nor was the physical evidence of much help. Ballistics tests performed on Rad's gun proved only that it was used to kill Enrille. Enrille, himself a professional killer, had just completed his own grisly murder of Rendt. A first-year law student could have hung a jury with a self-defense claim.

The police might have bundled it all into a salable package were it not for the ambition and incompetence of Detective Spiro Andersen, who still managed to climb over McCabe into the driver's seat. Andersen had O'Malley down to Parker Center, with Baird at his side, to ask every question he could think of. There weren't many and the ones he came up with were the wrong ones. O'Malley answered each question as asked, and as Baird ordered, didn't volunteer anything. At the close of the interview, Andersen still hadn't a clue what the whole thing was about.

That left Marks, who wasn't talking to anybody, and McCabe, who resigned in disgust after Andersen's ascension. There was a very good chance that Rad might have walked.

O'Malley couldn't let that happen. He sent Baird to visit Rad on his behalf, to play God, judge, jury, and jailer. Baird told her quietly that O'Malley's memory would improve if she didn't do as asked. Rad understood. She pleaded guilty to

211

two counts of first-degree murder in exchange for the DA's dropping the special circumstances allegations. She was sentenced by a kindly judge to concurrent terms. Nevertheless, she will be older than sixty and the gray-black hair will be all one color by the time she leaves the Sybil Brand Institute for women.

Marks pleaded *nolo contendere* to one count of federal securities fraud and was sentenced to eighteen months at the Lompoc farm—there to join famous politicians, businessmen, and attorneys—and was ordered to perform four hundred hours of community service at the Red Cross. The State dropped charges against him after his lawyers convinced the DA that "the man had suffered enough."

On O'Malley's last day in Los Angeles he met Baird for what they both knew would be a misty farewell at the Bonaventure. He arrived to find Baird staring straight ahead, rotating with the room on the axis of the building, a tall beer and a short glass with something brown in it sitting on the bar in front of him. The white tab already had four green entries from the cash register.

"Jack Daniels, rocks with a twist, please," O'Malley said. Baird didn't take his eyes off the wall. O'Malley lit a cigarette and considered how to cheer him.

"Don't take it so hard, pal. You did a great job, saved my ass, and all the bad guys have gotten their just desserts." Except Marks, that is, but some things never change.

Baird shrugged and for a while the two sipped quietly. Then Baird spoke.

"Any chance that you'll change your mind and stay? We could open up a practice together. Ever think of that?" He was slightly embarrassed and kept his eyes straight ahead.

"Baird, is it possible you're getting sentimental?"

A little laugh came through Baird's nose. "You know, it's probably true. Even though I know it could never work. I'd probably spend half my time playing Sancho Panza in your ill-advised adventures and the other half listening to the torturous details of your goatlike private life." He turned his head, the banter a defense, the eyes requesting a serious answer. "Nevertheless . . ."

"Of course, I've thought about it, thought seriously about it," O'Malley lied. "And the prospect of forming a partnership with a virgin mystic doesn't bother me at all. But it's time to leave this town. The Holy Grail, if it exists at all, is elsewhere."

Baird nodded. "I expected that. Where will you be going? And when?"

"Today, to the last question. And up north to Mendocino County to the first. My father has just been offered a job as chief of police in a little town up there. I forgot the name—something with a 'ville' on the end and the name of the local tree on the front. He's taking over from the chief, who got too old and will now be the deputy. The two of them will be the whole force." The chief and the deputy, making sure that nobody steals the trees. The old man didn't care. To him it was Hollywood.

"So what are you going to do up there? You'll go nuts—just you and the trees."

"No, it's all planned. I'm going to find some land by a river and build a house. Then I'm going to find a plump farm girl from Petaluma. She can tend the garden and I'll tend the stock. In about forty years the kids will bury us together by the side of the river."

Baird laughed, a good laugh. "Sounds idyllic. More than a little naive. Nonetheless, idyllic."

"You ought to come up. We'll practice tree law together. Maybe get together with the old man and open up a bar and grill for the loggers."

"I'll consider it, but I doubt it. I'm too perverse to enjoy pastoral settings and plump farm girls. It would take all the suspense out of life—like whether the woman I'm ogling is really a business associate in drag." He was right. They toasted his perversity.

"By the way," Baird said, "speaking about the perverse, I have a message for you from Bishop."

"Oh?"

"He wants to see you. To patch up the past. Wish you well in the future."

"Pass, thank you."

"Don't be hasty. There may be dollars in this in addition to his penitent outpourings."

"I'll leave you my address. The U.S. government has this service where they'll deliver checks wrapped in sealed containers for only fifteen cents. Just tell him—"

"Why don't you tell me yourself, Ben?" Bishop was there, all three pieces in place, just off O'Malley's right shoulder. Baird had a twinkle in his eye.

"That's why I brought it up. You see, I sort of asked Mr. Bishop—"

"Please, Armington."

"—asked, uh, Armington to join us here." Old Armington was staring at O'Malley waiting for a response.

"Well, Ben. May I join you?"

"Of course." Bishop sat between the two friends and ordered his Dubonnet. O'Malley was disgusted. He couldn't believe Baird would fuck up their last snootful together just so Bishop could play the good thief. He was full into a lovely sulk when Bishop spoke.

"I'm sorry I'm late, Jerome, but I've been locked in negotiations with a lawyer for a rather crazed drilling contractor in Louisiana who won't return my furniture." He stared at O'Malley pointedly and smiled.

O'Malley made no effort to hide his yawn. "Gee, that's real interesting, Armington. What other cases are you working on these days?"

The smile on Bishop's face faded and the expression darkened a bit. "Look, Ben, I don't expect you to like me. Or like my partners. Or even respect us. That's not why I'm here. I asked Jerome to arrange a meeting so that I might personally express my apologies for the way you've been treated."

"Baird said something about a check. Why don't we slide by the apologies and get to the money?"

Bishop stiffened at that. When he spoke again the voice was formal. "As you wish, sir." He reached into his breast pocket and pulled out two envelopes. "Mr. O'Malley, I have been authorized to extend to you a draft in an amount equal to two years' salary at J and D." He handed O'Malley an envelope. "I have also been authorized to extend a draft to Mr. Baird representing our estimate of the attorney's fees you have incurred as a result of this, uh, unpleasantness." He gave Baird the other envelope.

"Obviously, Mr. O'Malley, this is not charity. It is a sincere effort on our part to accept responsibility for events—Mr. Marks was, after all, a member of the firm acting in his official capacity—and to provide you some recompense for the monetary damage you have suffered. In addition to these drafts I have also been authorized to extend to you, although you may not be willing to accept it, the deep regret of Jenkins and Dorman for the injuries you have sustained as a result of your association with us. Finally, I wish to add a personal note. Your courage and resourcefulness throughout this matter have been exemplary."

It was quite a generous bonus, and pretty speech besides. But that didn't mean O'Malley was done needling. "Why only two years?"

It was apparently the question Bishop wanted. Smiling, rising to his feet, he downed his Dubonnet with a theatrical flourish. Then he spoke, high-pitched and soft. Vintage Bishop. "Because, sir, in the judgment of the partnership there was no possibility, even in the absence of these special circumstances, that you would have lasted more than two years at Jenkins and Dorman." Then he was gone.

What a great exit line! Baird and O'Malley stared at each other, then howled. Maybe Bishop was a white hat after all. They ran to the elevator and dragged him back, then made him drink Jack Daniels, pick up the check, and apologize some more. He took it all in good spirits, even when they told him he had to leave after two drinks because Baird and O'Malley had some serious reminiscing to do. Which he did. Which they did. Through dinner and lots of coffee for the road. Then all of a sudden it was over. Bishop was gone, Rad was gone, and Baird was walking down a dark driveway. Then he turned a corner and he was gone, too.

O'Malley passed the turn at Franklin and kept going to Hollywood Boulevard. A desert rain was falling in sheets, causing drivers familiar only with dry pavement to smash into each other. He hadn't seem him in months and didn't expect to find him doing business on such a night. He was there, however, huddled with the others under a cornice like a muddy lamb under a rocky overhang. He didn't recognize the van and O'Malley had to do a lot of honking and shouting before he came over.

"Nice car," he said. "But I liked the other one better." The Healey was now no more either, its sensuous curves and raucous Lotus innards exchanged for a square van with a heart made by Ford.

"So did I. But sometimes things change."

"I guess." The water had washed off the first layer of grime but hadn't done a thing for the smell. He sat in the back dripping, looking molted and slightly uncomfortable. The color of the eyes proved that he hadn't found religion yet.

"So how did things wind up?" he asked. "I never did find out."

"You mean your answering service didn't give you my messages?"

He laughed flatly and briefly. "Yeah, sometimes I'm hard to find. I guess you been cruising by here, right?"

"Not often. A couple hundred times maybe."

He shrugged. "Business has been good. I was probably on a house call." More like a car call. He looked around the van for awhile, avoiding O'Malley's face. "So what happened?"

O'Malley didn't think he really cared, but he told him anyway. There was more nodding and fidgeting but very little that might be called interest. O'Malley began to panic. The sick feeling each night would never go away if he had to leave the kid on this corner.

"Listen, I've got a proposition for you," O'Malley said. It was too soon, much too soon.

"Yeah, what? More baths?"

"In a way, yes. I want you to come up north with me."

"Up north? Where up north?"

"Way up. Past San Francisco."

"Why?"

So that O'Malley could sleep again at night. So that there would be one life saved to balance the others. "Never mind why. But come up with me and I'll guarantee you a job and a place to live. No rules. You can do what you want. You'll have a place all your own. Stay up there two years and in addition to the money you earn, I'll give you a check for five thousand dollars. You can take the money and stay or take it and leave. Up to you. No strings, no rules."

It didn't sound right at all. Tab was staring through narrow eyes, his mind working through the fog. O'Malley thought he was stoned and not listening until he spoke.

"You think that's going to make up for your girlfriend killing all those people, don't you?"

O'Malley opened his mouth to deny it but no sound came out. There was no percentage in lying. "That's right. And to return a favor."

Tab's head hung, bouncing slightly on his shoulders. For what seemed like a long time there was no sound in the van save for the clamoring rain beating a staccato report on the metal roof. O'Malley thought he had fallen asleep, or passed out, yet didn't want to disturb him for fear he'd leave, taking with him a last hope. Without him O'Malley would have to drive away alone, up Vine to the familiar freeway entrance. And alone past Laurel Canyon, which was the hard part. When Tab finally opened his eyes the yellow was crossed by small red lines.

"No."

"Why not?"

He spoke back into the floor again. "Because I been down that road. Lots of times. There's nothing in it for me. After a while you'll get bored with it and where will I be—up fucking north, wherever the fuck that is." He looked up. The eyes were pleading. "Don't you think I know about this trip, man? Don't you think I been to relatives' homes and foster homes and juvenile homes and all that shit? How the fuck do you think I got here, man?"

Then he dropped his head and began crying like a little boy.

O'Malley stared at the torrent falling through the black night, wondering if the kid was right, whether he would lose interest once they were up there, once they were away from Laurel Canyon and Sybil Brand. And of course he was. There wasn't any room next to the river for dirty-faced drug addicts. Yet that didn't mean he'd abandon him. It just meant that the most he could offer was a chance.

O'Malley tried to explain that, to convince the kid that this time it would be different. Tab was polite enough to listen but that was all. When the talking was finished he gave a weak smile as a wave. Then the door opened and closed and he was gone.

There was nothing to do or try. O'Malley engaged the clutch and moved into the traffic flow on Vine, inching through the wet to the freeway. He looked in the mirror one final time. The boy was still there, standing on the corner oblivious to the downpour, staring with calm eyes at the receding taillights of the van.